*Also by Philippe van Rjndt*


**THE TETRAMACHUS COLLECTION**

# BLUEPRINT

# BLUEPRINT

## Philippe van Rjndt

G.P. PUTNAM'S SONS. NEW YORK

**Library of Congress Cataloging in Publication Data**

Van Rjndt, Philippe, 1950–
    Blueprint.

    I.   Title.
PZ4.V276B3    [PR9199.3.V36]     813'.5'4     77-2934

SBN: 399-12002-5

# BLUEPRINT

BLUETHING

# CHAPTER ONE

## *The Interrogation*

THE CELL WAS A LARGE ONE, lined with dark-red brick. He guessed its length at about seven meters, the width four or five. He could judge only by the dimensions of the ceiling since he had been strapped to the table, faceup, from the time they had brought him here. He didn't know where "here" was. He heard no sounds, nor were there any windows to bring in natural light. It was very cold. Nor did he know what time of day it was. He had formed no internal measure of time such as touching his beard to check its growth. But he remembered exactly when he had been picked up: twenty-three minutes past one o'clock, Saturday afternoon, the sixteenth of November.

Hans Schiffer was twenty-five years old, a tennis player by profession, and they had come for him as he had been on his way to the indoor courts on Koblenzstrasse, in Bonn.

Schiffer felt particularly good that afternoon, rested and prepared for hard practice rounds with his partner. The satisfaction of having defeated the American at the European International last week was still with him. As he walked, he was conscious of a lightness to his step. He permitted himself a smile and savored his pleasure. After all, he was the first German to win the International since the war. There were high hopes for his chances at Wimbledon next year.

They were waiting for Schiffer on the corner of Koblenzstrasse. The black Opel passed him, pulled up slightly ahead, and a tall, elegantly dressed gentleman stepped out onto the middle of the sidewalk. Schiffer judged him to be about thirty-five, dark hair, very black eyes. Before he spoke, he showed Schiffer a police card which read "Assistant to the Chief of Criminal Investigations."

The detective apologized for detaining Herr Schiffer this way, but if he could spare a moment of his time, the police would be very grateful. The matter concerned a certain Frau Baun whose apartment had been broken into and systematically robbed. Yes, Schiffer remembered her. She was the widow who lived across the hall from him. Had she been harmed in any way?

The detective looked around and with an embarrassed expression led Schiffer to the car, indicating he would prefer to continue the conversation in privacy. Schiffer saw nothing wrong with this. The police were undoubtedly bungling the investigation and so wished to keep it quiet

He sat himself down diagonally behind the driver, a thickset heavy type with close-cropped yellow hair. The detective came around and also got into the back. The Opel moved off sharply from the curb, crossing two lanes and speeding down Koblenzstrasse. Surprised, Schiffer twisted his head in the direction of the detective. He was about to shout something when an arm swung across at him. There was sudden pain as the hard, bony hand smashed into the nerves under the ear. As his head rolled against the cushions, Schiffer's eyes lifted to the sky beyond the dirty window. The rotating clock above a pharmacist's shop read 1:23 P.M.

Schiffer was a courier. He had been trained to handle microfilm and, if need be, to operate a rado transmitter. No one had counseled him how to withstand torture.

There was a faint snapping noise somewhere in the cell, and the lights came on. On either side of him, parallel with his eyes, two high-beam lamps cut into his vision. He tried to move his head, but it was firmly held back by straps across the forehead. He moved his fingers, tapping them lightly on the wood. Suddenly he jerked his legs up, as though to roll over, and immediately the leather cut into his ankles. He relaxed and shivered, feelng sweat break out over his body. For the first time he realized that he was naked.

"Please open your eyes!"

It was the detective's voice. Schiffer obeyed; but the lamps were still on, and he closed his eyes at once.

The first blow was delivered on the bicep of the right arm. It came down with the full force of a man's body behind it, the knuckles searching for the bone under the muscle.

"You have a body any man would be proud of. Do not have us destroy it."

There was no melodrama to the words, but neither was the threat concealed. Schiffer opened his eyes and kept them open in spite of the red blotches that appeared before them. The pain in his arm peaked sharply and began to ebb as fear released his adrenaline.

"Thank you, Herr Schiffer."

He could not see the face behind the voice. The detective was standing somewhere beyond the lamps.

"Water. . . ."

He heard the splash of a container bringing water. A large freckled hand, calloused along the edge, bearing a white metal cup appeared before his eyes. He tried to remember if it was the same hand that had hit him in the car. Instinctively Schiffer raised his head to reach the cup.

"Lie still and drink very slowly. Otherwise, you will drown."

The water was warm and sweet, and it raised his thirst rather than quenched it. He could not get enough into his mouth at one time to rinse the palate or the gums. The water went over his tongue and straight down his throat.

"We must ask you several questions, Herr Schiffer." The cup was removed. "If you answer them, you shall be free to leave. If you pose difficulties, we shall be forced to abuse your body and you will still tell us what we wish to know. Is this clear?"

He didn't dare close his eyes although the pain from the light was becoming intolerable.

"Could you move the lights, please?"

"Not at the moment."

"Herr Schiffer, we understand you are a courier for Soviet military intelligence, GRU. Is this correct?"

A new speaker had taken over, possibly the driver of the Opel. His voice was guttural, the German heavy with a foreign accent Schiffer could not place. Slavic possibly, but he couldn't be certain. Schiffer could hear him breathing

10

deeply, the air whistling through his nostrils. Schiffer remembered him as a large, heavy man.

"I know nothing about military intelligence," he said slowly and distinctly.

"Herr Schiffer, we are the earliest stage of the interrogation. If we use force, what sort of man will you become in the end? You were not trained to experience torture. You know nothing about it. We are aware of this. Please remember the pain in your bicep and do not complicate the proceedings."

The heavyset man repeated his question.

"Who are you?" Schiffer blurted out suddenly.

The blow landed even before the words were fully from his mouth. The knuckles drove deep into the same place, the right bicep, and Schiffer's wrists and ankles dug into the leather straps as he tried to curl up.

The question was put to him again, and this time he nodded his head as much as the straps permitted.

"That is correct, Herr Schiffer. You are a courier. How long have you been working for the GRU?"

"Three years. . . . Almost three years."

"Close enough. Who is your control?"

"Code name Madonna."

"Yes. And who is Madonna?"

"I . . . I never knew his real name."

"But you did meet him."

"Twice."

"Where and when?"

"Bonn, twice in Bonn. In a theater. I can't remember the name. October and December of last year. . . . The lights, please!"

"Describe Madonna."

11

The pain was retreating again, but his arm had gone numb. He wondered how long it would be before he could lift a tennis racket again. Schiffer thought for the first time about how fragile his body was, for all its excellent condition.

"Madonna—he was tall and wore spectacles. He was over fifty, I think, and walked with a stoop."

"Your memory is excellent. When Madonna met with you, didn't he tell you about the operation against his network, the killings?"

He was sweating now, and the acid was running into the cuts the leather had made in his wrists and ankles.

"No, never."

"There was never any mention of the operation that was systematically exterminating his agents?"

"No, I'm certain."

"Do you know a motor mechanic?"

"I don't understand. . . ."

"No, I don't suppose you do. Madonna never allowed his agents to meet. To rule by division, that was his principle. But we knew a mechanic who worked for Madonna. His name was August. He worked out of Koblenz."

"I have never been to Koblenz."

"That is irrelevant. I know Madonna told you about the mechanic, that he and others had been killed. So Madonna must have told you what he suspected, *whom* he suspected of carrying out the executions. He told you all about this, didn't he, Herr Schiffer?"

Suddenly he felt too weak to bother answering these stupid questions. The pain was wearing off and with it the fear that his body would be destroyed. Although Schiffer did not know it, the pattern was classic: pain leading to fear, then to cowardice and then to a respite which produced anger.

12

"The mechanic told us you were the only one Madonna confided in. He told us Madonna trusted you above all others. He was telling the truth."

"He was lying! Whatever he told you was lies because I never knew any mechanic. Madonna never talked about any killings! Nothing about suspicions!"

"The mechanic is dead now. He told us a little about Madonna's thoughts, the suspicions that were growing in his mind. He said you knew more. Will you please explain?"

He closed his eyes, frustrated by the other's stupidity. His anger was pushing him to refuse them anything more. But then the interrogation began in earnest.

The third blow fell on his chest, directly over the heart. The heart muscle contracted, spasmed, then beat on furiously.

"What did Madonna say to you, please?"

A thick, heavy palm swung from the right side, hitting the upper portion of the rib cage. The heel of the hand broke three bones.

The question was repeated in a low, patient voice. Schiffer's eyes were wide open, staring blindly through the lights at the ceiling. He was not aware that he was screaming.

"Nothing!"

The next blow smashed the remaining ribs on the right side, and the interrogation continued carefully, precisely, without pause. Schiffer was never permitted to lose consciousness. The voice of the heavy man never changed. There was no strain in it, indicating that the physical task of beating did not tire him. Schiffer remembered smelling cigarette smoke. The detective must have lit a cigarette as he watched, listened and waited.

He did not know when the beating stopped or how long

13

they had been absent. But now he could hear them coming back. The lights had been left on, still trained on his face. He opened his eyes only to have them paralyzed by a red film that seemed to hang over his vision. He wondered if he were already blind. There was also a warm wetness under his genitals and a burning sensation along his thighs. He must have urinated on himself without realizing it.

They were back in the cell now. A finger touched his bicep, and he winced.

"You have had a respite," said the heavyset man. "Please tell us about the talk you and Madonna had, the one about the killings."

Schiffer shook his head. "Nothing to say," he muttered thickly. "Nothing."

"You are certain of that?"

"Yes."

"We have asked everyone—the mechanic, the woman of the air force man, the chemist. They told us you would know every detail. Madonna would not keep the information from you. What if something happened to him? He must have taken the precaution of telling you."

"I don't know any of them," Schiffer answered dreamily. "Not a soul . . ."

The interrogator stepped back from the table, turned, and whispered a few words to the assistant. What appeared to Schiffer as a grotesquely swollen face descended upon him from above, the eyes looking down impassively, pitiless. Then it was gone.

"Very well, Herr Schiffer," the interrogator said abruptly. "We choose to believe you. No man would be as stupid as to persist in denials, not under these circumstances."

Down the table two sets of hands began to undo the straps that held his ankles. Schiffer closed his eyes, and a

14

tiny smile appeared on his lips. They believed him. They were letting him go. He was being given back his life. He groaned hysterically and tugged at the wrist straps.

Two cement blocks were swung onto the table and set upright. His legs were raised so that the heels lay on the bricks. Schiffer was still moaning when two iron bars swung down simultaneously on his legs, just below the kneecaps.

After that they untied his wrists and flipped him over like a piece of meat. Then they broke his back.

Alexander Roy was waiting for Schiffer on the other side of the Wall, in East Berlin. The light was emptying from the sky and the wind had picked up in the last quarter hour. Soon it would be too cold to be outside.

"The troops have all been alerted, Captain. If the ambulance has to crash through the American checkpoint, we are ready with our support."

Roy looked at the man who had come up beside him. Lieutenant Kinzel of East German Security, SSD. He was probably not quite an idiot but close enough. If the Americans stopped the ambulance, what would the border guards, the Vopos, do? Nothing. They would not fire into the western zone unless the order came directly from the General Staff. The Vopo colonel in charge of this shift had probably told Kinzel a lot of lies about cover support, and Kinzel had believed him because he was nervous. Or perhaps he was trying to impress Roy, who represented SSD's big brother, Soviet military intelligence. Roy had requested an experienced coordinator for this operation, and the East Germans had given him Kinzel. He supposed it didn't really matter. The retrieval of Schiffer called for a bluff. The ambulance driver was to try to talk his way into the zone, using the papers he would get in West Berlin. Only in the last resort was the ambulance to attempt to break through the barrier. Roy's orders had been firm on that point. The Americans would hesitate to fire on a target moving into the zone. They had their orders as well. But neither should the driver give them cause by mowing down soldiers in his path. Roy knew the driver. He was a good man. He would get through on the bluff.

"Thank you, Lieutenant," Roy said and turned his back on Kinzel.

The operation had begun on Tuesday night, after Schiffer had failed to transmit at his usual time. The same night Roy had alerted his field agents in Bonn to Schiffer's possible disappearance or arrest. He was lucky. Within a few hours a male nurse at the Bonn hospital reported to his East Berlin control that the tennis player had been brought in over the weekend, badly beaten and very likely crippled. He had undergone initial treatmnt in Bonn but was, upon his manager's insistence, to be moved Wednesday to a special clinic in West Berlin. The nurse made a point of mentioning that no special security, no West German counterintelligence, had been placed around Schiffer.

Roy left Moscow at one in the morning, Wednesday, traveling to East Berlin aboard military aircraft. He arrived in the city at three, read the interim reports including all transcripts of West German broadcasts that had carried the incident and made contact with the agent who was arranging Schiffer's covert removal from the clinic and would get him to the other side of the Wall. Roy did not know how or why Schiffer had been picked up. Or by whom. It could have been Scharek of BfV counterintelligence, but then Schareck would have thrown security teams around Schiffer's hospital room. The alternative was someone's personal vendetta against the tennis player. Possible, although unlikely. Roy looked after his agents very carefully. He knew Schiffer did not mix with the elements of organized crime that worked the sports.

But motives and explanations could come later. It was important now to know whether Schiffer had talked and, if he had, to what degree. Roy was bringing the tennis player home to find that out.

Schiffer would be taken from the Berlin clinic in the middle of the afternoon, during the staff change. The orderly would help in his removal. The ambulance, specially reinforced with bulletproof glass and tires, would carry Schiffer and the orderly to the Wall.

The passage papers, forged in East Berlin that morning, would be with the driver. According to schedule, Schiffer should be in East Berlin one hour later.

Roy hoped the orderly had not been mistaken about the absence of security. But if Schiffer had talked and Schareck was onto him, an unguarded room was a trap laid by BfV for whoever might be coming for the tennis player.

Roy pulled up the cuff of his coat and looked down at his watch.

"Ten minutes to six, Captain," Lieutenent Kinzel volunteered.

"Thanks."

It was no use waiting outside any longer. Roy had forbidden radio contact with the helicopter because BfV monitored all SSD frequencies. There was no way of knowing if the operation was still running. If it was and the ambulance appeared, Roy could see it just as well from the Vopo lookout, a chicken shack on steel girders with an iron rung ladder running up one side.

17

The corporal handed Roy a cup of coffee as soon as he climbed up into the hut. The coffee was watery, but hot and sweet. On the table stood an open bottle of Bulgarian brandy. Roy was tempted by the silent invitation. But he had not slept in thirty hours. The brandy would do him no good. He sipped at the coffee and smoked in silence.

The telephone rang. At the same time a red bulb, the alert signal, glowed above the door. The corporal snatched up the receiver, listened briefly and began relaying the message.

"Two vehicles stopping at the American checkpoint. The first is a truck, medium size, three axles. The second vehicle is unidentifiable—too close behind the truck. . . .

"Truck driver escorted into the station for the document check. . . . Officers approaching the second vehicle—"

"What is that car?" Roy whispered. "Ask them what it is. They can see it from the tower!"

"Second vehicle now moving very quickly around the truck. It's the ambulance, Captain! He's in front of the truck, using it as cover, moving through the American—"

Even in the hut Roy could hear the dull snapping of wood as the ambulance broke through the barrier that separated the U.S. zone from the no-man's-land between the two sectors.

"Twisting sharply, but he's through," the corporal continued excitedly. "Approaching our zone. . . . No American fire. . . ."

Roy clambered down the ladder, jumped and began running. All floodlights had gone on maximum, bathing the entry lane in brilliant white. The ambulance, with its headlights gone, was roaring down on a squad of Vopos at the first barrier. They barely had time to clear the way before the car was on top of them. There was the dry squeal of brakes being pumped and gears grinding down as the driver fought to control the vehicle. But the car was home.

"Get the doctor!" Roy shouted to Kinzel.

The ambulance skittered to a halt behind the second post and rocked gently on its suspension. The driver jerked open the door and staggered out, supporting himself on the hood. Roy caught him by the shoulders.

"Not bad, eh?" The driver grinned, then coughed heavily. His eyes were blinking rapidly. "It's those damn lights up there. Hit me straight on as I came through—"

"Captain!" Kinzel was calling.

"You're all right?" Roy murmured.

"A couple of bruises. Not to worry. One of the Americans recognized Schiffer's face. Must have been a tennis buff. Otherwise, we would have made it through without any fuss."

Kinzel was calling him again. Roy came around to the rear door and looked down at the figure on the stretcher. Schiffer's face was deathly pale, with bloodied saliva dried to the side of his mouth. Both his arms were in casts, as were the legs, and the torso was heavily bandaged. The expression in his eyes was one of pure terror.

"The legs were in traction," the orderly explained. "We had problems with that. The pain he must have suffered." He shook his head and stepped back.

The doctor, an SSD man, bent over Schiffer. His hands moved swiftly over the broken body, probing, feeling, listening. Finally, he stood up and waved away the military ambulance that was waiting. He turned to Roy.

"They have delivered you a corpse, Captain," he said.

19

# CHAPTER TWO

## The Killing of Berg

"SO THE HEART OF THE MATTER is whether or not to take Berg out?"

"I believe it is."

"Has anything been found on Schiffer?"

It was well after three in the morning in Moscow, but even over the telephone General Mitko's voice sounded firm and alert. Mitko was chairman of Soviet military intelligence, GRU, and Roy's superior.

"The X rays showed nothing inside him. The body search yielded nothing," Roy said.

"When did he die?"

"Schiffer was still alive when they took him from the clinic. Sometime after that his heart gave out, perhaps during the crash."

"What will you do with the body?"

"Get it back to Bonn and have it placed in the river

20

where the federal police will find it in a day or two. This will cause complications for them. The BfV will wonder why we should have kidnapped Schiffer alive just to bring him back dead."

"And the driver?"

"He says no one had a clear look at him. He was wearing a wig anyway. He wants to go back in a few days. The same with the orderly, but he will need new papers."

"I am very sorry about this whole affair, Alexander. It didn't work for us, not at all."

"We needed to get Schiffer back. We had to know who had done this to him, if he said anything. . . ." Roy finished slowly.

"Which leaves us Berg."

"Yes."

"You want him to stay?"

Ever since Schiffer's corpse had been dispatched to the military morgue, Roy had been searching for alternatives. One man had already died violently that night. His decision could condemn another to the same end.

"I would have Berg stay," Roy said very quietly. He paused and repeated, "Have him stay. I can't get a message through to him until tomorrow. There is too much allied activity around the Wall. By this morning Berg will have heard of the incident at the Wall. When he hears about Schiffer, he may even ask us to bring him in."

"I think not," Mitko said. Roy did not respond. He too knew that Berg would never ask for help.

"I will stay here until Berg confirms receipt of the message," Roy said.

"Yes, you should," Mitko answered. "Do not blame yourself, Alexander. In time we shall know everything. It only takes time."

21

Roy replaced the receiver and walked over to the windows of the hut. To the left, in the American sector, he could see flashing red and blue lights, complemented by giant overhead searchlights that wavered in the darkness as the wind pulled at their riggings. The incident at the Wall had broken the tedium that weighed on both the East and the West. American security forces had begun their battle countdown but had stopped, predictably, at Alert Orange. The British and French were still running about in a mild panic, but the Americans knew it was too late to shut the barn door after the horse had bolted. The West German press, led by the Springer papers, would make a ballyhoo of it all. The chancellor would express regrets that such an affair had taken place after so long a period of calm. The East Germans would counter by accusing Bonn of disrupting traffic in the zone, and the matter would be forgotten within a week.

Roy lit a cigarette and leaned against the cold glass. He wondered if the memory of Hans Schiffer, destiny's darling in German sports, would last any longer.

"The chancellor will see you now, Herr Berg."

The voice of Cornelia Zolling broke his reverie pleasantly. The chancellor's chief security advisor looked up and smiled. He thought the chancellor's private secretary a very nice girl. Cornelia was no longer young and had a figure of matronly plumpness, but her face was shining and scrubbed and reminded Berg of his courtship days. Girls wore no cosmetics then, and many had their hair done up in braids, as Cornelia had hers, in two interwoven locks wound around her head. The braids represented an older fashion, an image from a time that had all but disappeared.

22

Berg gathered up the files on his lap and rose. He wondered if Cornelia Zolling affected the chancellor in the same way she did him and immediately answered his own question. Of course not. Cornelia Zolling directed the chancellor's office. She was indispensable in organizing his schedules, screening his appointments, procuring files and information from the ministries and listening for palace intrigue. She was both his protector and workhorse. In romance and midnight confessions the chancellor preferred spring chickens and men respectively.

"Thank you, Fräulein Zolling," Berg said courteously, bowing slightly from the waist. "I hope you are having a nice day."

Her face beamed.

Berg enjoyed the chancellor's office, a hexagonal room with windows on three sides. It was almost always sunny and very comfortable when the light warmed the old panels and ancient leather chairs. There had been some debate on the security problems posed by the windows, but the chancellor would not consider moving to another office and had personally defrayed the cost of installing bulletproof glass.

"Good morning, Otto."

The chancellor was standing in profile, hands behind his back. His face was squat and rugged, handsome in a hard way, suiting his short height. The single flaw was a nervous tic on the left side of the mouth, a reminder of the heart attack he had suffered six months ago.

"Those are the files?"

"On the three operations you requested, Herr Chancellor."

Berg sat down in his customary chair, an overstuffed

high-back, and spread out the files before him, pink, blue and dull green. The chancellor reluctantly returned to his seat in front of Berg.

"I have given my approval to the plan put forward by BfV," he said slowly, measuring his words as though he were saying something which might offend Berg.

"Has Schareck finished with the army?" Berg asked him.

The chancellor passed him a buff file with a single red stripe across it. "Schareck had this brought to me last night by courier. There is nothing wrong in the army. BfV only confirmed what MAD had already reported."

MAD—Military Security Service, the counterespionage unit of the German armed forces.

"Schareck will now proceed to the Foreign Ministry?" Berg inquired.

"He does not expect to find anything there. He thinks the civil service and the military are above suspicion. Schareck believes the leak is within the Social Democratic Party itself, Otto, among my own ministers and appointees!"

The chancellor's anger was masking his fear, Berg knew. To the world the chancellor was a legend—Nazi hunter, tactician, womanizer, opportunist, visionary. He was the personification of the New Germany, a bastard from the small town of Lübeck who had awakened one day to find himself on the national pedestal. Too late he realized he was out of his depth. He was best at infighting, charting party programs, drinking whiskey with women, then seeking refuge in their embrace. He is naked and cold on the pedestal, Berg thought. He has no confidence in what he has achieved. He relies too heavily on the party to support him, and that is why he is afraid. Were a traitor to be found anywhere else, he would go after him like a terrier. But not in his own party, his last refuge. He does not want to believe this is happening to him.

"Shall we begin with the Pantrax report?" Berg asked him. The chancellor nodded and slumped back into his chair.

"Pantrax A.G. Arms Company," Berg read out. "Subscription to the Social Democratic Party fund totals DM one hundred and forty-six thousand over a period of three years.

"The first conference concerning irregular sales by Pantrax was held in this office on November 17, 1960. The subject of cabinet discussion was Pantrax sales of aircraft and small arms to India, Pakistan and Saudi Arabia. Evidence of these sales was provided by the BfV, and the suggestion was put forward by Schareck that Pantrax should be kept under observation by counterintelligence until further information could be gathered on the resale of these arms to third parties.

"Schareck's suggestion was adopted. The chancellor ordered that no further funds were to be accepted from Pantrax until the outcome of the investigation was known. The meeting was classified as Most Secret, limiting access of the minutes to a dozen people in the ministries involved.

"On November 2, 1961, the Soviet news agency Tass reported accurate details of the Pantrax sales. The story was carried by all major wire services. All accounts of Pantrax were subsequently seized on November 3.

"A BfV report tabled by Schareck on December 21 alluded to the possibility that the Tass information had been based on the minutes of the Most Secret meeting. The Soviet Union scored a tremendous propaganda victory by publishing details of the Pantrax sales. It insinuated that the West German government, because it had accepted Pantrax funds as contributions, knew not only of the illegal sales but of the subsequent resales by the buyer coun-

25

tries. However, a full investigation of the departments and personnel that had access to the report revealed no irregularities nor any indiscretion. The matters of the leaks and the party's acceptance of Pantrax funds were brought up before a plenary session of the Social Democratic Congress in January. At that time the party organizers believed the political ramifications of the Tass revelations could be satisfactorily dealt with. In a subsequent by-election, however, the party lost two long-standing seats in Bavaria."

Berg paused. "The international repercussions are tabled in a separate report, including notes exchanged between Bonn and Washington and London. Should I include this?"

The chancellor shook his head. "I remember the rest well enough."

"Next we have the troubles over Lost." Berg looked down at the notes in the pink file and began paraphrasing them.

"In 1947 the West German government signed a treaty pledging abstention from the use, manufacture and stockpiling of atomic, bacteriological and chemical weapons. In March, 1963, the army depot at Münsterlager reported the theft of four cylinders of a highly toxic battlefield gas code named Lost. The investigation was headed by General Roenne, who was not unaware of the potential repercussions of the theft. The British and American armies had given Lost over to the new German command in 1948 with explicit orders that the gas be destroyed. This directive was never carried out. General Roenne understood that if the theft of Lost came to light, it would prove highly effective propaganda for the USSR.

"Lost was the subject of a full Cabinet discussion on

26

April 16, 1963. General Roenne and the chief of MAD, General Wicht, stated that no orders countermanding the destruction had been received from either the British or the American commands in the intervening years and that the army had all but forgotten the existence of Lost until the theft. Roenne suggested that army experts develop a means of neutralizing the remainder of the gas. He did not feel that dumping the gas at sea or burying it was a foolproof method of destruction.

"Army chemists started work on a method of disposing of Lost within the week. However, on May 1 the Soviet ambassador at the United Nations accused West Germany of violating the postwar treaty by stockpiling Lost. The ambassador gave the exact location of the camp in question, Münsterlager, the number of cylinders there and a description of the gas' effects on the battlefield. The ambassador accused Great Britain and America of secretly rearming West Germany in clear violation of the pact signed by the four powers. He added that this rearmament could be construed only as part of imperialist aspirations upon the sovereignty of the German Democratic Republic and Eastern Europe as a whole.

"As a consequence, the chancellor's office ordered BfV to determine how the Soviet Union received such precise information about the gas so shortly after the Cabinet meeting. The case has never been satisfactorily closed, and BfV has not ascertained the source which reported to the Russians."

"There was another meeting concerning Lost, wasn't there?" the chancellor asked sharply.

"On July 2," Berg said. "On that date Schareck voiced the possibility that the source of information for both the Pantrax scandal and Lost was the same. Unfortunately his department did not have any substantive evidence to support the thesis."

"Until. . . ."

"Until early 1967." Berg picked up the green file.

"On February 2 of that year the Norwegian Foreign Ministry informed BfV of the existence of a Romanian industrial espionage ring. Schareck passed the report to your office, and a meeting was held on the eighth of the month. Present were the chancellor, myself, the minister of trade, the foreign minister and Schareck. The scope of the alleged ring was great, covering not only Scandinavia but Belgium, France and Great Britain, as well as West Germany. One week later forty Romanian diplomats from various embassies and consulates throughout northern Europe were recalled. The defector who had supplied the Norwegians with their information was murdered in an Oslo hospital. His killer was never found.

"Acting on Schareck's proposal, the counterintelligence bureaus of the countries concerned gathered further details on the ring, basing themselves on the material provided by the defector prior to his death. Despite intensive efforts, no contacts of the Romanian diplomats were ever unearthed."

"And when news of the spy ring came into the papers, all hell broke loose." The chancellor shook his head as though trying to throw off a depressing thought. "The industrialists, who got wind of the investigation, accused me of snooping on them, and the press wanted to know where the BfV was all this time!"

He rang for some coffee and pulled a packet of cigarettes from his pocket. He did not bother to offer one to Berg, who did not smoke.

"I drove in with Schareck this morning," the chancellor

said. "British and Scandinavian intelligence have completed their internal inquiries. Their units are deemed secure. The defector was not murdered because of a leak in *their* organizations. Schareck is satisfied that this is so, and I suppose I must be also. Schareck has investigated everyone who has handled any information on the Romanian case, including the typists. Nothing. Certain members of the party have been screened but again, nothing."

The moon-faced Cornelia Zolling entered, carrying a tray of coffee, sugar and cream in silver service. She turned her perpetual smile from the chancellor to Berg and departed without a word. The chancellor searched in his drawer for saccharin tablets.

"I hate these things, you know," he said. "It was a choice—less alcohol or no sugar.

"We really cannot afford any more incidents like the ones you've mentioned," he continued slowly. "Schareck has convinced me of one thing: The Soviets have someone here in Bonn who is deliberately trying to destroy my policy of reconciliation with East Germany, the so-called *Ostpolitik*. They have no wish to see the two Germanies reunited. The Americans are reluctant to let me proceed too far too quickly, for fear I might jeopardize their détente overtures to the Russians. But East Germany *is* interested in reunification. That is why if we have any repetition of scandals or stupidities like the one at the Wall last night, it will do us in."

The chancellor kept stirring his coffee absently, blending in cream.

"I am inclined to agree with Schareck," he repeated. "There is someone in our circles, although I do not believe he is a member of the party, who is working against us. The nonconfidence in the government is spreading. If an

29

election were forced on me, the party would have to re-nounce the *Ostpolitik* program to survive at the polls. My own party would demand this!

"The Americans will not cry if *Ostpolitik* dies," the chancellor went on, his voice straining. "The British and French will be satisfied. The Russians will have kept their hold over their satellites. Only the two Germanies will emerge as losers, again."

Berg thought it pitiful that for all his connections within Washington and the Agency, the chancellor could not gather enough foreign support for his beloved *Ostpolitik.* Berg knew it had been Czechoslovakia. The chancellor's life dream of reunification had been wounded by the scandals, but it had bled to death when the first Soviet tanks crept on Prague, followed by East German soldiers. After that, how was he to explain to his Western allies that the basic interests of the two Germanies still coincided or that East Berlin could deal as a sovereign government?

"I had ordered Shareck to use all resources at his disposal to identify the leak," the chancellor said suddenly. "All resources," he repeated.

"That was agreed upon three weeks ago," said Berg. "At the security colloquium."

"Yesterday Shareck told me that a highly placed double within the Soviet Union has come into Bonn. Wessel brought him in after much ado."

"There was no mention of such an arrival on the day security sheet," Berg objected.

"Wessel insisted on that. He also asked that there be only one copy of this report concerning Iron Mask." The chancellor pulled a buff file from underneath his blotter and passed it to Berg. The file was stamped with the personal seal of the president of the BND, West German intelligence, Gerhard Wessel. Its contents were meant for his eyes only.

"This is the original typed by Wessel himself. I must ask you to read it here."

Berg took the file and let it lie in his lap. "Is my name now on the circulation list for this dossier?"

"It is, as is my name and Schareck's, and that is where it stops. As you will see, the information on Iron Mask is scanty enough, Wessel made certain of that. Iron Mask is so important he is not run by BND control. For security, Wessel himself controls him. You can understand why. Iron Mask is a highly placed double within the Soviet government. He can travel at will. From his information it is evident he meets with the Politburo at frequent intervals. He is one man in a thousand, Otto, one in a thousand. . . ."

"And Iron Mask is here to pinpoint the source of the leaks on the operations we have just discussed—Pantrax, Lost, the Romanian affair?"

"Schareck is certain Iron Mask will make the identification."

Berg shifted in his seat and fingered the file. He had not yet opened it. "May I ask why, if the investigation has proceeded to this stage, you are telling me this? It does not appear there is any role for me to play."

"Ah, but there is, Otto," the chancellor said harshly. "I want you to meet with Iron Mask. I want him to tell *you* the identity of the double."

"But Iron Mask will tell Schareck whatever he wants to know."

"Suppose the leak is not within the government? Suppose it is within the BfV itself? Will Schareck still tell us the name Iron Mask provides?"

31

So this is the whole of it, Berg realized. He has reached the point where even his own chief of counterintelligence is suspect. Berg wondered if he had completely misread the seemingly light and cordial relationship that existed between the chancellor and Schareck.

"Do you really believe Schareck will not tell us if the leak is within his department?" Berg said somberly.

"I cannot answer that," the chancellor replied. "Because I don't know. It appears inconceivable even to think such a thing about Schareck . . . yet there is a great deal at stake. BfV is already suspect in the eyes of the Americans and NATO, especially after the Romanian setback. Schareck would find himself in a very embarrassing position if after all this time it was his department that was responsible."

The chancellor leaned forward on his desk. "*I* must know what is going on, Otto. I must have an independent source against which to measure Schareck's information. Just this one time. . . ."

"So Schareck is not to know about my meeting Iron Mask, assuming a meeting can be arranged."

"Schareck is personally responsible for Iron Mask while he is here. It will be difficult to see him without Schareck's permission. If you cannot gain access, I will issue the necessary authorization—without giving Schareck prior notice."

Berg looked down at the buff file on his lap, then at the chancellor.

"Who is Iron Mask?" he asked softly.

"Iron Mask's arrival in this country coincided with that of Sergei Bibnikov, head of Soviet Special Investigations. Who do *you* think Iron Mask is?"

Berg opened the file, and his eyes flinched as he read the name of Iron Mask.

Otto Berg left the chancellor's officer ten minutes later. Upstairs, in the room directly above, Colonel Schareck removed his earphones and switched off the tape recorder. He reached for his cigar and delicately rolled the ash into a cut glass tray. He was pleased with the way the chancellor had conducted the meeting, exactly as Schareck had coached him. Now that Berg believed in the existence of an Iron Mask dossier, Schareck was very curious to see whom Berg would share his information with.

Otto Berg escorted Cornelia Zolling downstairs. They parted at the front doors, she going out to lunch, he continuing downstairs to the BND transmission and communications center.

Berg told the security at the door that there was a tape to be played for him. The guard escorted him to the soundproof studio and locked Berg inside. But instead of listening to communications, Otto Berg constructed two messages. The first was about ten minutes in duration. After he had passed it through a scrambler and reducing machine, his monologue was reduced to no more than nine or ten seconds. He placed this message at the beginning of a cassette tape.

The second message was untreated. It did not pass through the scrambler or the condenser. When Berg was finished, he placed the cassette in a small jeweler's package, wrapped that in brown paper and addressed it to a Geneva bank. He rapped on the door, and the guard opened up immediately.

* * *

From there Otto Berg went directly to the mail room at the rear of the building, arriving just as the noon post was being loaded into sacks. He dropped the package into an international delivery bag and left the Chancellery through the postal depot.

Otto Berg was fifty-six years old, tall, gangling, with a freckled balding scalp and rimless glasses. An electrical engineer whose family had come from Leipzig, he had lived in East Germany after the war. The repression of the East German uprising of 1953 destroyed his hopes of fashioning a new life in yet another "new order," and in the heyday of the cold war he established contact with the Gehlen Org, West Germany's fledgling security service.

For the next three years Berg sent a steady stream of intelligence to Bonn, dealing mainly with the industrial sector of the German Democratic Republic's economy. He traveled to the Dnieper hydro dam site in 1954 and across Poland as an adviser on power plant construction. In the spring of the following year his only son was killed when a Vopo lorry, hurrying to arrest an enemy of the people, crashed into the boy's bicycle. On August 24, 1956, Berg and his diabetic wife, Martha, disappeared into the American sector of Berlin.

Berg now began to collect the dividends from his association with Gehlen. After a two-day meeting with Berg, Gehlen recommended him to the head of counterespionage, responsible for operations in the East German zone. Following one year's service, the department waived the usual three-year waiting period, and Berg was given citizenship for himself and his wife. With a letter of recommendation from Gehlen, both joined the Social Democratic Party. Within two years Berg was established in Bonn.

34

He rose quickly within the party machinery, from campaign worker to secretary. In 1959 the man who was now chancellor accepted the post of foreign secretary under the German National Coalition, and Berg, vetted by the Americans through Gehlen, became his chief adviser on security affairs.

Berg nudged the Volkswagen out of the Chancellery parking space, drove north for three kilometers and swung out onto the autobahn. It had been very cold during the past week. The dead gray shade of winter had driven autumn from the countryside. It was the limbo season, no whiteness, no color either. But the garden had turned out nicely, with plenty of canning for Martha. The squash had been particularly good. This afternoon he would spread a few more bags of leaves at the foot of the hedges for the winter. His thoughts came much more clearly when he worked with his hands.

One of the cars that overtook the Volkswagen before the suburban exit was a large black Opel. Berg did not notice it. The Opel took the ramp quickly and braked hard at the intersection. The driver made a right, and the car roared off in the direction Berg was to follow a minute later, toward the new annex, where the roads were still unpaved. The driver of the Opel made his way carefully around the potholes, slowed down as he passed Berg's home, then continued over the hill and down.

The assassin got out and headed into the pine forest that surrounded the annex. His shoes sank into the wet, half-frozen earth as he made his way up the hill, ducking under branches and brushing dead wood from his path. When he reached the top, there was a thin stream of blood near his temple where a branch had hit him, snapping back unexpectedly.

35

Berg's house, a small prefabricated Finnish design, was one of two dwellings at the bottom of the hill. There was no car in the drive of the other house, so the assassin assumed the neighbors were absent. He brought out his gun, a long-range weapon with a slender eight-inch barrel. The rooms he was looking down on were Berg's kitchen and bedroom. Berg would probably go into the kitchen first. The distance between himself and the kitchen window was only thirty meters, but the silencer would diminish his velocity and accuracy. He chose a tree against which to balance himself for the shot.

He waited. There was no sound save that of the winter sparrows and the soft dripping of moisture from the pine needles. The assassin's hands were wet under the chamois gloves. He brushed at his close-cropped hair, a nervous gesture, and hoped that Berg would come soon.

Berg did not bother to put the car in the garage. He might need it later on. He opened the door and deposited his overcoat on an ancient coat tree, dropped his rubbers in the plastic stand and padded in his stocking feet into the kitchen. Under the bread box lay a note from his wife. She had canned pears that morning and had left a few out for him. Berg smiled to himself and went over to the sink to wash his hands. Suddenly he was very hungry.

The first bullet hit him low in the throat, just above the breastbone. It shattered the window above the sink, and splintered glass fell into the stainless steel tub, sliding around and around until it collected in the drain catch. Berg fell back, his head smashing against the door handle of the dishwasher, and slid forward, his stockinged feet providing no traction on the waxed floor.

The assassin's target was minuscule now. From where he stood, he could see only the crown of Berg's head. He aimed very carefully and fired the second shot, through the hole the first bullet had made.

Satisfied that Berg was dead, the assassin unscrewed the silencer and slipped it into his pocket. He was still watching the house when he realized he had made an error. He turned around abruptly, moving very fast for a man of his bulk, the gun arm swinging wide, his other hand coming up under the barrel.

The boy standing behind him was ten or eleven years old. His high rubber boots and trousers were caked with mud. The face was punctuated by two very large front teeth. He was wearing a child's glasses—clear hard plastic frames—and was smiling nervously at the assassin with an expression half curious, half afraid as though he knew he had stumbled on a grown-up doing something no little boy should see.

"Are you a policeman?" he called out, trying to smile even more.

The assassin knew he should kill the boy now. But he had removed the silencer from the gun and could not take the time to fix it back on. He would kill the boy with his hands. Slowly he lowered the weapon and stood up.

"You are a policeman, I know it. Only policemen carry guns like that."

The boy was afraid because the man said nothing. He was going to punish him.

"Yes, I am a policeman." The assassin smiled and stepped forward, tucking the gun away. "You're not a bad detective to have found me."

Somewhat reassured, the boy came forward. "Were you shooting at Herr Berg's house?" he demanded boldly. "I heard you smash a window."

"No, I wasn't doing that. Some of my friends are down

there, shooting at targets. We come up here sometimes, for practice."

"With your guns?"

"With the guns. You must know this land very well," the assassin added.

"I live over there." The boy answered happily, waving a grimy hand in the direction of the road. "Sometimes I go down into Herr Berg's garden."

"For the apples?"

"No, to help him with the leaves!" the boy scolded, embarrassed.

"All right, all right." The assassin laughed.

He placed one hand around the boy's shoulder, the thumb sliding to the base of the neck, the forefinger curling around the other side. The boy's skin was very soft.

"Do you know a trail that leads back to the road?"

"There are two," the boy answered, looking up. "Come on!"

He broke free and started down the hill, using the heel of his boots against the slippery ground.

The assassin decided not to kill him. When Berg's body was found, the boy might hear the news and tell his mother about meeting a detective near Herr Berg's house. The mother might pass on the information to the police. That was doubtful because she wouldn't want the boy involved, but even if she were willing, the child would be frightened and confused by police questioning. He would not be able to identify the assassin from photographs since none existed. The boy would do no better with a police artist.

"We can come out here!"

The boy was waiting for him by the shoulder of the road. The black Opel was only a few meters away, and the assassin cursed softly at missing the trail on the way up. He felt inside his pocket for a coin.

"This is for you, for showing me the way out."

"Will you take me to Herr Berg's house now?" the boy asked, clutching his coin. "I know he's home. I can help him with the leaves."

"My friends are with him now. Police business, you know."

The boy hesitated, then nodded solemnly. "I'll see him tomorrow then," he said. "Good-bye!"

Pocketing the coin, the boy ran down the road. Suddenly he stopped and turned around to wave, but the policeman was in his car. The boy remembered his father's saying a driver shouldn't turn his car around like that, in the middle of the road. He supposed policemen had special privileges.

# CHAPTER THREE

## *GRU Center, Military Intelligence*

THE CLERK AT THE GENEVA BANK recognized the client as soon as he stepped up to the wicket. He was a man of about thirty, medium height, with a brisk military stride. The clerk remembered the coat as well, beige, elegantly cut, with wide lapels that were the season's fashion.

"Good morning, Monsieur Roy."

Roy acknowledged the greeting with a distracted nod.

He is subdued, the clerk thought. A bad investment, more than his account could absorb? Perhaps he will be closing altogether. It happened too frequently these days, what with the markets languishing.

"Please deposit this in my account." Roy pushed a fat white envelope under the grille. "And I expect there is mail for me."

The clerk was pleased about the money, disappointed that he had so misread his client's intentions. He tore open

40

the envelope, quickly stacked the U.S. dollars by denomination, counted them and signed the chit. He placed the money and one copy of the chit into a pneumatic tube.

Excusing himself, he left the wicket and walked to the end of the counter. He squatted before a row of pigeonholes and ran a finger along the oiled walnut edge. He returned, carrying a small package, about the size of a necklace case.

"This is all."

Roy glanced at the postmark and dropped the packet into his pocket. "We'll be seeing you then."

The clerk nodded conspiratorially. Roy might come back in a fortnight or perhaps not for several months. Unlike most of the bank's clients who had well-defined deposit-withdrawal schedules, Roy visited the bank erratically. There was no pattern. Whatever Roy's occupation was, the clerk was certain it was not quite aboveboard.

The LOT Polish Airlines plane banked sharply to the left, circled the city and made for the east. Roy unbuckled his seat belt against regulations and stretched out his legs. He was very tired from last night's journey—Berlin to Stuttgart, from Stuttgart by train to Geneva, where he had arrived at six in the morning. Now this flight, which was to land in Moscow shortly after three in the afternoon.

The younger of the two hostesses came by and looked disapprovingly at the unbuckled seat belt. She could look pretty, Roy thought, if her hair were not in a tight bun. He supposed she was an apprentice working the shorter routes to gain experience and be vetted for political reliability. Much good that procedure was. Three weeks before a senior LOT pilot had defected in New York.

"Would you like something to drink?" she asked. She

was still looking at the seat belt, hoping he would oblige her without a reprimand.

"Juice. Any kind of juice."

She thought he was good-looking. A strong, handsome face, old somehow, too serious for his age. The green eyes held hers, and she was conscious of a blush spreading across her cheeks.

"There is tomato and apricot. I can bring you ice if you like."

"Tomato, with plenty of ice."

She began to move down the aisle, then turned around, thinking he was staring after her. But he had turned to the window, and in the reflection she could see him biting his lip.

Alexander Roy was thirty-one years old. He had been an orphan for twenty of those years, after his mother died in 1948. After passing through five state orphanages, he entered Moscow's Frunze Military Academy in 1956 and became its youngest graduate. After two years with a combat unit he was taken into the GRU, doing courier work and surveillance first in Vienna, then in Berlin.

Roy lived alone in a three-room flat on Kutuzov Prospekt. He had few friends and was more often a guest than a host. Through Mitko he was on familiar terms with most of the General Staff. Their wives welcomed Roy as an eligible young man with excellent connections, so there was never any lack of dinner invitations. There was also a girl, Anna, whom he had been seeing regularly for almost a year. But even her he kept at a distance. During the last five years Roy had been building up the GRU network in West Germany. Five years. It seemed a very long time, now that they were all dead.

* * *

Roy didn't know if Berg had received the message about Schiffer's death and, if he had, whether it had made any difference. Berg had been the last of the network in Germany. The end had begun with the shooting of the mechanic from Koblenz. He had been on his way back from Luxembourg after completing a dead drop. According to the rules, they should have picked him up going there, when he was carrying something. But they had hit him on the return trip.

After the mechanic came the woman Roy had recruited in West Berlin, whose husband worked as liaison with the American air command. The official report stated it had been a traffic accident which did not account for the fact that the body seemed to have been tortured beforehand, and neither the truck driver nor his vehicle was ever traced. She had been a good agent. The husband drank and carried on, and she listened. That was how Center had come to know of the new fighters the Americans were building specifically for the German air force.

The last two had been working around Berg. They had been his personal satellites, the chemist at Essen and the tennis player, Schiffer. The chemist had been found dead in his laboratory, an "industrial accident" the press had called it. He had been working with toxic serums and had accidentally inhaled some vapors.

They had been cruel to Schiffer.

Like five little "niggers," eliminated coldly, methodically. It made no sense at all.

When the mechanic was killed, Roy thought Schareck was onto the network. But why kill the man? If you knew he was a courier, you would pick him up on the way to Luxembourg and get hard intelligence. But this killing was wanton, not Schareck's style at all. The same for the others, especially Berg. Dead, they were of no use to anyone, no information, nothing to trade. But they were dead all the same.

And there had been no outcry at Berg's killing. He had been the chancellor's adviser on security affairs, and the flap must have been terrific when they found the transmitter in his house, the one he used to communicate with Center. But nothing leaked out. Was it possible they hadn't found the transmitter? No way of knowing. The West German government was playing this one very close to the chest. The usual eulogies about service to the fatherland, but not a word about the bullet in the head. Even the press was subdued. Perhaps it had been warned off.

There was also the problem of Martha Berg. She should have contacted Center by now. Yet three days had passed, and still there was no word from her.

Roy adjusted the seat, and its back pressed against someone's leg. His operation in Germany had been the pride of the GRU's European theater, and now it was in shambles. That meant the whole GRU was in trouble. General Mitko had investigated the first killings but had not got conclusive results. After the third death, the chemist, the attitude of the Politburo had shifted from impatience to suspicion. Bibnikov of Special Investigations had been ordered to begin a parallel inquiry. The Politburo was not at all satisfied with Mitko's efforts.

Roy knew all about Bibnikov. A tall, heavy man with cruel, watery eyes and florid, sagging face, Bibnikov had been a weight lifter in his youth. He was still very strong.

Bibnikov had been one of Beria's inquisitors, until Stalin died and Khrushchev had had Beria shot. He had fought World War II against his own side, in a special SMERSH security unit that rooted out treason, real or otherwise,

44

among Soviet troops. In 1954 Bibnikov had fallen from favor, and he packed himself off to West Berlin, where he ran a string of minor agents. Then he moved to Munich, where he infiltrated the Russian Patriotic Society. Within three months Bibnikov had personally eliminated twelve people, among them the head of the White Russian monarchy group, NTS. The last had been a good job, and his star again began to rise.

Roy didn't know whether it had been in Munich that Bibnikov had obtained his information on Yuri Popov, a highly placed double in the GRU apparat. Bibnikov traveled about a great deal in Germany, moving into and through émigré groups and relaying information back to Moscow. Someone in one of these enclaves might have boasted of hearing about Popov. However it happened, in 1958 Bibnikov was suddenly back in Moscow and Lieutenant Popov was exposed. On October 12, the eve of the Revolution's anniversary, Lieutenant Yuri Popov was executed at the Lubyanka. Khrushchev personally rewarded Bibnikov by making him deputy director of Special Investigations. It was a new organ, nominally under the control of KGB Chairman Serov, but in reality it was an independent investigative body which had a mandate to search for treason within both the KGB and the GRU.

Bibnikov did his job well, almost too well. Four years later he caught another fish, bigger than Popov. Oleg Penkovsky, colonel in the GRU, was blown as a joint agent of the CIA and British Secret Intelligence Service. The case implicated Serov, Khrushchev's favorite drinking partner, because Penkovsky had been sleeping with Serov's daughter. He stayed with her at Serov's flat when the old man was away, ate his food, drank his liquor and microfilmed all secret memoranda Serov brought home from the office.

Serov resigned in disgrace, and an angry Politburo widened Bibnikov's authority. Special Investigations would be responsible to the Politburo first, the KGB second.

Roy did not know why Bibnikov hated the military. Perhaps it had to do with the whole history of civilian mistrust of the army. The Revolution had been preserved by the Red Army but afterward its leader, Trotsky, had his back broken by Stalin. Stalin purged the officers corps in 1937, but then had to haul czarist generals from Siberian prisons to win the war for him. The Great Patriotic War it had been called. But at its conclusion the soldiers who had given Stalin his victory disappeared into the camps. The Great Father was afraid of them, afraid they would make some claim on him for their suffering. So he banished them, with the help of sycophants such as Bibnikov, who spent the war at the rear lines where soldiers returning from the fire sometimes cursed the stupidities of Stalin's military tactics. That was what Bibnikov waited for, the wrong word spoken to relieve embittered feelings, a phrase said in anger brought on by fatigue, a careless opinion nurtured by the presence of death. Like a vampire, he waited, and when the word had been spoken, he took the soldier aside and accused him of treason. He had done this to Roy's father, late in 1944. His father had struck Bibnikov, fighting with all the insane fury of the tired, the desperate and the condemned. Bibnikov had had to return to Moscow to have his teeth replaced but not before Roy's father had been court-martialed in the field by a special NKVD tribunal and sentenced to death. Bibnikov himself had carried out the execution.

That was Roy's reason for hating Bibnikov. He thought it sufficient.

* * *

In two months a network that had begun five years before was destroyed. Berg had been running longer than any of them, ever since 1956, when he first arrived in the West. Initially Mitko had been Berg's control, but after Roy had set up the auxiliary agents, Mitko had given him the deep penetration man as well. Now they all were dead. The money Roy had deposited in Geneva was GRU funds, to cover the expenses of starting another ring. Mitko had been adamant on that point. Even a setback of such proportions must not leave the GRU European theater paralyzed. A new operation was to be organized as quickly as possible.

If Bibnikov permits us, Roy thought.

Roy tapped the outside of his coat pocket, feeling the small package he had received at the Geneva bank. Unless something else had gone wrong, Berg's last tape recording should be inside. It was an emergency procedure Roy had had Berg adopt. Should it prove impossible to get to a dead drop or keep a radio date, Berg was to record his information and simply drop it in the mail. The package was the other reason Roy had traveled to Geneva. He was hoping that Berg could help him now, even from beyond the grave.

Ivatushin from Bomber Command, Overflight Reconnaissance met him at the airport and drove Roy into Moscow. Ivatushin had been brought into the GRU to piece together the latest data on the German air force.

"Are you going to salvage anything?" Ivatushin asked him.

"I don't know. Any reports from Sister?"

"Nothing."

"Any political reports?"

Ivatushin shook his head.

"Has there been *any* transmission from Germany?" Roy snapped.

"Nothing, Alex. I'm sorry."

Roy swore under his breath. So Berg's wife hadn't called in. She was a trained radio operator, a shrewd strong-willed woman whose pleasant fussiness was a perfect mask for her work. Martha Berg forgot nothing. A conversation could rest in her mind for a year, and when she repeated it, she even remembered the speaker's stress on particular words.

"Have a look in the rear view, will you?" Ivatushin said quietly.

A blue Volga was keeping pace with them, not bothering to be subtle.

"They trailed me from headquarters straight to the airport," Ivatushin commented. "I found this under the steering column."

From the breast pocket of his uniform he brought out a small circular microphone.

"When did Bibnikov begin this?" Roy asked him coldly.

"I think this is the first sign," Ivatushin said. He made an illegal turn in full view of a policeman and gunned the engine. "The old man will brief you, but I think the Politburo has already decided who will clean up the shit in our nest."

"What does Bibnikov hope to achieve by tailing us?"

"To achieve? It's standard procedure. He will start shredding our nerves by spot surveillance in the hope someone makes a mistake."

Roy stared at him, incredulous.

"Oh, yes!" Ivatushin laughed. "I have it on good authority Bibnikov is after a double—again!"

General Nikolai Stepanovich Mitko was a short man, five

feet six inches, with the mustache and ramrod stance of a Semeonovsky Guards officer. The eyes were a deep brown shot through with green; the silver hair was swept back; the hands were soft and freckled, lined with blue veins.

Mitko had turned sixty-eight three days before. A small dinner party was organized by a few of his surviving friends, but it had just gotten under way when word of Berg's killing reached Moscow. Mitko had gone back to Center at once. He had not moved from his office since.

"Berg was one of the best," Mitko murmured. He reached for his glass of cold tea and squeezed more lemon into it. "You worked him very well."

Roy stirred and put out his cigarette. Daylight had gone, but Mitko didn't bother to turn on the lights. Worn by fatigue, he preferred the comfort of darkness. Roy wondered how he could keep up such a pace at his age.

"They have drawn our teeth," Roy said. "We have nothing left. Not even Berg's wife. She was reported at the funeral the day after he was killed, then disappeared."

"I know," Mitko said. He paused as though searching for his words. "But who are 'they,' Alexander? *Who* has drawn teeth?"

Roy looked at him helplessly.

"The silence in the West continues," Mitko said, thinking aloud. "Berg was an important man. They gave him a small state funeral. But obviously BfV knew nothing of Berg's activities because the chancellor still reigns. If Schareck had been responsible for Berg's death, *Ostpolitik* would be a dead issue. That has not come to pass."

"So Schareck wasn't the one who destroyed the network."

"No," Mitko said with finality. "It wasn't him." He drank the remainder of the tea and set the glass down gently.

49

"It's possible both Schareck and the chancellor knew what Berg was doing and are simply keeping it quiet," Roy said. "The state funeral could have been the last touch in the camouflage."

"I have considered that theory and discarded it," Mitko said. "Look around you. Everything is a mess, as Tolstoy so correctly observed about the Oblonsky household. Here, too. Files, computer data, notes, personal letters from Berg, I have been studying all this for two days. Nothing. The Americans, whom I first suspected of doing a little dirty work behind Bonn's back, have not run a major operation in the last six months. Nor could they have executed such a precise operation on such a scale without BND or BfV help. Besides which," Mitko added, "they trust their Teutonic allies too much."

"If not the Germans or the Americans, then that leaves only one other party, doesn't it?" Roy said dully. "Ivatushin mentioned that Bibnikov suspects a double in our apparat."

Mitko looked at him and smiled sadly. "You were only twenty-six when I gave you West Germany. I should never have done that, no matter how well you performed. It was too sensitive an area, too easy to make a mistake, the penalty for error too heavy. Now Bibnikov will set his inquisitors on you. He will try to do to you what he did to your father."

"Will Bibnikov be able to convince the Politburo of a leak in our apparat?"

"Results," Mitko said softly. "The whole world lives by results in one fashion or another. We have had negative results. We have lost not one agent or two but an entire network. I think Bibnikov has already convinced the Politburo, yes. . . ."

50

"Berg aside, the German network had only a string of minor agents before I took it over," Roy said slowly. He was angry, and his voice was flat, hard. "We were getting the better part of our information from Sister. But within four years all that changed; Andropov began feeding off *us*. Those are results too, Nikolai Stepanovich! If I had wanted to sell my own men, I would have made arrangements to watch the slaughter from the safety of either Langley or London!"

"That is what Penkovsky said before the first interrogation, almost the exact words," Mitko observed. "Before Bibnikov had a chance to work on him. He may get you to sing a different tune."

"Bibnikov cannot put lies into my mouth!"

"Bibnikov lives on lies!" Mitko retorted. "They are his life's blood. He obtains *results* by them." The general stopped and shook his head. "Bibnikov was twenty, only a boy, when he interrogated me. But he has learned well. He was tough and very hard. He came close to breaking me in '37."

This was the bond between Mitko and Roy that spanned two generations. They both had suffered under Bibnikov's hand, and the suffering united them.

"Bibnikov thinks there is a double in the apparat because we haven't a satisfactory explanation for what has happened. The Politburo believes him because Bibnikov has had results in the past. In fact," Mitko added carefully, "I happen to agree with them. There is a ferret."

The words jolted Roy. His reaction was to disbelieve what he had just heard. But Mitko had spoken quietly as though he were certain of the truth.

"How long have you suspected this?" Roy asked finally.

"How long?" Mitko was looking away from him, speaking to the dilapidated walls. "Since the first killing. Even before. The death of the mechanic confirmed my suspicions."

"Then couldn't we have stopped this?" Roy said savagely. "Couldn't we have warned the others?"

"As much as I wanted to, no. I had only a feeling then, an intuition. But there was no face behind it, no identity. How can you warn men against something or someone you cannot see?" He paused and looked directly at Roy. "How many people knew the full details of the German network?"

"Yourself, I, Marfa Petrovna in Communications, Arkadei Ivanovich in Finance, Kominev in Special Investigations, who makes certain our agents aren't doubling. . . ."

"Since the death of the mechanic I have run security checks on all of us. I will show you the files later. I think you will find them extensive and conclusive. The result is nothing. I have found nothing out of place in our apparat."

"And Special Investigations?"

"You will see. You have the recording Berg sent you? Put it here in the cassette. If I remember correctly, Berg preferred the cassette to the reel-to-reel."

Roy removed a stack of papers and dossiers from Mitko's desk and dropped them in a chair. He brought a tape deck from the cupboard and placed it in the cleared space.

"Wait a moment."

Mitko leaned over and pressed two buttons on a control panel on his desk. The first was a light switch. The second activated the electric jamming device. A slow hum sounded throughout the room as the motors wound up to maximum revolutions.

"You can never tell, can you?" Mitko laughed softly.

"Ivatushin found a microphone in one of our cars," Roy said. He slid the cassette in and snapped down the plastic cover. Mitko did not seem surprised at this piece of news.

The tape added its own minuscule contribution to the hum in the room. It spun on without a word coming through. Suddenly a sharp electronic whine burst from the speakers.

"Must have had the radio on,' Mitko murmured. "Or the microphone was too close to an electrical instrument. . . ."

There was a click, and Berg's voice, faint at first, came through. Roy pictured the dead man adjusting the volume control on the tape recorder. He had the ghoulish feeling that he was listening to a corpse.

Berg began speaking.

"Twelve thirty, November 18, the Chancellery office.

"A quarter hour ago I completed a meeting with the chancellor concerning security dossiers code named Alpha, Delta and Omega. According to the chancellor, Schareck is seeking a high-level leak responsible for the dissemination of details of the said dossiers to the Soviet Union. Schareck believes the source lies somewhere within the chancellor's ministerial appointments.

"In addition, I believe Schareck has already investigated a number of people without the chancellor's knowledge or authority. I received word of this from Jaunich in the Foreign Ministry yesterday. Because nothing was mentioned on this point, I believe I am above suspicion. It is almost certain that thus far Schareck's investigation has yielded nothing. However, the inquiry into the leaks has been stepped up.

"The appendix to day security sheet Friday, November 15 indicates that Schareck was in Luxembourg that day. His presence seems to have been accounted for by the arrival of Flight Two Thirty-three, Aeroflot, which carried Sergei Ivanovich Bibnikov, chief of Special Investigations. The report states that Schareck subsequently lost track of Bibnikov once the latter had crossed the border from Luxembourg into West Germany. But the appendix does not explain why Bibnikov's arrival *necessitated* Schareck's presence in the first place. Routine surveillance of Flight Two Thirty-three is carried out by junior officers. Nor is it mentioned how Schareck knew Bibnikov was coming. His pending arrival was not mentioned in any prior security memoranda.

"The day sheet Monday, November 18, passed to me by the chancellor during our discussion, was appended by a note concerning Iron Mask. As my previous reports have indicated, Iron Mask is a highly placed double within the KGB or GRU. At today's meeting the chancellor named him. He is Sergei Bibnikov of Special Investigations and is run by Wessel himself, as I had suspected. Schareck, having failed in his previous efforts to locate the leaks on Alpha, Delta and Omega, convinced Wessel to bring in Iron Mask so that he might identify, if possible, the Soviet Union's source. He is a major threat to all Soviet security operations in the West, and his arrival in the West may be the signal for the final phase of destruction of our network."

There was a pause, followed by a series of clicks as though the dead man were adjusting the microphone stand. The voice picked up again. This time Berg was speaking rapidly, chopping his words. He was afraid. He was smelling his own death.

"The appendix on Iron Mask, until then known only to Wessel, Schareck and the chancellor, was shown to me for the following reason: The chancellor strongly suspects that the leak is to be found within the BfV itself, *not* in the government. The chancellor has therefore instructed me to meet with Iron Mask, without Schareck's knowledge, and get the name from him. The chancellor is concerned that if the leak is within BfV, Schareck will withhold this information in order to stave off embarrassment and so as not to have BfV considered a security risk in the eyes of other Western counterintelligence services.

"The day sheet of November 15 is therefore partially inaccurate for the sake of security. Bibnikov arrived, but he did not disappear. According to the appendix, he is currently at a safe house in Friedrichstrasse Seventeen."

There was another pause, Roy could sense Berg gathering his last thoughts.

"Because of the unquestionable danger which threatens the surviving members of the network, my wife and myself, I cannot wait for Center to issue directives in this matter. It is obvious Bibnjkov was responsible for Schiffer's death. Therefore, I must attempt to gain entry to Iron Mask before he talks. When I do, I shall kill him.

"I will try to have the execution appear an accident. This will be very difficult, but if I succeed and am suspected, though not apprehended, then it may be difficult to prove my complicity. I am, after all, a security adviser to the chancellor, and my clearance is one of the highest.

"Center will know immediately if I should fail in my task. Quite simply, Bibnikov will get to me first.

"In the event of my death, nothing will be discovered about the operations I have carried out. The transmitters have been removed from my house. All code books have been destroyed. I have also made separate arrangements for my wife. She will contact Center within a few days of my burial.

"My final request, should it be final, is that my wife be

looked after by Center and provided with the compensation that befits a loyal citizen of the Soviet Union."

The tape spun on for another few seconds, and the cassette switched off automatically.

"So there we have it," Mitko said softly. "It has cost us the network, but we have it."

Roy slumped back in his chair and looked at him stupidly.

"What do we have?" he asked hoarsely. He lifted his head and cleared his throat. "What in God's name do we have?"

"A traitor. Our traitor."

Roy said nothing. Berg had known of Schiffer's death, probably from the local newscasts since there had been no mention on the tape of a BfV investigation. He could have fled then. Even if Berg had never received Roy's message, it was possible to run. Berg knew the avenues to the East. Instead, he had chosen to stay. He had found his traitor, and he wanted him dead.

"You knew about Iron Mask," Roy said at last. "You suspected a double."

"Yes, for a long time."

"And we couldn't have warned them, not any of them?"

"No."

Roy got up and searched in his pockets for some cigarettes. "Did you ever think it could be Bibnikov?"

"The thought crossed my mind," Mitko admitted. "I investigated elsewhere first, to make certain neither we nor Sister were infected."

"And this," Roy gestured at the strewn papers. "Does this tell us how often Bibnikov went to Germany, whom he saw, under what circumstances? Does it tell us anything?"

"Bibnikov was in Luxembourg when Berg said he was."

56

Mitko paused and added, "He returned to Moscow last night, the early flight from Frankfurt."

"So we know Iron Mask is Bibnikov. We also know he's been feeding the Germans for God knows how long. Why he's been doing this is another matter. But that can wait. What I want to know is why so suddenly the killings?"

"You are not thinking." Mitko shook his head reprovingly. "Except for the last two, the killings were carried out over a period of time, periods which incidentally match Bibnikov's presence in West Germany. On the surface the executions appeared nothing but credit to Schareck's good work, if one could believe that Schareck had some valid reason for deliberately killing our people instead of arresting them. And that is where the problem comes in, do you see?"

"No."

"We know that Schareck is not a sadist," Mitko explained patiently. "He is a policeman, a detective really. The killings were not his style, and I think it is very important to remember that. Bibnikov, on the other hand, is a man well versed in wet affairs. He was and remains a torturer, and I believe he enjoys the sight of blood. He is also a man with an exceptional sense of security."

Mitko rose and picked up the kettle from the window ledge. There was some old water sloshing around in it, and he emptied that into the sink, refilled the kettle and set it on the two-plate burner in the corner of the office.

"Consider Bibnikov's dilemma," Mitko said. "He is a double agent. Yet he is also head of the department which concerns itself with double agents. So he is safe. He does not have to investigate himself. Nor will Sister move against him if we go to Andropov. Bibnikov has Politburo protection, and Andropov will not touch him without the strongest evidence. Until now Bibnikov has made certain there can never be any such evidence.

"Nor has Bibnikov anything to fear from us. In the past he has discovered two traitors in our apparat. He has climbed to where he is over our backs. He believes we are still whimpering. No, there is no threat to him from inside the services."

Mitko stopped to stroke his thick nicotine-stained mustache. Against the glare of the table lamp he appeared very frail and vulnerable.

"Bibnikov has only one fear, and its source is beyond even his control. He is afraid of the agents we and Sister have placed abroad, the senior men such as Berg. They are Bibnikov's greatest threat. He could destroy them. But in turn, their seniority could finish him first!"

"As Berg tried to do."

"That is correct," Mitko said softly. "Berg had access to material which mentioned Iron Mask. Bibnikov, at the beginning of his German adventure, would have planned for the eventuality of Berg's one day discovering the identity of Iron Mask. Special Investigations would have kept Bibnikov up to date on our deep penetration men, as well as those of Sister. Once he started his killings, it was only a matter of choosing when and how Berg would be eliminated."

"Why the others?"

"I don't know, Alexander," Mitko said softly. "God help me, but I do not know. We have only begun to work on Bibnikov. What motivated him to become a traitor, so very long ago I would think, is beyond my comprehension. Perhaps all the killings were really because of Berg. Assume Bibnikov felt or was warned off that Berg represented a threat, a real threat to his operation. That being the case,

Berg could have passed his suspicions to others in the network."

"Or to us," Roy cut in.

"Yes, or to us," Mitko agreed. "But Bibnikov has an excellent sense of security. He eliminates that which is readily within his grasp, in this case the West German network. He accomplishes two things by doing this: First, he eliminates the possibility of anyone talking about Iron Mask; secondly, he in effect silences us because even if we suspected him of being a double, how much weight would our word carry in light of our failures? It was a brilliant stroke, I admit.

"Bibnikov also knew that even if Berg suspected him, he would not inform us until the time was right. Berg could voice suspicions, feed us whatever slender clues came his way, but he could not break Iron Mask until he was absolutely certain and could document his identity. Berg was a deep penetration man. If he acted too soon and broke his cover and was wrong, then more than ten years of preparation would have been wasted."

"So Berg waited, and in the end he waited too long."

"He took that risk," Mitko said. "And I believe that had it not been for circumstance, Bibnikov's moving very, very quickly, the chance would have paid off. Bibnikov must have known BfV was investigating the leaks into operations Alpha, Delta and Omega and was in fact on Berg's tail. If this was the case, what did Berg have to lose by doubling his efforts to secure the identity of Iron Mask? Even if Berg's information could not destroy Bibnikov, there could well be enough to discredit him. And Berg had nothing to lose if he was about to be blown anyway. This is how Bibnikov must have been thinking.

"So Bibnikov, to ensure his security, began the killings.

He went after the minor agents first, allowing enough time to pass between murders to have it appear the BfV was doing a very efficient job of rolling up our network. He gambled on our leaving Berg in Germany since he was the only one who could possibly tell us who was engineering the massacre. At the appropriate time Bibnikov, always moving closer to his goal, killed Berg as well. I think the incident at the Wall forced his hand. Bibnikov had to go after Berg immediately after Schiffer was dead, and Bibnikov probably believes that whatever Berg knew about Iron Mask died with him."

The kettle whistled faintly. This time Roy got up. He turned off the gas and brought the kettle over to Mitko, who was holding out a stained brown and white teapot.

"The lemon is between the windows. They still haven't come with that refrigerator."

Roy opened the inside of the double windows and took out a half lemon, shriveled from the cold. Outside, on Quai Maurice Thorez, he could see lamps trailing a reflection off the ice-laden Moskva. There was the faint crackle of frozen branches bent by the wind, pushed to and fro throughout the night. The odor of stale putty mixed with lemon came into his nostrils, and he closed the window abruptly.

"That is not enough," Roy said at last, watching the tea swirl in his glass. "The tape is not enough proof. We believe Berg, but who else would—without corroboration, hard evidence? Even the word of his wife, assuming she could be found, will not be enough." He paused. "I wish Berg had told us more about motive, why Bibnikov would betray and how long he's been at it. . . ."

"We can speculate if you like," Mitko said. "But it won't do us any good. A traitor is a very complex animal, driven

60

by extremely powerful hates and loves. I doubt if even Bibnikov could understand, much less explain, the true depth of his feelings. And we could not presume to have any idea of his commitment to our destruction and whatever it is that feeds it. But now, tell me, how do you feel, now that you know?"

Roy looked at him, helpless, frustrated.

"I don't know." He laughed. "Helpless, I suppose. Bibnikov is big, too big to go after. Christ knows how we'd get to him. He's after us now. He'll be on his guard. Still, a long-range shot might do it. . . ."

"Are you tired?"

"I suppose I need some sleep."

"Are you defeated?"

Roy looked up, trying to fathom what the old man was driving at.

"My network is finished. Five, probably six people are dead. I don't know if that's what you mean by defeat. It comes very close."

"I could arrange for you to take a rest, to get away from all this." Mitko gestured at the papers.

"I don't want a rest."

"But do you need one?"

"No!"

"You think you murdered Berg, don't you?" Mitko said suddenly. "You think that by failing to bring him home, *you* might as well have put that bullet into his throat."

Roy was very tired now. Exhaustion swept over him as he shifted in the chair. He was failing to make any sense of what Mitko was saying.

"I let Berg stay. It was my decision. They were my people, my network."

"Your people, your network," Mitko echoed softly.

"Agents are sources of information, hard intelligence, rumors, hints, possibilities, and so they are not just people! You acted correctly by not bringing Berg in!"

Mitko's eyes were glittering, the head thrown back haughtily. Suddenly Roy understood how Mitko had survived. It was his spirit which rose again and again when everything else, every belief, hope and last ounce of strength, had been expended. He demanded to survive, using all the discipline and courage he could command. He was an old man, but he would never talk of defeat.

"What is it you want now?" Mitko demanded.

"Bibnikov's head."

"As much as he wants yours?"

"More. Bibnikov has no revenge in the back of his mind. I do. I owe something to my murdered people!"

Mitko squeezed his piece of lemon too tightly, and the juice spurted across the papers, a seed spinning to the floor.

"It is incongruous to be fighting one's own brother," he said slowly, "yet that is the way of the world."

"You want Bibnikov as well," Roy almost shouted. "You must!"

"Oh, yes, I want him," Mitko said patiently. "But we must never strike out of revenge. It distorts the image of our work. We might land one blow or two, but that is never enough. And we are very close to the edge now. We cannot afford to fail. We cannot because we will be dealing against our own people."

Roy fished out another cigarette and lit it. "If you want Bibnikov, I'm game," he said slowly, exhaling through his nostrils.

"There are a number of people who can help us," Mitko said. "Koldakov, the psychiatrist, is one. I would like you to

62

speak with him. Possibly Golosov of Kremlin security as well. They know what I have in mind. I am flying to the invisible city tomorrow and will return at the end of the month. I hope that gives you the time you need."

The invisible city, Leninsk. Its name did not appear on any map, and outside the military and security ranks its existence was only rumored. Leninsk was the secret site of the country's space program, and it also served as the command center for the eastern bomber fleet and the missile systems.

"To work what happened to Berg and the network out of your system, I want you purified, clean. I don't want you to go into this out of revenge."

Roy reached for his coat.

"One more point," Mitko said. "You are now considered a failure. You have lost an entire network and a very important one at that. People will expect you to bear certain consequences. There is no need to contradict their assumptions."

# CHAPTER FOUR

## *Pawn Sacrifice*

"'WE WANT ROY OUT," Bibnikov stated.

He shifted slowly in Mitko's direction, the chair creaking under his weight. The ugly thyroid eyes were watery and pale.

"We feel you were wrong in giving Roy the West German sector," he continued. "It is true certain results were obtained from his operations. We do not discount these. In fact, it is only because of these that Committee One is willing to be lenient. But while the investigation into the destruction of the network is under way, my department wishes that Roy be removed entirely from active operations."

The meeting fell on a frigid December day, the first of the month. Mitko had been summoned from the invisible city the evening before, a day before his scheduled return. He had expected something like this, a decision made in

64

his absence. To see Andropov's car waiting for him at the airport did not surprise him either. The driver politely refused to take the general to his offices first. He would be arriving late as it was.

Committee One was a special board which overlooked the security performances of both apparats, KGB and GRU. The chairman, Yuri Andropov, had brought with him the chiefs of Departments Three, Four and Five, responsible between them for all KGB operations in Western Europe. Bibnikov came alone but carried a thick dossier bearing Roy's name across the front. He had taken charge of the meeting, obviously with Andropov's consent.

Bibnikov lit another cigarette. He was a chain-smoker, and his fingers were always damp from yellow tobacco juice.

"Committee One," Bibnikov continued ponderously, "is prepared to separate Roy's incompetence from the general activities of the apparat whose results over the last years have been very good. I see no reason for an inquiry by Special Investigations into the GRU, and I would prefer to recommend to the Politburo that the GRU be allowed to continue its work unimpeded."

So, Mitko thought, they *have* been thinking of appointing an overseer!

"However, this recommendation is contingent on Roy's transfer to a far less sensitive post."

Bibnikov sat up in his chair, his hard belly pushing against the side of the table. He was looking directly at Mitko, his mouth working as though he were chewing on straw. There was silence in the room. The GRU librarian, Tamara Maslova, who doubled as stenographer of the committee, was watching Mitko closely.

"I appreciate your position and the Politburo's concern," Mitko said at last. "I assume the KGB shares the feeling of Special Investigations."

"It does," Andropov said tonelessly.

Mitko curled his lip and carried on.

"That Captain Roy's network has met with this is regrettable, not only because we have lost a primary source of high-grade intelligence, but also because Captain Roy is an excellent security officer. I would not employ the measures you suggest." Mitko did not address Bibnikov by rank. He never did. "I would let him finish the investigation the GRU has already begun."

"Unfortunately, Nikolai Stepanovich, we cannot afford such luxurious, even noble, sentiments," Bibnikov said with finality. "To coordinate our investigations, Departments Three, Four and Five of the First Directorate will pass you information which is extremely sensitive. Only the most trusted officers will be permitted to see it. I believe you understand that the scope of the inquiry has now exceeded the traditional apparat borders. As you yourself mentioned, the West German network was important to us all. Its destruction may be a signal for a general offensive by Western security. Since we are all concerned, we cannot take even the slightest chances, can we?"

"Are you saying that Captain Roy is under suspicion of treason?" Mitko asked softly.

"Not at all," Bibnikov smiled. "I am saying he has failed in his duties. As a soldier he must expect to be disciplined. Part of that discipline entails removing him from his present posting in which he is privy to classified documentation. That is all."

"That is the position of the KGB as well," Andropov said, even before Mitko had had time to put the question to him. Andropov, like the stenographer, was watching Mitko's every move.

Mitko waited a moment, then turned to the girl.

"Would you be so kind as to include this in the formal transcript? As head of military intelligence I shall act on the advice of Committee One and discipline Captain Roy for dereliction of duty. This discipline shall consist of demoting him, not in rank and equivalent privileges, but only in duties attached to intelligence operations. As of this moment, Captain Roy's security rating is diminished to D, the lowest in the apparat. He will be assigned to activities which require no higher clearance. Since Captain Roy has been involved in active operations from the start of his career, it is conceivable he will ask to be relieved of these lesser duties and transferred to an active army unit. Such a request will be granted, provided his future work requires no higher security clearance.

"Upon execution of such an action I will request from Committee One the following: complete reports from all intelligence cells in West Germany, freedom to continue the strictly GRU inquiry which has already begun, finally, the complete support of Committee One for such an independent inquiry."

Mitko addressed Bibnikov: "I trust that is fair."

"I applaud the clarity of your proposal," Bibnikov said dryly. "I have no objections to these conditions."

"Committee One is in accord with your requests," Andropov said. "Other details can be worked out at a later date."

He gave Mitko a curious look, surprised that Mitko had dropped Roy so quickly, without much of a fight. Perhaps he had neither expected nor found any other alternative. Or else age had finally caught up with the old man and he was too tired to fight. Andropov was surprised to find himself disappointed in Mitko; but he had bowed out, and there was nothing more to be said.

Mitko was the last to leave when the conference was over. As he headed for the door, he heard the stenographer call out his name.

"Why did you do that?" Tamara whispered. "Why did you let them destroy your man?"

His first reaction was to try to justify himself in front of her. She was so young, and the words had come from her heart. Instead, he turned on her.

"Because there was no other way," he said cruelly. "Do not meddle in things which do not concern you!"

Word of Mitko's capitulation filtered down to Quai Maurice Thorez by the end of the afternoon; but Roy wasn't there, and he did not hear of it until the next day.

He arrived at the office early, as was his habit, and found a two-paragraph letter on his desk. He read it through once, crumpled it and threw it away. He was grateful there was no one about to witness his humiliation. Quickly he went through his drawers, gathered personal items from his desk, locked up the files and left. He was going to see Ivatushin.

"Did you know of this?"

Roy arrived at the flat as Ivatushin was in the proces of shaving. Tea had already been made, and Ivatushin, with cream over half his face, brought the pot into the living room.

"You look terrible," Ivatushin grunted. "Give me a few minutes, will you?"

The living room was larger than the one in Roy's flat. That was because Ivatushin claimed his mother was living with him, a barefaced lie since his mother left Odessa to visit Moscow only twice, perhaps three times a year.

Roy brought his cup over to a small table by the window

and made room for it among Ivatushin's plant collection. There was a spider, a couple of avocadoes in wooden crates that had once held oranges, an azalea and some potted vines Roy couldn't identify. He wondered how the leaves managed to survive Ivatushin's cigars.

When Ivatushin returned, he was dressed in full uniform, the tunic marred by a small jam stain.

"What do you mean you've been sacked?" Ivatushin asked him.

He sat down beside Roy, picked up a lump of sugar and crunched on it.

"There was a letter on my desk this morning," Roy said. "The usual runaround—policy changes, security reviews, not a word about the German fiasco, not a word. Then the kiss-off."

"Why don't you take your coat off?" Ivatushin suggested. "You're starting to sweat."

"The old man's signature was there, right above the transfer sheets to a new job," Roy finished. His voice was low and soft, as though he could not believe what had happened. "A new job. A bloody clerk's job."

"Go slow," Ivatushin commanded. "And take your coat off, for heaven's sake. Did you bring the letter with you?"

"Threw it away as soon as I read it. Didn't seem any point to keeping it."

"So you left, just like that?"

"What the hell did you expect me to do?" Roy flared. "Stay around and wring my hands?'

"There was a meeting of Committee One yesterday," Ivatushin said slowly. "But I was certain the old man would stand up to them, whatever they wanted—which was probably your head. I was certain of it!"

"Well, think again, chum." Roy laughed. "One lamb—

69

eviscerated, skewered and ready to be tossed on the coals. Mitko was quick about it, too."

"Where are they transferring you?"

"China Section. But not active, oh, no! Analysis—can you believe it? I'm going to sit and pore over bloody books!"

Abruptly Roy stood up and crossed over to the glass cabinet. He pulled out a bottle of vodka and jerked out the stopper.

"I really need this today, really do."

"You haven't spoken with Mitko? The transfer could be temporary, you know, until tempers cool."

"No." Roy held the bottle with both hands, his thumbs rubbing the neck nervously. "Mitko's dropped me, very clear. I have no intention of crawling back to him."

"What?"

"That's right. What the hell is there left to say? West Germany blew up in my face. The network all dead. That's it. The whole world lives by results, that's what he told me. And we have had 'negative results.' I should have known then, Christ! The way he was going on, it was so obvious he was setting me up. No chance for an investigation, no reports from Sister, just a quick clean exit for Captain Roy and let's pray the Politburo is satisfied with his head."

Roy pushed the bottle away and dropped his head between his hands.

"I want you to stay here," Ivatushin murmured. "Stay until I've had a chance to look around. I can't believe this is all there is to it. I knew about the Committee One meeting, but this. . . . Will you stay?" he repeated.

"Why not?" Roy smiled crookedly. "I deserve a holiday."

* * *

By eleven o'clock Ivatushin had confirmed what Roy had told him. Center was alive with rumors and stories of the West German debacle.

In the canteen the physical security officers congratulated one another that they had only headquarters to protect, and the colonel in charge suggested that this might be the time to increase vigilance. He ordered a double check of all passes for the building.

At the other end of the cafeteria Tamara Maslova was sitting alone. She had been the center of attention all that morning as the girls in the typing pool and library research gathered around, insisting Tamara tell them *everything* that had gone on in Committee One. Tamara recounted her story simply, without exaggeration, and of course, her listeners were not satisfied. They demanded a tale of scandal from her in which men threatened and cursed one another. Hadn't Roy been present? Why hadn't he entered the meeting halfway through and presented secret evidence of his innocence? Wasn't there even a *hint* of blows?

These girls lived and worked in the antechambers of a mystery world. They could enter the doors closed to them only through their imaginations, and they nourished their daydreams in a desperate attempt to keep the shabby reality of their duties at bay. They were often reminded by their superiors of the importance of their work, but if they could not from time to time touch those who held the keys to the mysteries, enter into their terrible secret lives, this duty had as much meaning as a street sweeper's job.

So they badgered and cajoled her and in the end gave up on Tamara, ridiculing her and accusing her of holding something back. She, who could have satisfied them at this

71

moment, instead gave them nothing. The girls retreated into their cabals and wove a heroic story from the threads of their own needs.

Tamara sat alone, half ashamed of having failed them. She never seemed to be able to give enough, and she was relieved when the time came for her to return to the safe confines of the library, where she was invulnerable. But all the while, she too thought of Captain Alexander Roy.

Ivatushin encountered the same atmosphere of curiosity and anticipation in his bomber command group.

"Roy? Forget him, Oleg," Ivatushin's senior advised him. "He's death to the touch now. Can't say I blame Mitko, though. The network rolled up and so on. Roy should have played his cards a little more wisely. As it is, he hogged the show in Bonn and now has a flop on his hands—with nowhere to spread the blame."

Ivatushin's request to see Mitko was turned down flat. The general was seeing no one today. He wasn't even taking appointments. Ivatushin went down to Roy's office on the second floor and found Baidakov from the French networks rummaging through the desk drawers. He was visibly upset.

"You don't understand what's happened," Baidakov moaned. "The whole department has gone crazy. I was checking my own files—there's a security alert on all sections, you know—when the old man called down and told me to cart Roy's files up. I've sent him a dozen boxes already, but he says there's stuff missing. Have you seen Roy today? Something is missing. I can feel it myself. The stupid bastard was probably taking classified material home with him."

Baidakov continued his search in the filing cabinets,

dumping out reams of multicolored folders onto the floor. He turned to Ivatushin.

"Will you help me?" he asked plaintively. "Together we can get this over with quickly. I'll tell you what to look for. And with you here, I have a witness. . . ."

"Go fuck yourself!" Ivatushin said coldly and walked out.

Ivatushin returned to his bureau on the fifth floor and called home. There was no answer. Roy had either left or—Ivatushin remembered the vodka—drunk himself into oblivion. For good measure he called Roy's flat. There was no answer there either.

He arrived at Center late in the afternoon, after three. He was in civilian dress, the tie hanging limply to one side, the collar and the jacket both unbuttoned. Security at the door didn't recognize him until he held out his pass.

"Registry would like to see you, Captain." The guard averted his face from the vodka fumes. "At once," he added.

Roy grunted and made for the staircase leading down into the three lower levels. He almost tripped on a discarded cigarette pack and cursed. By the time he reached Registry he felt dizzy and nauseated. He turned off into the toilets and closeted himself in a cubicle. Sticking two fingers down his throat, he forced himself to vomit.

"Captain Roy reporting as requested!"

The fat woman behind the counter stared up at him as though he were one of the dead. His breath was vile now, sickness mixed with alcohol.

"Your security pass!" she demanded.

He fumbled through several pockets before producing it, and she snatched the card away as though he might damage it.

"Wait here."

Roy leaned against the counter and watched the clock at the end of the room, staring at the sweep of the second hand. The fluorescent lights burned into his eyes. He brought his head down and belched.

The fat woman returned after what seemed an eternity, but she did not come all the way up to the counter.

"You will be issued a new pass next week, at your new posting."

"Security rating?" Roy croaked and cleared his throat.

The woman turned her back.

"I asked you for the security rating!"

The typewriters in the room ceased their clatter, and ten pairs of eyes shot up at him in defense of the fat woman. She swung around at him, livid.

"D! And get out—the armorer wants to see you!"

"Thank you, madame!" Roy raised his hand stiffly in a mock salute and slammed the door behind him.

The armorer's quarters were at the very bottom of the building, next door to the firing range. Roy negotiated four more sets of stairs, his head reeling from the stink of cordite.

The armorer was Andrushin, a thin beanpole of a Ukrainian with spectacles and very large soft hands. Roy wondered how a man who handled so much killing machinery could have hands like that, as tender as a child's bottom.

"I'll have to have your guns now," Andrushin said. He was wearing denim overalls smudged with oil and grease around the waistline. Beyond the doors Roy could hear faint popping noises.

"I have only one issue."

74

"You have the Czech Stag and the Japanese Hanyatti, which I gave you without authorization," Andrushin corrected him.

"I didn't bring it," Roy mumbled.

"I will expect both of them tomorrow."

"I have only the one gun," Roy insisted stubbornly. "That's all I signed for."

Andrushin gazed at him through the thick lenses. He liked Roy because Roy cared about the guns he handled. He was also very good with them, much better than most. Andrushin felt a twinge of pity for the man swaying before him.

"You can have the Stag. I'll turn it in on Monday."

"Alexander, please. . . ."

"Thanks, Andrushin, thanks very much. Am I still permitted to practice?"

"Per diem pass."

"Weapons?"

"Whatever we have unless I hear otherwise."

Roy grinned lopsidedly. "You're a good man, Andrushin. I won't forget that."

"I still want the Hanyatti."

But Roy was gone, and the thick cork-lined door hissed to a close behind him.

He left through the back way, not wanting to meet anyone he knew. He was frightened, and like a tracked animal, he was raging at creatures smaller than himself but was unequal to confronting his equals. He desperately wanted a drink.

Roy walked up Herzen Street to the Nationale Hotel. The wind had picked up, cold and slashing, and he had forgotten to wear his coat. Outside the Tchaikovsky Conservatoire he stopped to count how much money he had left. As he was counting, the clocks struck five. Anna would be finishing her classes at the university. He would take a cab and go pick her up. What he really needed was a woman and some good food.

She was very beautiful, tall, with a long, purposeful stride. Her hair, unfettered by a hat, fell around her cheeks and onto the shoulders. He watched her until she passed Lenin's statue. Then he called her name and smiled as her gray eyes darted among the knots of students, looking for whoever had called out to her. Then she saw him, and a wide smile broke on her lips. She waved, and he waved back.

But suddenly Roy wished he hadn't come. Only for him had things changed. The rest of the world moved on at its own pace. He wanted desperately for someone else to understand how he felt, and he was afraid Anna would disappoint him in that. But it was too late.

"What are *you* doing here?" she asked. Her arm circled through his, and she pressed against him.

"Dinner," Roy mumbled. "Where do you want dinner?"

"But I can't," she protested. "You know I have music lessons tonight."

As a general's daughter Anna's contribution to the proletarian cause consisted of giving piano lessons at a Moscow orphanage.

"Listen, it's important," Roy said. "You can miss it for once. I've got a taxi waiting."

"Alex, please." Her gloved hand came to his cheek, and her fingers were pressing against his face. "What's the matter? You've been out on a binge?" She was standing very close to him now. "You have, haven't you?"

"Let it go, will you?" he said viciously.

76

"The children will be waiting. Can't we do it later?"

"For the love of God, can't you change it this one time?" he shouted at her. "Is it every day that I ask you to break your precious schedule?"

"There is no need to yell, Alex." She let him go. "I don't have to be home until six thirty. Let's go somewhere. You're going to catch cold standing there like that."

They said nothing to each other in the taxi, as though acknowledging that words would be futile. Anna should have known better than to argue with him. This one time she might have held back until he explained what it was that had driven him to that state. But Anna was a headstrong woman, proud and impatient. She jealously guarded the routine she had carved out for herself. She was also confused by his drunkenness. Roy had never been without his calm and reserve, and she did not believe he needed the comfort other men did. She could not recognize the signs of that need in him.

They walked into the bar of the Metropole, and the steward gave them a table at the back, casting a long glance at Roy's shabby dress. Roy glanced up at the clock and figured that if Anna were leaving, she would have to go in twenty minutes. That would be enough.

"Will you stay?" he demanded.

"What's happened to you, Alex?"

"If you're staying, I'll buy you a drink."

"Nothing for me, thank you."

He signaled the waiter and gave his order of vodka.

"I got the boot today, that's what," Roy said, sticking a cigarette between his teeth. "Nice, eh?"

"You were fired?" The men at the next table glanced in her direction. Surprise had made her voice too loud.

"You don't have to tell the whole bloody world," he

77

snapped. "That's right, though. The old man gave me my walking papers, without so much as a thank-you."

"But why?"

"They rolled up my network, blew my entire German organization."

"I don't understand."

"They killed my men, the agents I was running in West Germany! They got to the best one two, three days ago, can't remember. So the old man was hauled up before Committee One, and Bibnikov, the hatchet boy, demanded someone's head. Mitko gave him mine. Very simple."

"Was it your fault? I mean, did you make a mistake?"

In the past he had spoken only vaguely of his work, and she had known better than to ask questions. Now she did not understand what he was trying to tell her.

The waiter arrived with the vodka and stood waiting to be paid. Roy reached for the ice-cold carafe and poured half of the contents into a small tumbler. He paid the waiter then and added a niggardly tip.

"Cheers! He who does not work neither shall he eat. Will you stay for dinner anyway?"

"What will you do now?" Anna asked him.

"Oh, they've given me a desk job. Frittering about with China stuff. Very dull, very very dull!"

"At least there is that," Anna said carefully. "Perhaps it's not as bad as you think. After all, you haven't been demoted, have you?"

"It's as bad as that! I'm not a bloody clerk."

"Alex, you've lost your job, but they have given you another. Is that so bad? No, let me finish. Perhaps it is, but you haven't explained how. You're sitting here feeling sorry for yourself and insulting the whole world. What has come over you?"

78

"Is it so bad to ask for a little compassion?' he demand-ed. "A little caring? Small lot I've gotten from you these past weeks!"

She knew he was right. For the last month most of her time had been taken up in preparation for the Conser-vatoire competitions. But although one part of Anna whis-pered that she should go to him, another bridled under his attack. She found herself disgusted by the alcoholic slur to his words. Finally, he answered for her.

"All right—get out of here!" he whispered. "Run back to your precious kiddies!"

He slumped back in the chair, staring mindlessly at the burning cigarette. She wavered again, then suddenly de-cided he would not treat her like this.

"I'll call you tonight," she said and rose. Roy didn't both-er looking up, but the men at the other table were staring at her. The fatter of the two ogled her shamelessly.

"I'll call," she repeated tightly and walked out.

Roy consumed another three carafes of vodka, but the bartender, smelling a mark, charged him for four. Not to be left out, the waiter snatched the last five-ruble note on the table while Roy was in the washroom. He knew the money would not be missed.

Roy staggered from the Metropole and managed to flag a cab immediately. When the driver insisted on seeing pay-ment beforehand, Roy swore at him and handed over a couple more notes. Once the cab got under way he fell asleep.

The fare came to two rubles. The driver half carried, half dragged his passenger into the foyer of the apartment building and left him tottering on the stairs. He walked away pocketing a handsome tip.

It took Roy ten minutes to climb up to his apartment. He swung back the door and went through the living room directly to the toilet. He swayed but managed. After knocking the telephone off the hook, Roy made it into the bedroom and collapsed on the mattress, not bothering to undress. He remembered nothing after that.

She found him in the unmade bed, curled up like a small child, his shoes soiling the sheets. His face was a mass of sweat, the odor blending in with the stench of vodka. One pillow had been flung across the floor as though he had swung at it in his sleep. For the first time she heard him snore.

Anna had tried to call several times, once in the course of her lessons, when there had been no answer, then again later on, and the line had been busy. Finally, she had decided to come down. Now she stood at the doorway of the bedroom, looking at him thoughtfully, almost critically. She had intended to sleep with him tonight and try to wean him from his anger. Except for the last month, they usually stayed together two or three nights a week. When she wasn't there, the bed went unmade and the dishes piled up until his better sense of order took over. The flat was dusty now, and the kitchen stank of putrid garbage. In the meantime, her lover snored in an alcoholic daze.

She looked at him once more and walked to the door. She would speak with him tomorrow or Sunday, when he had got whatever it was out of his system. She didn't think she could help him now. Her father had suggested that she stop seeing Roy for a while, that there had been some trouble for him at work. She closed the door softly and turned the key, wondering what it was that had really happened to him.

# CHAPTER FIVE

## *China Section*

He SPENT THE WEEKEND ALONE, taking his meals out, not bothering to answer the telephone or the door. After the debauch on Friday night he retreated into his territory to nurse himself on hot soup and tea and prepare for the next week. He had been tempted to call Anna but didn't. There seemed no point to it.

Instead he went for long walks along the Moskva, loitered at the Tretykov Gallery and tried some of the newer restaurants that had opened up along the Arbat. By Sunday evening a veneer of calm had settled over his anger and restlessness.

On Monday he rose early, showered, brushed his uniform and set out.

China Section was not housed at Quai Maurice Thorez but on Arbatskaya Ploshchad on the opposite side of the Kremlin from the Lubyanka. It was a dreary two-floor affair, its corridors were constantly overheated, and there was no ventilation in the windowless cubicles. The walls were painted an ugly lime green so hideous one only wondered what malice was responsible for the choice.

But China Section, at least the top echelons, was becoming an increasingly important component of Center's operations. It was the clearinghouse for all intelligence originating in the East. The section also prepared for the General Staff game plans on preemptive attacks on the People's Republic. In conjunction with forward operations, the section had drawn up a precise timetable, supplemented by details on manpower and weapons systems, for a possible Soviet offensive against China early in 1969. The plan had been demanded by Marshal Turchevsky. The marshal's chief evaluator and critic of the plan was GRU chief Mitko, who had code named the proposed operation Blueprint.

The trouble started at the door. Security asked for his pass, but Roy had not been issued a new one. Nor was Roy's name on the day sheet, so technically he had no business being at Arbatskaya Ploshchad. Security telephoned upstairs, but it was a full half hour before the department head appeared.

Yarmolai Lazarovich Panev, a Jew, was the boyar of China Section. A thin, tall man with a perpetually pained expression, he walked with his legs close together as though he had done it in his pants. His voice was a persistent whine, the words accentuated by rapid, slicing gestures. Yarmolai Lazarovich was a very nervous man.

He looked at Roy distastefully. Roy stared back, and the two loathed each other on sight. Doubtlessly Panev had been told he would be receiving a leper he couldn't refuse to take on.

"Good morning," Panev said. He consulted his watch and pronounced Roy fifty-five minutes late. He was certain Roy would not repeat such a performance. Roy said nothing. Panev gave him another moment, then turned and led the way up to the fourth floor, down the lime green corridor lit by overhead bulbs and into a small cubicle at the rear.

"This is your bureau," Panev announced. "Your primary concern is the industrial section of the People's Republic economy. From your record I gather you have no experience in this particular field"—Panev stressed the word "particular"—"but that you have some knowledge of heavy industry."

At Frunze Roy had specialized in naval warfare. He could not make the connection between that and heavy industry.

"Our special interests," Panev continued, "are as follows: the republic's ability to construct hydro-power dams, control floods and supply necessary irrigation; the industrial sectors which rely most heavily on water or steam power; the exploitation of this power for atomic purposes. The material passed to you will give you an accurate idea of the scope of your work.

"The intelligence you will use"—the emphasis, this time, on "you"—"will be declassified. Periodicals, journals, newspapers and the like will have been translated from the original. These will be supplemented by satellite and overhead reconnaissance reports.

"Section units meet twice a week, Tuesdays and Thursdays, to discuss progress in various sectors. I require a written report from each unit at that time. Any unusual developments within your area will be brought to my attention immediately. Is that clear?"

Roy pursed his lips and frowned. "Were you ever at Frunze?" he asked.

Panev gave him a frigid look. "*Avant le déluge*," he said and left.

Roy muttered an oath under his breath. So Panev was one of those Jewish instructors who had been hustled out of the academy in the "restructure" that had taken place during the fifties. Roy hated the thought of working for an academic. They had no imagination, and those with chips on their shoulders, like Panev, were sticklers for rules and regs.

By Thursday Roy realized he hated not only Panev, but the job as well. Panev checked on him every day. At the Tuesday meeting he had had nothing to say, although Panev obviously expected him to file a report after only a day's work. He didn't present anything on Thursday either, and the thirteen other analysts clucked their disapproval. Roy's failure to contribute meant that Panev scrutinized the other presentations more carefully.

The eight or nine hours of the day became endless. The procedure of initialing a chit for every periodical he received from the library drove him mad. On Wednesday he had signed himself "Beethoven," and the librarian, Tamara Maslova, promptly called him up to ask who Beethoven was and what kind of security clearance he had been issued. He was rude to her, yelling about the stupid bureaucracy she was running up there, and ended up disconnecting the line when she tried to talk to him reasonably.

The others who worked in Analysis were all young. Most of them had done their military service on the Chinese border, manning the electronic listening posts or sifting through information brought in by the patrols. Roy wondered what had made them give up active operations for a desk job. Perhaps it was a different breed of soldier coming up, the bureaucrat instead of the fighter.

He tried to strike up a conversation with one of them but was rebuffed. That afternoon he overheard a pimply analyst describe how the "new man" had been broken in active duty and that his posting in the section was only a stopgap before he was cashiered altogether. After that Roy avoided them all.

His new security pass arrived at the end of the week. It was good for only three months, with no space for renewal stamps. What the analyst had said was true. He was on the way out.

Roy worked late Friday night. He decided to call in sick the first of the week and stayed to get ahead on reports that would fall due. Shortly before nine o'clock he went up to the library on the sixth floor.

Behind the wire mesh which surrounded her desk like a cage Tamara Maslova had fallen asleep in her chair. She was slumped forward, her head cradled in her arms. Roy came over and quietly opened the small window grille. He hesitated a moment, looking at the sleeping girl. His hand came down on her hair, and he pressed gently until she awoke.

"What is it? What—" She reared back instinctively, her eyes growing large with fear.

"It's Beethoven," he said.

"Beethoven. . . ."

She stood up and gazed at him, blinking rapidly to focus her vision.

"We quarreled over the telephone."

She was wide awake now. "Yes . . . yes, I remember. Why were you so rude?"

"It goes with the job. A bad day. They're all bad days."

Unconsciously Tamara ran a hand over her hair, wondering if she looked all right.

"I'm sorry," Roy said, "for the argument and waking you up now. Why don't you just go home?"

"The library doesn't close until midnight," Tamara said. "I couldn't leave."

"Who would be the wiser?" He shrugged. "Surely I'm the only idiot who comes creeping around at this time of night."

"Actually you are." She laughed. "So if for no one else, I must be here for you, mustn't I?"

She caught herself immediately, realizing the innuendo in her words. Roy did not let it pass.

"Yes, you must be here when I come." He reached across and handed her a slip of paper. "I need these references."

Tamara almost snatched the paper from his fingers and glanced at it. "Everything you want is here. It will take only a minute."

Tamara walked off quickly, without bothering to close the grille. Roy reached through the grille window and picked up her keys. The files he had requested were at the other end of the floor, on the top shelves. It would take her at least two minutes to return with them. Quickly he selected three keys and took out a mold. He pressed the keys carefully into the wax, wiped them and returned the whole ring to her desk. One of the three keys he had copied would open the cabinet marked "Sensitive."

Tamara came back and handed him four worn files which he duly signed for. Slowly Roy walked over to the row of benches and desk tops that served as desks and chairs and sat down. For a moment he did nothing more than hold his head in his hands and gently massage his temples. Then he looked around, swiftly.

Tamara had been watching him, and he had caught her. He held her eyes with his own and, despite her embarrassment, would not let her go. Finally, he smiled, to reassure her, opened his files and turned to read.

One of the few personal effects his father had left behind was an appointment calendar. The covers were bound in good leather that was wrinkled from age and very soft. Roy had brought the calendar with him from his old office.

There was an entry in it for that weekend, a Saturday afternoon party at the German embassy. Members of the Soviet scientific community were invited, and Roy, who spoke German and could conduct himself among diplomats without offending, had been slated to attend as part of the GRU surveillance team. Since he also controlled the German network, Roy could handle a potential defector more deftly than anyone else.

Roy decided to go, even though a replacement would have been assigned for him. There would be an inevitable fuss when Internal learned he was still stepping out socially. But he owed nothing to anyone. Center had put his head on the block and slammed down the lever. He was on his own now.

The German embassy was a four-story house built of new stone, the kind that absorbed rain and dutifully turned gray as a result, a hundred years before its time. There was a tall hedge planted around the building to prevent cameras from peeking into the ground floors. Beyond the shrubbery stood a black iron-spiked fence, broken at the path to the front doors and garage entrance.

Roy had the taxi deliver him directly to the gates. He noticed a couple of men across the street quietly talking by the side of a blue Volga and dismissed them as KGB on routine embassy surveillance. He did not make the connection between one of the men and the taxi driver who had taken him home the night before.

A very large majordomo greeted him at the door and looked down inquiringly. Roy passed him the embossed invitation and was permitted as far as the antechamber. The majordomo did not ask for Roy's coat.

From what he could hear Roy thought the party was moving along quite well. Contrary to their reputation, the Germans usually had the gayest affairs. They seemed to have recovered nicely from Stalingrad and the Wall.

The majordomo returned with the ambassador's personal secretary, a thin young man, immaculately tailored, with sandy hair and sharp blue eyes. His name was Hans Boysen and he knew Roy well from other occasions.

"It was good of you to come, Captain," he said formally. He turned to the majordomo and dismissed him.

"May I take off my coat?"

"Yes, of course," the secretary said hastily. "But I should like a word with you before we go in."

Roy shrugged and sneered at the German. "It has come down, hasn't it, Hans? The word is I'm untouchable."

The secretary did not shy away from Roy's glare. "It has, regrettably."

He beckoned for Roy to follow him down the hall into a small private sitting room. Passing the central parlor, Roy caught a glimpse of two cultural "attachés," liaison officers working for the Third Department. They made a point of looking into the hallway to register the new arrival.

Hans Boysen closed the door and motioned Roy to sit. "May I get you a drink?"

"Thanks."

"Scotch or vodka?"

"Scotch."

Hans poured out a small tumbler's worth of whiskey and passed it to Roy. He took nothing for himself and remained standing.

"We have been given to understand you are no longer with your department."

"Who said so?"

"Major Kominev."

"Ah, yes. I know him. He's first-rate pig. Be careful of him, Boysen."

Roy took a long reflective sip of whiskey.

"Major Kominev believes some time is needed for you to . . . adjust to your new circumstances," Boysen said carefully. "He has therefore suggested that during this transitional period you not be included at our gatherings, the issued invitations notwithstanding."

"He was always blunt, that man."

Roy swallowed the rest of the whiskey and reached for the decanter.

"So I get kicked downstairs and suddenly I'm a pariah. A security risk. That's what Kominev really told you, wasn't it? Stay away from Roy, or else surveillance on your people will triple and life will become very hard. Hard because I'm a beaten man and losers often get strange ideas into their heads. Such as defection, right?"

"Times will change," Boysen said. "In a little while—"

"But until it changes, I'm out, no matter how much you love me!"

"I must ask you to observe some protocol," the secretary said stiffly. "I have been more than honest with you. There is nothing that can be done. I'm sorry, but I have recommended to the ambassador that we do as Kominev suggested."

Roy reached for his glass and brought it to his lips. For a moment it appeared he would crush the tumbler in his grip, but then he very deliberately drank the remainder of the whiskey.

"Thanks for the liquor," he said, choking back a cough. He raised his voice for the benefit of those beyond the door. "And you tell Kominev that he doesn't have to worry. I'll get his balls first before I have to run to the Hun!"

Roy took out the invitation, scribbled a few words on the back and handed it to the diplomat. Then he left.

He went up Bolshaya Gruzinskaya Street in search of a cab but had to walk three blocks before spotting a rank. He gave the driver the address of a pool hall on Gorky Street and upon arrival proceeded to get very drunk on the hundred rubles he was carrying. After thirty were gone, the first shark drifted in, judging that Roy was far enough gone.

"Would you be interested in a little game of *zhelezkha*, friend?"

It was the standard gambling game of Moscow hustlers, using the serial numbers on ruble notes. The highest digit in a given column won.

Roy shook his head and sipped the vodka. Another hustler came up.

"Perhaps the gentleman is more amused by cards," he said sarcastically. "All kinds of games here, even baccarat played to international rules."

"It must have been a bad day on the market," Roy said, without bothering to turn around. "Even scumbags like you can usually take a day off."

The barkeeper picked up a cloth and moved down the counter. Very few people besides the regulars came in here. If they did, they left quickly enough. This end of Gorky Street was not polite.

"You might reconsider, friend," the first shark said smoothly. "After all, it's not likely you're going to drink that pot away."

He laughed at his own wit.

"I think you should just bug off," Roy said very gently. His palms were sweating from the alcohol, and he slurred his words.

The shark standing beside him, a fat youth with greasy hair and the wild eyes of a hophead, reached for one of the bills. "Now this one, for example, if you had played this one then—"

The shark screamed as the palm of Roy's hand smashed into his nose. Blood spurted on the counter and over the bills. Roy swung himself around, knowing the other operator was still behind him. But the alcohol slowed him down, and the blow went off the other man's shoulder, giving the shark time to drive a punch into Roy's midriff.

There were four of them around him now, one for the money, the others to get him out of the hall. Hustlers didn't want any more trouble from the police than they already had. They were not fighters at heart. It would be enough to take Roy's money and get him out of there. If the shark with the smashed nose wanted revenge, there were ways to arrange for that—outside their safe territory.

While two grabbed Roy under the shoulders, another took hold of his hair, forcing his head back. They steered him out the back way. Someone kicked open a door, and he was shoved into the alley. The whole incident came off very smoothly and took less than a minute.

Kneeling in a pile of garbage, Roy groaned and forced himself to stand up. He waited a moment, then began to stagger down the alley, lurching from side to side. He stopped short of the street, out of breath and stomach heaving. When the world stopped spinning blindly, he stepped out and immediately bumped into a young couple. The man, sharply dressed, cursed at him and drew the girl protectively to his side.

"Drunken bastard. They're all over nowadays. He'll fix him."

The couple hurried away toward the comforting form of a policeman who was moving up the street. Roy stared after them stupidly.

"Problems, friend?" said the policeman.

"Taxi . . ." Roy croaked.

"Which cesspool did you crawl from, the pool hall?"

The policeman, a big, heavy brute, gripped Roy's arm tightly. "Start something with the barkeeper?"

"Let me be . . ." Roy gasped. "Want to go home!"

"Let's go in for a minute and see if there's anything that needs looking after, eh?"

The policeman started to lead him away when Roy, using the last of his strength, pivoted and kicked the man heavily in the groin. He went down, and the heel of Roy's boot caught his cheek, cracking the bone.

For a moment Roy stood over the curled-up body that was grunting in pain at his feet. Then he backed away and tripped. His head caught the edge of the sidewalk, and the full impact of the overhead lights cut into his eyes. The last thing he remembered was the sound of footsteps running up to him.

It was all very elusive, Bibnikov thought. He poured himself another brandy and chased it down with tepid mineral water.

Like Andropov, he had been surprised at Mitko's willingness to ditch his West German control. True, Mitko would have received no concessions from Committee One had he fought against Roy's demotion. He probably considered that sacrificing Roy was worth it if the move meant keeping Bibnikov off GRU territory. But Mitko was old school; he lived by the code of one officer's loyalty to another. And Mitko liked Roy personally. Bibnikov found the general's actions out of keeping with his character.

While the GRU, KGB and Special Investigations all looked into the destruction of the West German network, Bibnikov had quietly arranged for Special Investigations to cover Roy. His men had followed Roy and his girl to the Metropole and overheard their quarrel. The taxi driver who helped him home also worked for Special Investigations. To Bibnikov had come word of Roy's behavior in the Personnel Section and his reluctance to give up his weapon to the armorer. Panev, head of China Section, sent in abysmal reports of Roy's non-progress within the unit. Bibnikov also knew of Roy's visit to the West German embassy and the subsequent argument with Boysen, the substance of which had been overheard by Internal's man when Roy began shouting. Tonight the team that had trailed Roy to the pool hall had been responsible for getting him away from the scene before the stricken policeman could summon help. Special Investigations had also asked the Moscow police not to make an issue of the matter. The injured policeman would be compensated in another way.

There was very little Bibnikov did not know about Roy's movements. Yet the reason why Roy was acting in this fashion escaped Bibnikov, and so he found it unsettling. A man who believes himself unjustly slighted would nurse his anger for a few days, perhaps a week, but he would not continue to feed off it as Roy was doing. He would have, after a time, attempted to make some sort of contact with the people he had known in Center, Ivatushin, for example. Roy might even have gone to see Mitko. One disciplinary action seldom erases ten years of friendship. If for no other reason, Roy could have seen Mitko to get himself transferred to a different posting. It was obvious he was unsuitable for China Section.

Too many question marks, and a smell about the man Bibnikov did not like. Yet if nothing turned up by the end of the month, he might have to admit that he had been mistaken about Roy. Perhaps he was at last showing his true colors. After so much success one failure had been enough to reduce him to a vicious, self-pitying neurotic. It happened like that sometimes. In any case, Roy wouldn't last very long in China Section. Panev had made that clear. The skids had been well greased, and Roy would be out of the service by the New Year, latest.

# CHAPTER SIX

## *Crossover*

DEFECTION, FOR ANY REASON—FEAR, "rebirth," change of conviction, discouragement, revenge—is based on one fundamental often invisible or unspoken premise: a response to the death wish.

Even a man who has come to despise the land that has nourished and shaped him, who is prepared body and soul to go over to the opposition, discovers that a little part of him dies as soon as the conscious decision to defect has been taken. The longer he continues to live in the society he seeks to destroy, the more of him dies. The defector finds himself in a limbo between the world he seeks to run from and the one that awaits him. He must wait and suffer alone. He must always be on guard against the whispering voice which suggests that he give up this madness. To survive, he must be prepared for the subtle psychological tricks his mind will indulge in. Fear will mushroom out of nowhere, fear of being tailed or watched or that his friends have been recruited against him. He cannot succumb to the delusion that his scheme is known to the enemy and that this enemy is merely toying with him, waiting for the right moment to spring the trap. If fear should get the better of him, he will begin to make mistakes. He will start looking for tails or guard his conversation, signs which will surely betray him to experienced counterintelligence. The waiting may become intolerable. Out of a human need for reassurance he may foolishly contact the party that is to bring him out. And at heart there is always the possibility he may be betrayed by those whose sanctuary he seeks.

So which act is justified for self-protection and which will be the one to cast suspicion on him? The defector can never answer this question to his satisfaction. He never knows.

Nothing happened to Roy on Sunday. He remembered that he had hit a policeman, but there were no visitors from Moscow central headquarters. No one from GRU Internal Affairs called up for an explanation, assuming the police had allowed the military to look after its own. It was as though the incidents of Saturday night had never taken place. Yet they had and whoever had brought him home and ensured his privacy thereafter had been with him the whole day. Bibnikov was stalking him.

Roy did not leave the flat that day. He remained in the kitchen, reading, smoking cigarettes and drinking endless cups of coffee. In the afternoon he brought out his gun and cleaned it thoroughly. But Bibnikov did not come.

The week at China Section was predictably rotten. His position papers were condemned not only by Panev, but by his gaggle of hissing geese. Panev acidly suggested that Roy try to concentrate a good deal more on his work, and Roy snapped back that he was sick and tired of the whole department. Panev smelled the alcohol on Roy's breath and dismissed him from the room. Roy did not show up the next day.

"They come looking for you sometimes, during the day," Tamara said.

In a half hour the library would close. She and Roy were sitting at his workbench, a piece of honey cake lying between them on grease-proof paper. Beside the cake was a small bottle of rum, which Roy tipped into their teacups from time to time.

"Who comes?"

"The people from China Section. Twice Panev himself has been up."

"Bully for him."

"Where are you during the day, Alexander?"

"Usually sleeping."

"No, I'm serious!"

"So am I. Why do you think I work here? Because I can't do anything during the day, not with those shits on my back. Here, in the evening, I can get two days' work done in one sitting. And I like it here. It's quiet. I like the smell of the old sweat benches, rotten though they may be. I feel safe here . . . away from everything."

She smiled at him and said, "I'm glad you're here."

He laughed and lightly pinched her cheek, and they laughed together because this library had become their private world. No one could intrude on them and destroy the small pleasures they found in each other, pleasures which were very simple and to which they returned night-ly, drawn by an instinct which each obeyed unhesitatingly. All this made Tamara very happy, and she would let no one come and take this man from her. She had lied when Panev asked if Roy came here at night. She would lie again, if need be, to protect Roy.

"Go home now?" he asked her.

At first she did not understand what he meant, but when she looked at him, it was clear. Carefully she gathered up the crumbs on the wax paper and went to fetch her coat while he packed his briefcase. That evening Roy had coded a full volume of security material labeled double A. He did not tell Tamara, and he knew she never suspected a thing.

Contact was made one week later, on a Saturday.

He was a nondescript little man, neither young nor old, with a grizzled beard, two, perhaps three days' growth. The eyes were bright and lively, those of a good-humored jester. The clothes, however, were odd: a shiny blue suit, well worn and ill fitted, and a dirty white shirt, open at the neck. The shoes were scuffed and a cheap Soviet make.

He had gotten Roy out of bed.

"What the hell do you want?"

The man blinked rapidly and whispered in German, "Get me out. I don't have much longer."

Then he raised his voice and immediately continued in Russian. "I am sorry to have interrupted your bath," he said politely, although it was obvious that Roy had not been in a bath.

Roy seized him by the lapels and hauled him into the flat, kicking the door shut. He was gripping the German very tightly, and his other hand was in position, ready to strike at the neck.

"Where did you hear this?" he whispered.

"That is what you wrote on the invitation, Captain. . . ."

Only then did Roy release him. He led the way to the bathroom and turned on both faucets. Roy sat down on the edge while his contact remained standing.

"Shall we begin with the obvious?" Roy asked him.

"That is not necessary," the little man replied cheerfully. "You will never meet me again, not here that is. There will be someone else the next time."

His Russian was flawless but too correct grammatically.

"To make matters simple," he continued, "I should tell you that you will be moved out on the twenty-third of the month."

"That's impossible!" Roy whispered. "You couldn't be ready that soon."

"Please do not question what I tell you," the German said, always smiling. "It must be then. Even now the arrangements are being effected. The question is," he asked urgently, "can you last until then?"

"I suppose so," Roy shrugged. "You must have done a good deal of work in the past week, checking me out."

"We know you very well," the little man said matter-of-factly. "We have worked very hard to move you out quickly, but that is because we need you. We have waited a long time for someone of your standing."

Need. The principal guiding light of intelligence. If a man, a piece of machinery, a plan, a photograph, was needed, all stops were pulled out. Risks and potential ramifications which otherwise would have been the subjects of debate were dealt with quickly: acceptable or not acceptable, usually the former. In a major operation politicians were never told of it unless it was unsuccessful. Then apologies would be tendered and scapegoats offered up. But the operation always had its justification—need.

"Who else is in on it?"

"No one."

"Strictly BND?"

"All the way to Pullach."

Roy smiled at the thought. Pullach, six miles outside Munich, was the headquarters of German intelligence. A few times Roy had tried to get agents into the camp. Nothing had come of it.

"Method?"

"That is for the next time," the little man said. "Will you be carrying anything?"

"Possibly."

"Paper or microfilm?"

"Paper."

"Dimensions, weight?"

"I don't know yet."

"Contents?"

"That is for the next time."

"Coded?"

"Yes."

"Your next contact will take place on Friday, the twentieth, at the Arbat Restaurant. Please come at eight thirty. You will be joined shortly thereafter."

Quickly he explained the code that would be used, made Roy repeat it back and rose to offer his hand. The first rule of intelligence had been followed: The initial meeting was to be as brief as possible with the primary purpose of setting up another one. That much and more had been accomplished.

"Good luck, Captain. We will see each other on the other side. You had better destroy this." He handed Roy the invitation.

By the time Roy had seen him out, the tiny pieces of paper were swirling toward the Moscow sewers.

The following Monday Roy made formal application to terminate his duties at China Section and be forwarded to active duty. Panev said he would issue the recommendation but that Roy was expected to continue his work, for what little value it possessed, until clearance came through.

The next day Roy threw the cafeteria harpies another succulent morsel to chew on. Tamara, prettier now with makeup and a bright dress, appeared on his arm at luncheon. Both were conscious of the eyes upon them as they filed down the food counters. Twice Tamara caught girls staring at her, some smirking, others incredulous. She felt at once proud and embarrassed. Sensing her confusion, Roy took a table well away from the coteries.

"I'm sorry we came here," he said. "We could have gone out."

"No, it's all right, really," Tamara answered quickly and covered his hand with hers. "What is there to be ashamed of?"

Roy paused and looked directly at her. "Nothing," he said. "There is nothing to hide."

When she smiled at him and pressed his hand, Roy knew he had deceived her very well.

Over the next twelve days Roy cut afternoons to go to the firing range. He had prepared the excuse that he was returning to the military proper and needed the practice. But Panev, if he knew of Roy's absence, never referred to the truancy.

Andrushin, the armorer, made no comment when Roy began to appear regularly at the weapons room, each time on a per diem pass. There was no mention of the Hanyatti

Roy had never returned. Twice a week Roy also spent the early evenings at the central gymnasium, at an unarmed combat class. Then he would return to the library.

His days were thus completely filled, as he wanted them to be. Most nights he would fall asleep quickly before his mind would lead him into introspection and the guilt feelings that followed. Several times, when sleep proved impossible, he went to Tamara and passed the night in her bed.

On the nineteenth Ivatushin came by unexpectedly. He found Roy in his cubicle, doodling aimlessly on graph paper.

"Business is slow, I gather," Ivatushin said. Roy stiffened and turned around slowly.

"It's you. I thought Panev might be doing a spot check."

"Does he?" Ivatushin perched himself on one corner of Roy's desk. Roy sounded irritated and did not look happy to see him.

"He likes the personal touch," Roy said vaguely as though his mind were elsewhere.

"You look as though you're bored beyond belief."

"So would you be," said Roy. He stopped fiddling with the pencil and looked up. "Speaking of boredom, are things so quiet at your end that you have time for social visits?"

"Just wondered why you haven't called," Ivatushin said lightly. "It's been almost a month. We still haven't found a replacement for you at the German desk. Mitko's handling it himself. Some think you might be brought back in."

"No chance." Roy laughed softly. "My security card has a three-month limit. You know what that means."

Ivatushin knew.

102

"Any idea of what you will be doing?" he asked at last. He took out some cigarettes and handed one to Roy.

"Not yet. First I've got to get out of this place. If I can, I'll try to head for the navy."

Ivatushin raised his eyebrows. Any operational posting in the navy required an excellent security rating. With his D standing, Roy would have no chance. He must have known that.

"Yes, I know," Roy said quietly. "It mightn't be possible. Still, I've got to get out of here. . . ."

"Koldakov called up at the department. Apparently he couldn't get hold of you anywhere else. He'll be wanting to see you," Ivatushin said, "at the end of the month. He left this number."

Ivatushin fished out a piece of paper from his pocket and laid it on the desk.

"Roy looked up at him sharply. So this was why Ivatushin had come. Mitko hadn't told him Ivatushin was in on it.

"Are Bibnikov's people still bothering you?" Roy asked.

"As usual. You?"

"I don't know. There's not much to be done if they are, and I can live with it until the transfer comes through. Do you want to eat?'"

"No, I don't think so." Ivatushin smiled. "Anna is waiting for you at the Neopolitain."

"What a coincidence," Roy murmured.

"I tried to reassure her you hadn't taken up with anyone else"—Ivatushin laughed—"but I suppose she wants to hear it from the horse's mouth."

He walked up Gorky Street to Kalinin Prospekt and found her at the café, sitting at one of the front tables by the window. She waved, and he raised his hand wearily in return. Roy pushed his way past the queue, ignoring the dirty looks of the headwaiter, and settled in the chair opposite her.

"I was beginning to think Ivatushin hadn't reached you." Her words carried a none-too-subtle reproach.

"Obviously he did," Roy said.

Her long hair was piled up the way she knew he liked it. Her eyes were warm, holding his gently, fingers running over his hand. Roy would have seen her before he left, but he had wanted to be ready. Now he was unprepared, and Anna made him remember how much he was leaving behind.

"What do you want to eat? They really do rush you, but the food is good." Her eyes shifted between the menu and the hovering waiter.

"Whatever you like. Order for both of us."

She was about to say something but thought better of it and asked for two salmon salads and some beer.

"May I have a cigarette?"

He gave her one, lit it and sat back as the beer was set down. She blew the smoke through her nostrils, nervously tapping the cigarette against the rim of the ashtray, then moving the glowing end around the bottom.

"Why haven't you called?" she asked blankly.

"There wasn't any reason." His voice was low and indifferent.

"I tried to call you," she said defensively. "You've been out a lot."

"I work late, at the library. When I get home, I sleep."

"That simple?"

"Yes."

Again—the intake, the smoke coming through her nos-

'trils and the cigarette being nervously tapped against the edge of the tray.

"I finally got it out of my father what it was that had happened to you," she said. "I'm sorry about the other time, Alex. But you were difficult. You weren't making any sense."

"It's all right. It doesn't matter now."

"Yes, it does!" she said fiercely. "It matters a hell of a lot. I want to know what your plans are—what we plan to do!"

He could not help smiling. Anna was too lovely when she was angry. And knew it. But women liked to be taken seriously when they were upset.

"My career at Center is finished," he said quietly. "I've applied for active service."

"But your job!"

"My 'job' will be over within less than three months. It's only a stopping post, the laxative to help ease me out of the system altogether. Your father must have known that—or didn't he tell you?"

Her silence confirmed what he said. Her father had insisted she drop Roy as quickly as possible. It was that bad.

"Have you no feeling left for me?" she asked him quietly, grinding the ashes into fine powder.

"That's not what we were talking about," he answered harshly.

"Then let's talk about it!"

The waiter came by and dropped off two plates of food. Anna's question was left unanswered as Roy set into the fish. She looked at him for a time, but when it became clear he wouldn't say anything more, she too began to eat. They finished very quickly.

"What's happened to me has nothing to do with you," he said, wiping his mouth and throwing the napkin to one side. "You must let me take care of what happened my way. I won't be in Moscow much longer, and in the time that's left . . . well, there won't be very much I could give you. You should not call me again."

Her hurt was unmistakable, but she covered up quickly. She drained her glass and reached for her purse.

"Anna, I'm sorry. . . ."

"Go! Just go, will you?"

He looked at her for a long time as though fixing every detail of her in his mind so he would never lose the image. He dropped some notes on the table and elbowed his way to the door.

"I assume they have made contact with you."

"They have."

"West Germany?"

"Yes."

"When are they bringing you out?"

"On the twenty-third."

Koldakov's great head shot up in surprise. He was a mammoth man, over six feet six inches with the physique of a wrestler. Running his fingers through his black beard, Koldakov surveyed Roy through thick-lensed spectacles that had slid halfway down his nose.

Koldakov was probably the most eminent psychiatrist in the Soviet Union. He worked mainly, though not exclusively, with the military, training cosmonauts to withstand the psychological pressures they would encounter in outer space. For the air force he had developed the stress evaluation tests to determine the mental fitness of technicians operating the missile silos and pilots who would fly the lead attack bombers.

"That gives us very little time," Koldakov said thoughtfully. "That is, if you need any special arrangements. Is there anything you want?"

"Why wasn't I told Ivatushin was in on this?"

"You have not been told a great many things," Koldakov said. "In time you will know everything. We all have our reasons for involving ourselves in this enterprise. Bibnikov touches every one of us. Perhaps I should tell you how I see him?"

He took Roy's silence for an affirmative reply.

"On December 1, 1934, S. M. Kirov was murdered at the Bolshevik headquarters of Smolny. His assassin was L. Nikolaeev, a young party member. At the time of his death Kirov was a member of the Politburo, secretary for the Central Committee and first secretary of the Leningrad regional committee. But he was more. Kirov was Stalin's chief opposition for the seat of the secretary-general of the party, occupied at that time by Stalin.

"The Eighteenth Party Congress, 1934, was held to demonstrate support for Stalin and his policies. What happened in fact was quite different. An antiparty sentiment arising within many committees hardened into a resolution that Kirov should be nominated for the chair. Support was also forthcoming from members in the Central Committee itself. The mood of the party was definitely identified when Stalin received fewer votes than any other candidate for a position he already held. It was clear that Stalin's influence was on the decline.

"But Kirov was not quick to bid for the leadership. Perhaps he was confident that Stalin's policies could be realigned in a democratic fashion. Kirov also controlled the powerful Leningrad party, and that, although it caused a lot of friction between himself and Stalin, afforded Kirov a measure of protection. He was simply too popular a man to get rid of. Whatever his reasoning, Kirov felt no need to move against Stalin. Oppose him, yes, but not dislodge him.

"Stalin, as you know, worked the other way. He recognized the threat Kirov represented and acted to quash it. You are familiar with the details of the execution blueprint. A highly unstable young man was found and carefully indoctrinated against Kirov on the supposition that Kirov wanted to destroy the party. He was armed and set loose. Twice this man, Nikolaeev, approached Kirov's office, gun in pocket, and twice Kirov's bodyguards intercepted him. On both occasions Nikolaeev was handed over to the NKVD, and both times he was set free within a matter of hours. The third time he succeeded in penetrating the defense and killed Kirov. Stalin's principal rival was thus eliminated. The course of his death was plotted by the psychiatrist who had primed Nikolaeev, the guiding hand was that of the NKVD, and the whole action was legitimized by Stalin's personal order for the murder."

Koldakov stared at his huge hands, then removed his glasses and rubbed his eyes. It was obvious the memory of that killing had never left him and that it had great personal significance.

"Perhaps I exhibit too much emotion for an event I neither witnessed nor participated in," he said, shaking his head. "But the killing of Kirov was, for our country, the crime of the century. It was a signal for the terror which followed. I was a first-year medical student then. My chief professor was Dr. Chapaev. He performed the autopsy on Kirov and subsequently on Borisov, Kirov's bodyguard, who had supposedly died of a heart attack when the van carrying him for interrogation swerved into a wall. Chapaev made the mistake of telling Stalin the truth: that Borisov had not died of a heart attack, but that he had been systematically beaten by blunt, heavy objects. Thirty years later Khrushchev identified these objects as crowbars, in his secret speech to the Politburo and Central Committee. Dr. Chapaev was arrested within three days of filing his report. I never learned what became of him."

Koldakov sat back and smiled. But his obsidian eyes were glittering.

"The killing of Kirov ignited the terror," he repeated slowly. "I cannot tell you what it was like. You know a little of it, I suppose, from your father. Each man has his story, and it is no worse, no less frightening, than anyone else's. But I believe there was a common thought in every mind at the time: If by reason or chance we survive, we must never allow such a thing to happen again. Thirty years later I see history repeating itself.

"Yes, Bibnikov must be stopped. Not only because he is a traitor, but because he is too close to the apex of power. He has too much influence over the Central Committee. There will be no one left to help us if he manipulates a seizure of power." Abruptly, Koldakov got to his feet.

"I'm sorry," he said. "It is not often I speak of these things. But sometimes it helps to know one is not alone."

"I have one request," Roy said, walking slowly to the door. "Tamara, the girl at the library, I've been seeing her. There may be consequences for her when I leave."

"You've gone beyond using her, is that it?" Koldakov inquired.

"Sometimes these things get away from you," Roy said harshly. "She was my cover for the nights at the library. Everyone thinks we are having an affair. So let them. It's perfect."

"It *was* perfect," Koldakov corrected him. "Until you became involved with her."

"A shy little girl hidden away in the library dust." Roy

laughed suddenly. "She shouldn't have touched me, eh? Yet she did. She cared for me."

"We all care for you," Koldakov said softly. "You know that."

"Then make certain Bibnikov doesn't touch her," Roy said. "You can do that for her."

"For you," Koldakov answered. "I shall do that for you."

Koldakov nodded his great head and rose, holding out his hand. "Good luck, Captain," he said softly. "From all of us."

As Roy left, the snowflakes of the eternal winter were falling over Moscow.

On the evening of the twentieth Roy went out for supper. He wore his uniform, freshly pressed, instead of a civilian suit.

The Arbat was one of the newest restaurants in Moscow, modern, spacious, with efficient service. Designed to serve senior party members and important foreign visitors, the Arbat quickly became the unofficial club for the city's underground millionaires, the high-volume black-market speculators. After nine o'clock it was impossible to get a table without the help of twenty rubles to the maître d' or a nod from one of the "specs."

Roy arrived at eight thirty, was shown to a table and ordered his meal. Forty minutes passed, and he had completed only the first course, eating very slowly. The restaurant had filled up, with a line forming out the door. The maître d' started doubling up the tables, seating single people or a couple with someone else eating alone at a table for four. As Roy's entrée of scallops was served, the maître d' appeared at the table with an anxious-looking foreigner.

110

The maître d' offered a sugary smile and asked if Roy would mind having this gentleman sit with him. It was unusually busy, and the gentleman, a visitor to Moscow, might have to wait quite a long. . . . Roy gave both a frigid look and said, "Not at all."

The diner thanked the maître d' in precise but heavily accented Russian and scraped his chair closer to the table.

"Very kind of you to have me," he said. "My name is Giering, West German trade mission."

"The food is good here," Roy said noncommittally. "You will enjoy it." He spread some more sauce on the scallops.

Giering was about forty, a compact man with wide shoulders and heavy thighs. His eyes, flitting across the menu, were a dark amber; the hands, hairy with short, stubby fingers. Giering caught a waiter by the sleeve and ordered in laborious Russian.

"It is very cold in Moscow, no, even for December," Giering said. He was leaning across the table toward Roy.

"It sometimes happens that way."

"I was hoping to go to the Bolshoi to hear the orchestra tonight, but it looks as if I have too much work to do."

"There is no orchestra tonight."

"Oh, but you are mistaken, there are two," Giering said emphatically.

Kiering had used the German word for "orchestra" *Kapelle*. The *Rote Kapelle* had been an extensive underground network of Soviet agents, scattered throughout Europe, even in Berlin itself, during the war. In this instance *Kapelle* referred to the Soviet internal security men who were shadowing Giering. Roy hadn't spotted anyone, but if Giering said there were two orchestras playing, then there were a pair of tails in the restaurant.

"Yes, I am certain of it," Giering declared. "The perfor-

111

mance which was scheduled for last Monday was canceled."

It was elementary code, the past meaning the future, a name taking the place of an entire action.

"I myself am waiting for the Tchaikovsky series," Giering said. "The one on the twenty-third."

Giering's potage was served along with black bread and butter, and he began to eat with the appetite of a hungry man.

"I understand von Karajan will be coming for that," Roy said. "It's been a long time since he's conducted in Moscow."

"Well, it's really to return a compliment," Giering said confidentially. "The Kirov Ballet will be coming to Munich. I understand they will even give a matinee performance."

Roy refused the cheesecake from the sweets trolley and sipped his coffee.

"Now that I'm sure he's coming I shall have to get tickets," Roy said. "Will you be in Moscow for the performance?"

"Alas, no." Giering sighed. "We leave at half past twelve on the twenty-third, can you imagine? And there are so many last-minute arrangements to be made. But it will be good to get home for Christmas."

Roy gestured to the maître d' to keep the change and rose.

"It was pleasant to have spoken with you," he said. "I compliment you on your use of the Russian language."

"One tries!" Giering said gayly and raised his hand in farewell. *"Au revoir!"*

The transfer to active service came through on Monday.

112

In keeping with procedure Roy went up to Panev and had him sign the severance slips. That afternoon he handed in his security pass. Personnel informed him that his last pay would be ready at the end of the week. He needn't call for it since it would be mailed directly to his new posting.

On his last night in Moscow Roy asked Tamara to come to his flat for dinner. It was the first time he had laid open the privacy of his home, and Tamara eagerly accepted. Roy had released in her feelings she scarcely knew existed. Sometimes their intensity threatened to break through and demand more of him, of his time and his love. At such moments Tamara disciplined herself, forcing herself to wait until Roy came to her in his own time. He gave slowly, with deliberation and care. He took the passion of the moment and, when that was spent, gently retreated into that private world he inhabited, which lay beyond the silence of their embraces or the quiet, regular breathing of his sleep. There he dwelled alone, and as much as she wished to follow him, Tamara understood that such a place belonged only to him. She would wait until he called for her.

She appeared at his door on the dot of seven, nervous and laden down with packages. Earlier he had given her money to do shopping and told her what to buy. She wondered where he had got so much money that they could afford a fine heavy chicken with giblet sauce and fresh fruit for dessert. But she had bought what he wanted and brought it to him.

He led her into the kitchen, poured out the sweet Bulgarian wine, and together they began making supper. Tamara found some favorite selections in Roy's record collection, and they ate to the gentle sonatas of Beethoven. When the wine began to take effect, she suggested they go to bed. But first she washed him, tenderly, and then drew a bath for herself. It was eleven o'clock, when, after being loved, Tamara slept.

Roy rose at midnight and changed into clothing he had left in the closet in the front room. From the bookcase he selected the four volumes, all dictionaries, whose pages had been removed and in which the coded double A security material had been inserted. He packed them into a tote bag.

Roy did not bother to look out the front windows. He took it for granted that Bibnikov's men were out there. They would have seen Tamara arrive, carrying food parcels. Since they knew Roy had a liaison with her, Tamara's coming was not unusual. When the lights went out, they must have assumed the night was over. Roy had invited Tamara over to create exactly that impression. He would find out now if he had succeeded.

Roy went out the front door, closing it gently behind him. Quickly he made his way to the basement and forced the rickety door which opened on the storage room. Light filtered in from the streetlamps. He made his way around the ancient crates and bits of rusted machinery to the windows, which were level with the sidewalk. Taking a knife from his pocket, he scraped away the loose putty around one frame. Then he stepped back and, placing his hands on either side of the frame, pushed. The window opened with a crackle, and the night air blew icy dust into his face. He tossed out his bag and crawled out into the snowbank, trying to stay in the shadows. He wriggled his way around to the side of the building, to the street which ran along the opposite side to his flat. He jumped over the low iron fence and made for the avenue.

They picked him up three minutes after that, as he was crossing Kuibyshev Street.

# CHAPTER SEVEN

## *Pullach*

THE GATES OF THE GERMAN EMBASSY were opened electronically from the inside. The Soviet militia guards standing vigil at the residence scattered before the onrushing headlights. As the car passed through the gates, one of Roy's escorts leaned out a window and, in a drunken voice, bawled a Russian obscenity at the detail.

The driver slowed down only when they were well inside the compound. The garage doors slid back, and he coaxed the machine into an empty stall next to the ambassador's Mercedes. Roy's pickup had taken less than four minutes to execute. Tomorrow apologies would be tendered to the duty officer of the militia for the unseemly behavior of some of the junior embassy staff. No insults had been intended. The intoxicated staff members would be disciplined, and there the matter would end.

"Good evening, Captain."

Roy stumbled from the rear seat, his eyes shielded

against the yellow lights. Before him stood Hans Boysen, the ambassador's secretary.

"Christ, I thought it might be you," Roy muttered. He reached for the tote bag, and Boysen saw that his hands were shaking. "Your people might have told me who they were."

"May I take that, Captain?" Boysen offered. "The bag."

Roy handed it to him slowly, his eyes narrowing suspiciously. "It's in—"

"We needn't worry about that now," Boysen cut him off smoothly. "There is very much to be done before you leave. If you will please come this way. . . ."

Roy stepped over and took him by the shoulder.

"Just wait a bloody minute," he said softly. "*How* do we move? They've been watching me, you know. I left a girl at the flat. When she wakes up and finds me gone. . . ."

"Yes, we know about her," Boysen said calmly. Deliberately he removed Roy's hand. "There is a Lufthansa flight to Frankfurt at seven o'clock this morning—five and a half hours from now. You will be on it. That is why we must hurry. Please." He gestured at the door.

Boysen led the party through the kitchens and into the main hall. There were no lights burning. Roy stumbled on the carpet and cracked his elbow on something hard. At the foot of the stairs Boysen turned to the two other men.

"See him to my room. I will be up directly." He might have been the concierge of an exclusive Swiss hotel.

There was a wedding picture of Boysen and his bride, a short, dumpy-looking woman, on the dresser. The bed had not been slept in, and Roy doubted Boysen would be using it tonight. The room was lit, but the windows had been carefully blacked out by thick velvet curtains. It was sparsely furnished—a wing chair, small carpet and book-

116

shelf with official-looking ledgers. A bottle of whiskey stood on the bedside table, along with an ice bucket and tumbler. Roy didn't know how he had missed him at first glance, but there was someone waiting for him, in the corner by the closet. He was a rotund gentleman, pink cheeks and very prominent ears. He was standing beside a covered trolley and looking at Roy very carefully, the blue eyes examining him critically.

"Could you stand in profile, please?" he asked suddenly.

Roy did as he was bid. There was an undertone of authority behind the courteous words.

"Excellent . . . yes, certainly it can be done. You're a little heavier than your photographs show, but that is of no importance."

He came over to Roy and ran a very soft hand over Roy's face, beginning at the temple.

"Will he do?"

Boysen had come in and locked the door behind him. Under one arm he was carrying several glossy photos.

"Why don't you introduce us?" Roy said sarcastically. "Your pansy friend here has obvious intentions on me."

The tubby man blushed and turned away.

"Whatever Herr Heilmann's sexual proclivities may be, the fact remains he is one of Germany's great theatrical makeup men." Boysen retained his official tone but permitted himself a smile. "When he is finished, this is how you will look."

He handed Roy the photos. They showed a man of about Roy's age, slightly taller, leaner, with features not unlike Roy's.

"Who is he?"

"Gerd Roeder, second secretary, Commerce. Today, when part of the embassy staff leaves for its Christmas holiday, Roeder will stay behind. You will take his place."

Roy stared at him incredulously, then began to laugh, a harsh grating sound tinged with fear.

"Simple as that?" he said, reaching for the whiskey. "We're all going to walk by the frontier police as though off to a picnic? You're mad, Boysen!"

"Consider," Boysen said carefully. "The KGB has been notified to expect a group of German diplomats at Sheremetevo Airport later this morning. Surveillance will have the names and photographs of every person leaving. Roeder's name is on their list. But instead of him, you will be there, carrying his passport, bona fide, and traveling papers. You will be given his bags and be dressed in his clothing. Everything has been arranged, to the smallest detail, I assure you."

"What about the others in the party?"

"They have been briefed as much as was necessary. Fortunately it is only a small group, twelve. They will not ask questions but treat you as one of their own. One embassy person has been specifically assigned to you. You will not be expected to talk very much. You see, Roeder's mother died three days ago in East Germany. The frontier police will doubtless know this. If you are upset or agitated, it will appear natural."

"And Roeder?"

"He will remain here at the embassy, under quarantine. Naturally he won't be permitted outside, not even at night. As soon as you are in Pullach, he will be brought out another way."

Roy sipped the whiskey and paced.

"It might work," he muttered to himself. "It just might work."

"There is no reason why it shouldn't," Boysen said. "After all, you do have diplomatic immunity with Roeder's passport. There won't be any difficulties. And now I suggest we start. Herr Heilmann is a meticulous man. I will get your clothes."

Heilmann began with the wig. He covered Roy's short hair with a length of dark-brown ersatz pile and trimmed it in the fashion Roeder wore. Roy's mustache was carefully shaved and replaced by a false one, light blond and longer. The makeup itself was applied layer by layer. Roy's nose was filled out under the bridge; the eyebrows were trimmed and lengthened, the forehead was smoothed out. Heilmann, no longer nervous, proceeded silently and quickly, with full concentration. He did not touch Roy any more than was necessary. He must have studied the photographs of Roeder beforehand, for he scarcely glanced at them in the course of his work. The job was finished in three hours.

"Tired?"

Hans Boysen had returned, carrying a gray woolen suit, white shirt, blue tie and fresh underwear. He glanced at the whiskey bottle and noted that Roy had been drinking steadily as Heilmann worked on him. He took the tumbler from Roy's fingers.

"Coffee is being sent up, as well as some breakfast. It wouldn't do to have you drunk, would it?"

"Leave me alone," Roy snarled. "How do you think I've managed to stay awake through this?"

"Another thing," Boysen reprimanded him sharply. "From now on you will speak only German."

Roy grunted and stood up. When he looked in the mirror, he did not recognize himself.

"Very neat, very very neat," he murmured. "My compliments, maestro."

119

Heilmann beamed and began packing his equipment.

"You don't wear rings or jewelry, do you?" Boysen asked.

"No."

"Good. This belongs to Roeder. He's married." He passed Roy a slim gold wedding band. "Change now. Breakfast will be up in fifteen minutes. Is there anything else you want?"

"Some cigarettes and an amphetamine capsule. I won't make it otherwise."

"I'll send for the physician."

The suit had been let out at the seams and fitted Roy snugly. He went through the pockets, but they were empty. Roy also checked the labels on all the clothing. They were West German except for the tie, which carried an Italian mark. He checked the mirror once more, then compared his reflection with the photographs. Not identical, but very close, enough to get by.

The breakfast trolley arrived and, just behind it, a young man carrying a doctor's bag. If the doctor was surprised at seeing a facsimile of Roeder sitting before him, he gave no sign of it.

"Are you in good physical health?" he asked without ceremony.

"Yes."

"Have you taken amphetamines before?"

"Of course."

"No adverse reaction?"

"None," Roy said irritably.

From his bag the physician removed a vial of red capsules and shook out two into the palm of his hand.

"After you eat, wait one hour, then take these. They will

activate in less than ten minutes and will continue to work for three to four hours. During this period you must not imbibe any alcohol."

He nodded to Boysen and left.

"I hope you like poached eggs," Boysen said, sitting down to the trolley.

Roy speared his egg clumsily and yellow yolk splattered on his tie. His hands were still shaking.

"What happens when we reach Pullach?" he asked.

Both of them had finished, and Boysen was pouring out the last of the coffee.

"You will be debriefed, I suppose," Boysen said. Evidently what became of Roy once he was out of the Soviet Union did not interest him.

"They must have told you."

Boysen passed him his cup and declined the proffered cigarette.

"We should understand each other, Captain," he said quietly. "I am a diplomat. As a rule, I do not engage in espionage activities, which, I may tell you, are distasteful to me."

Roy snorted, but Boysen continued.

"I was tempted to burn that note you passed me. I had no wish to start an enterprise that could destroy the work of our people. The rebuilding of relationships between West Germany and the Soviet Union has been going on for almost fifteen years. I weighed the possible outcome, the reprisals your government might make and whose careers, indeed, life's work, would be destroyed because of you. I thought very carefully before acting.

"With the ambassador's permission, I flew to Pullach myself. There I spoke with Wessel and Schareck. I did not

121

disclose your name until I was satisfied that the embassy would not be damaged by this operation. Only then did I reveal your name and position."

"Wessel must have loved you for that." Roy laughed.

"Wessel had little choice, which was exactly the position I meant him to be in," Boysen said. "I tempted him by saying you would be an important man for the BND. Wessel was intrigued. Given the political state of the BND, he also needed a successful operation. You see, I held all the cards."

"You must have been bloody sure of yourself," Roy said. "No matter who you *think* you are, Wessel could have had your balls."

"You are the expert on West Germany, Captain. Tell me, do you really believe he would have asked for them? Would *you* have?"

"I'd get them after." Roy grinned wolfishly.

"Therefore, as I was explaining, the plan which is in motion at the moment really had nothing to do with me," Boysen said. "I am, to the best of my ability, fulfilling the role which Wessel prepared for me. After our conversation he did not feel it prudent to elaborate on whatever would be waiting for you on the other side."

"Why did you finally agree to play with the BND?"

Boysen set his cup down and leaned forward.

"Because I honestly believed you were in difficulty," he said. "In spite of your occupation, you always behaved like a gentleman at embassy functions. Oh, yes, I understand your purpose for having been there, but even so, I believe you are a decent man. We have our sources in the city. It was not difficult to see what your lack of fortune was making of you."

"And what was that?"

"An alcoholic, possibly a suicide. You were being broken by the most efficient method I have ever witnessed. They stripped you of your pride, Captain, and trampled on your dignity. The punishment far exceeded whatever crime you might have committed in their eyes. They were wasting a good man."

"I don't think Wessel has run this operation out of pity," Roy said savagely. "He'll milk me for everything I'm worth."

"You have no doubt expected that," Boysen said. "It is part of your profession, the hazards of the trade, no?" There was a pause, and then Boysen turned to him directly.

"Do you have any doubts, any regrets about what you're doing?" he asked suddenly, as though everything before had been a preamble to this question.

"I have no doubts," Roy said slowly. "There was no other way. But I'm frightened. There's no backup. I'm in someone else's hands, yours. I hate it."

"Would you serve Wessel against your homeland?"

"I've already begun, haven't I?" Roy said fiercely. Then suddenly, the energy seemed to go out of Roy. He pushed the trolley away and went to sit in the wing chair, his back to the secretary.

"I have no country left to sell," he said dully. "I did what I did for revenge and to save my own bloody skin. That's all there will ever be to it. So don't look for any noble sentiments or any psycho crap. Deceit is never as complicated as one would like to believe."

Roy reached inside his pocket and brought out the red pills. He poured some water into the dirty tumbler and swallowed hard. For a moment he closed his eyes.

"Good luck, Captain. I will see you in a half hour."

Boysen had been good, Roy thought sleepily, damned good. He was the front line, the gentleman, still a useful tool in a practice which has no manner to it, never did. Boysen was the kind you sent in first, the quiet sympathetic face, alert eyes, diplomatic cover. Even now, Boysen would be on the radio to Pullach with the full report: surveillance on Roy's flat, the pickup, lack of opposition. He would tell them about the books Roy had brought, and the cryptographers would be alerted. Boysen, who had probed lightly and delicately, would give Pullach its first close-hand assessment of Roy—his temper, his fears, his egoism and arrogance. Still, he had been easy. The subsequent inquisitors would be quite different.

Roy was the last to get on the shuttle bus to the airport. He seated himself immediately behind the driver, dumping Roeder's suitcase on the empty seat beside him. Most of the passengers were half asleep. Some looked up at him, uncertain, embarrassed or simply curious, it was hard to be sure. They would have to perform better than this at Sheremetevo. It wouldn't look good if he appeared ostracized from the herd.

The bus moved out of the compound, cut through the dark Moscow streets and headed for the perimeter of the city, where they would get onto the narrow highway that led to the airport. Roy stared out the window, watching the bluish lamps of the city illuminate the façades of the houses and shops. Occasionally the string of lamps would abruptly end, and the outside world would be plunged into darkness. In the east a false dawn was breaking, the reflection of the moon off the clouds. The amphetamine was taking hold, shifting his mood between euphoria and depression. He was filled with sudden horror as his land, that quintessential amorphous "land," a tiny grain of which remains forever in a man's heart, was slipping by his eyes, to be gone perhaps forever.

Yet he also felt a surge of exhilaration. He was now taking out his revenge on Bibnikov. Roy stared greedily at the reflection of a face that was not his, and he wanted to laugh. Soon, Bibnikov, very soon, I promise you! His thoughts raced on, crowding and tripping over each other. He was drunk on vengeance, desperate for its execution, unafraid of anything that lay between it and himself.

He fumbled for a cigarette and lit it, closing his eyes, trying to concentrate on the soothing motion of the bus. The airport, he thought, can't be too far away.

The last of the suburbs passed behind them, and dark, shapeless woods appeared, lit up by the headlights of the bus. Roy looked back, straining for a final glimpse. Suddenly he pictured Tamara in his bed, alone. She would have discovered his absence by now. She held him when they slept and stirred if he left the bed during the night. He wondered what would become of her and if Koldakov would be able to help her. Roy knew he owed her more than he could ever repay.

The foul odor of travelers' sweat hung over Sheremetevo. The terminal was filthy from the traffic that had poured through it during the night. Beer and snack kiosks, littered with bottles, cardboard plates and greasy wax paper, were still offering herring and cold chicken bits while at the same time organizing for a new day. Domestic flights from all over the country had arrived in the last few hours, disgorging coal miners from the Donbas, oilmen from Siberia, diamond diggers from Yakutia. All of them panted after Moscow, that swollen whore whose exclusivity was protected by limited residence passes. But she welcomed them all, for business or pleasure—the difference was blurred.

And the sharks were there, looking for country marks whose fat billfolds could be painlessly slimmed in the space of forty minutes. The police, yawning and moving slowly, concentrated on the hustlers rather than on the victims. They patrolled the main hall carefully, checking to see who was fleecing whom and what the probable take would be. The police rate was ten percent of the night's work in return for the blind eye.

The German delegation, led by a matron with heavy shoes and a Prussian stride, proceeded through the terminal in one large group. The talk picked up now, as they tried to settle their nerves. A few of the younger staff members were looking around in innocent bewilderment. Obviously this was a side of Soviet life they had missed seeing on arrival.

Roy was in the center of the group, walking slowly beside two girls who were chatting away to each other. He had unbuttoned his overcoat in the stifling, fetid air of the terminal, but he was still hot. His eyes were constantly roaming the area, searching for signs of surveillance. It was there, he knew. As the party approached the counter, the watch was obvious. Four men, all smartly dressed, disdaining to pretend, had taken up positions on either side of the entrance. They belonged to the Tenth Department, Surveillance Directorate, which covered foreign embarkations, and would complement the usual customs personnel.

The stout woman leading the party halted before the counter and held up her passport like a shield. In good Russian she explained who everyone was, where they were going and that the party was already a quarter of an hour late. The customs officers began taking the luggage and stacking it on carts. There would be no inspection since it was all covered under the diplomatic seal. An officer from the Tenth produced a large plastic-bound book, asked the group members to arrange themselves in an orderly line and began checking. The book contained a list of all those in the party—names, ranks, reasons for exit, durations of absence, plans to return or not and photographs. It was standard procedure.

Roy dropped his cigarette to the floor and reached inside his coat pocket for the passport. When his turn came, he handed it over, swinging his bag onto the counter.

The man from Tenth looked at the photograph in the passport, then compared it with the one in the book. His eyes looked over Roy's face very carefully, without embarrassment. Finally, the passport was handed over to a customs man for stamping. As Roy moved on into the waiting room, the man from Tenth called out softly, "I'm sorry you must leave us under such circumstances."

He had spoken in quick Russian, and Roy, who had turned around, was caught. He stepped back to the counter and grasped the man by the arm.

"If you know so much," he whispered in Russian, "then you know my mother died of a broken heart. She was sixty-three years old, but no, you bastards wouldn't let her come to the West to die!"

The man from Tenth appraised him coolly. He looked at the German woman who was coming to Roy's side and ordered her to sit down. Then he turned back to Roy.

"Go and sit with the rest of your kind, pig," he said softly.

The remainder of the delegation was processed very quickly and without incident. There was another twenty-minute wait until departure, and at five minutes after seven the Lufthansa flight was taxiing down the runway.

Roy ignored the doctor's orders and drank brandies on the plane. He was consumed by a rage that was as futile as it was unextinguishable. The affair at customs had unnerved him, and his fear had broken open like a swollen bubble of pus. It didn't matter that he had understood what the man from Tenth had said. Roeder spoke Russian well, and Tenth would have known that. But he had made a mistake in turning when the security man called out. He had drawn attention to himself. The incident would be remembered, and Bibnikov would hear of it. He could not have done worse if he had told Bibnikov beforehand where he was going.

The flight lasted two and a half hours. No one approached him or sat down and struck up a conversation. He wondered who the surveillance was or if there was anyone at all. All the time he kept on drinking.

It had snowed in Germany. The Frankfurt airfield was covered with a light fluffy layer of powder which the winds shifted into small lazy drifts. When the aircraft rolled to a halt, Roy let the rest of the delegation file past. Someone had to contact him now. Looking out the window, he saw a small Mercedes sedan, the engine running.

"Those are our people. Please come with me."

It was the girl with the long black hair and smart blue eyes, one of the two who had walked beside him at Sheremetevo.

"God help us," he muttered, "for polluting innocent minds."

But she only smiled and led him to the aircraft door. He stumbled on the slippery metal steps of the ramp; but she caught his arm, and he followed her docilely into the rear of the car.

"Where to?"

"The other side of the airport. We shall be going directly to Pullach."

Roy wiped the moisture from the glass, and his eyes followed her gaze. Across the field stood a large military helicopter, its rotor blades spinning lazily.

"Do they serve whiskey on board?"

The girl smiled noncommittally and said he would have to wait until they reached their destination. "Merry Christmas," she said.

Pullach is a small compound about six kilometers south of Munich, on the banks of the Isar River. Built in 1936 for Rudolf Hess, it was once the residence of Martin Bormann and served, in the last days of the Reich, as field headquarters to General Kesselring. In 1945 the U.S. Army Postal Censorship Bureau had moved in.

Pullach comprises some 150,000 square yards of parkland, surrounded by a wall that runs around the perimeter. Inside the compound are a number of one- and two-story dwellings, huts, bunkers, a gymnasium, a cinema, community center and even a school.

In 1947 Pullach received its fourth and last guest: Reinhard Gehlen, former intelligence general who had, in the course of World War II, controlled all German espionage activity against the Soviet Union.

Long before the collapse of Berlin, Gehlen had predicted that after the Allies were through dismembering Germany, there would arise the inevitable conflict between the Americans and the Soviet Union. He realized that his information and expertise could be used as bargaining chips to save himself and his staff when the time came. In the last days Gehlen buried at Miesbach all the intelligence documents related to the Soviet armed forces that his organization had gathered since early 1940. To Miesbach he also removed his chief staff officers and Soviet experts. Then he went to the Americans and made them see his worth.

On December 16, 1947, Gehlen and his officers occupied the Pullach compound, nicknamed St. Nicholas in acknowledgment of the season. From the ashes of a Germany destroyed came forth a new all-German espionage unit, experienced, dedicated, geared against the Soviet Union and fueled with U.S. dollars from the hand of Dulles and the CIA.

The helicopter approached the compound from the east, flying low so that only part of Pullach was visible. Roy did not doubt this was being done for his benefit. They would not show him more than was necessary. The Germans were like that—too strict in some respects, stupidly lax in others. Roy already knew Pullach's layout very well from photographs taken by Soviet aerial reconnaissance.

The girl pushed open the helicopter door, shielding her face from the snow blown up by the rotor blades. Roy climbed out, and she led the way, leaving small, precise footprints on the snow-covered earth. There was no reception committee.

She led him to a small single-story maisonette, standing alone by a cluster of slender oaks. The door was unlocked, and they went in.

"You will be very comfortable here," the girl said matter-of-factly. She stepped inside and turned to face him, like a real estate agent dealing with a client. "The sofa opens into a bed. Sheets in the drawer there." She pointed to a long, low dresser. "It's only eight o'clock our time. Would you like to sleep or do you want to proceed?"

"Leave me be," Roy said quietly. "Is there a telephone?"

"Behind the counter. You are connected directly with the switchboard. There is no need to dial."

"Then I would like to rest."

"Very well." She turned to leave.

"It was a good job," Roy called after her. "Tell them they did a good job."

She glanced over her shoulder but said nothing.

As soon as she was gone, Roy began examining his quarters. He did not bother with the microphones, knowing they were there and not caring. The video cameras, one in the ceiling of the main room, the other in the bathroom, didn't bother him either. He walked around, examining the books in the case, touching the cold smooth walls, white, broken with framed cheap prints, checking the cabinet which held liquor, glasses and dishes, going over the kitchen appliances and utensils. Like an animal, he was smelling out this new territory, making certain he knew where everything was. A territory was divided into offensive and defensive positions, and he took note of where possible weapons lay.

When he finished, he stripped and showered, letting the hot water run over him until he was weak from the steam. The makeup clung stubbornly at first, but he managed to scrub most of it off. He stumbled into the main room and, without bothering to make a bed, wrapped himself in a blanket and fell asleep almost immediately.

# CHAPTER EIGHT

## *The First Run*

ROY SLEPT FOR TWELVE HOURS. He stirred briefly in the late afternoon, wanting to get up, but the amphetamine had worn off completely and left a well of exhaustion behind it. When he at last awoke in the evening, he was very hungry. He rang up the operator and asked for some food. Then he changed into fresh clothing from Roeder's suitcase, poured himself a whiskey and settled down to wait.

Ever since he awakened, Roy's mind had been at work, concentrating on and planning for the first meeting with his inquisitor. Roy was eager to meet this unknown man. Because he feared him, he wished to make him his friend, and to gain that friendship, he was prepared to reveal every piece of intelligence he knew. He wanted to be honest so the interrogator would trust him, for he believed this trust would protect him. What he had before forced himself to experience now became the real emotions of a defector—the passion for survival, the frightening unfamiliarity of an alien land, the fear of his interrogators—and his mind demanded that he take the surest way of saving himself. He would commit treason quickly and completely, and, in so doing, deliberately cut off all possible retreats.

Roy sat in the chair, quietly sipping his whiskey, his face expressionless. If he did not give rein to these feelings now, they would surface in the course of questioning when he could not control them. He would have to be hard during the interrogation, truculent and argumentative. He would lie to the inquisitor, not in so many words, but by omission, and the only fear he would permit himself to show would be a grudging one, born of respect for whoever questioned him. He would act exactly opposite to the protective fantasy his mind was weaving for him.

He sat in the chair until he had formulated the safest plan, the plan by which he was to humble and corrupt himself. Once this was fully worked out in his mind, he brutally shoved it aside.

The man introduced himself as Thiess, no first name, no rank. His long leather coat had long ago lost its sheen and was worn in places where brick, shrubbery and wire had torn and rubbed against it, leaving it a composite of a thousand tiny scars.

His was the face of a Teutonic warrior—used, sad, yet still defiant. The eyes reflected the spark of battles already endured and looked ahead steadily to new conflicts to be engaged in. Yet for all the horror, the face had the imprint of culture. It was long and aristocratic, with an aquiline nose and thin, trimmed mustache. The man was tall and striking, the effect heightened by his heavy gloves and high black boots, soldier's boots. Roy knew him to be fifty-three, a professional at ease in his surroundings. He represented Wessel and the BND rather than Schareck's outfit, counterintelligence. Schareck, Roy thought, must be very annoyed at having been shunted aside, even if only temporarily.

Behind Thiess came an orderly carrying a covered tray. He set it down on the counter and departed without a word.

"Welcome to West Germany," Thiess said. His voice was ironic, or perhaps it was just sarcasm. "May we speak in German or do you prefer Russian?"

"German will do," Roy said.

"Then I suggest you eat." Thiess motioned at the tray. "We can talk later."

There was a cutlet and fried potatoes, pickled beets and string beans. A half liter of burgundy shone dully in the glass carafe. Roy settled himself at the counter, his back to Thiess, and ate silently. Thiess brought out a pipe and scraped inside the bowl. He stuffed it carefully with pungent tobacco and lit up slowly. Roy thought the pipe a nice touch. It suggested informality and ease. But he couldn't say yet whether Thiess was a hard or soft man.

When he was through, he excused himself and went into the bathroom to rinse his hands. He returned to find Thiess settled in the one armchair, pencil and pad beside him on the table. He was waiting.

"I trust the meal was good."

"Very good," Roy said. He was pouring himself a stiff after-dinner chaser.

"Let us begin then. What is it you want from us?" Thiess asked directly.

"Sanctuary."

134

"And what else?"

"Compensation—money. Then travel papers, new identity . . . a new life."

"Do you have any specific identity in mind?"

"I don't know yet," Roy answered vaguely. "I want to set myself up here. It will take money."

"Here in Germany?"

"Possibly. . . ."

"But you don't have any definite plan in mind, what you want to do?"

"I didn't have time to think of that," Roy snapped.

"Quite." Thiess paused. "The books you brought with you, they have coded material in them, do they not?"

"You know they do."

"Is it a difficult code, one which you will have to work on yourself or can our people dismantle it?"

"There wasn't time to be fancy," Roy said. "It's the structure we rigged up for Felfe. I used only the first two tiers. You have the entire plan from the time you ran Felfe in."

Thiess rose and went over to the telephone. He asked for an extension and began speaking immediately. The conversation was one-sided and very brief. Roy guessed that the decoding room had been waiting.

"They will bring you the first few pages, to make certain the work is satisfactory," Thiess said. "Out of curiosity, what is the material?"

"Mostly China stuff. A few odds and ends about Germany. Some naval intelligence."

"Shall we talk about China Section?"

He's warming up, Roy thought. He wants to get into the German material, but he won't risk spooking me. So he will go easily, slowly, let me talk about this and that, get me comfortable, let me hear the sound of my own voice.

"It's all in the books," Roy said. "A complete list of units

135

stationed and in action along the Ussuri River, including those comprised of the Border Guards Directorate. Casualty rates, reserve strength, armament—light and heavy—deployment of tank regiments and fighter-bomber squadrons. I have also listed the position of the tactical nuclear task force."

Roy had thrown out the first of the bait. He was certain the Germans knew next to nothing about the Soviet nuclear arm in the east. The generosity of American intelligence agencies did not extend to sharing information of that importance.

Thiess, who had been making swift, short notes, looked up sharply.

"Could you be more precise about the nuclear arms?" he asked. "Are you speaking of missiles, short-range?"

Roy shook his head. "Warheads which can be delivered on something like the Scud rocket, only in this case the projectile is smaller, much faster, with a very sophisticated teleguidance system. It can be fired from mobile launchers which bear an uncanny resemblance to tanks, and the warheads themselves are covered by lead. American satellite reconnaissance probably mistook the launchers for conventional armor."

"Their number?"

"Launchers . . . about four hundred, with an equal amount in reserve some sixty miles back. Each launcher can fire two projectiles at a time, six projectiles per launcher."

"Deployment?"

"Along the Ussuri River between Vladivostok and Khabarovsk, then west along the Amur. In the event of a Chinese advance, the plans call for a wastage of the area forming a rough triangle between those two cities and Nerchinsk farther east."

136

"After that?"

"If the war does not terminate there, the rocketry in the Stanovoi Mountains will be released into the area three hundred miles south of the triangle, into the north-central part of China. Submarines in the Sea of Japan and the Yellow Sea will have Peking and Tientsin targeted. The Backfire bombers have standing orders to remove the Chinese missiles in Tibet, as well as the atomic installations in the Himalayan foothills."

Roy sat back and lit a cigarette. He had spoken quietly and fluently, as though reciting an academic exercise.

"And the Mongolian border?" Thiess asked him.

"Our strategy is to create a *cordon sanitaire* at the Chinese border. By devastating the area beginning at the border and running fifty to sixty miles into the interior, we would block off all possible traffic. At that point the major cities would still be spared. There will be no immediate invasion of the country, for we know that it is impossible to occupy China in the traditional sense. Yet the atomic sanitization of our common borders would guarantee that she could not invade us—and Bomber Command would make certain her nuclear arm has been completely and utterly broken."

Thiess looked down at his notes, which now covered a full three pages. He had noticed how Roy had slipped from the dry academic third person into the possessive, nationalistic "we."

"For someone who worked in the industrial sector of China Section, specifically on hydro power and dams, you have a very accurate—I assume it is accurate—assessment of an area which was not part of your responsibility."

Roy reached over and poured himself more whiskey.

"You know what it is like," he said softly, "to be trained to deal in death, to run operations. A coil is built inside

137

you. All the energy, time and precision which have been devoted to a single act stay pent up inside. You can live with that coil only if release comes from time to time, when you use your talents. When they put me in Analysis, they screwed the spring on tight. They left me no room. I have been trained for active reserve, and they were asking me to rot. The stuff I brought, that helped me stay sane; to work with it was a challenge. It kept me going. . . ."

He stopped himself and took a drink. "Look at what I brought you," he repeated roughly. "Check with the Americans if you like."

"You are a proud man," Thiess said. "You are right: They were stupid to do that to you."

"Since you have so much sympathy for me," Roy said quickly, "perhaps you will tell me what the BND has to offer. Tit for tat, I want to hear something from you."

"The sum will be substantial, enough for you to have a start—"

"How much, Thiess?"

"I am recommending DM fifty thousand. If your information is exceptional, the figure will naturally rise."

"Naturally."

"If you want further assurance, I can have a financial statement for you within the week, the money on account in Geneva. I assume you will want a Swiss bank."

"Yes."

"There are other possibilities, too. But there will be time for them later."

"Oh, Christ," Roy muttered. "You love to indulge in mysteries, don't you? You and your whole little service."

"We are very careful," Thiess conceded.

"And what would you like now?"

"Germany. Everything you can tell me about your old network in Germany."

Roy nodded and fetched another packet of cigarettes. He had not expected Thiess to go for the core so quickly. Perhaps Thiess believed preliminaries to be unnecessary. But under the soft, modulated tone Roy had detected a sense of urgency. After all, they had not brought him out so neatly and quickly for nothing. It would be a long night.

"I began building the network in '63," Roy said. "That was after training with Gorshkov's fleet in the east."

"You studied naval warfare and technology for three years," Thiess commented. "Obviously you were very good. Why did you give it up?"

"I learned German at Frunze. Picked it up easily and kept on with reading papers and whatnot. Then I realized that what interested me was the whole German mentality, the peculiar way you people speak and act, the gestures and nuances, the schizophrenic split in your nature. As it turned out, I had an instinctive feel for things German. In '61 I was seconded to GRU's European theater. A year and half later I was running agents out of East Berlin."

He stopped abruptly, remembering the room was wired. He was speaking of things he should not speak of, and he could not comfort himself with the thought of the fallibility of Thiess' memory. Somewhere in the house, in a hidden basement or a barrack well away from the cottage, an anonymous tape recorder was cementing his treachery on dark-brown ribbon. That he would never escape.

"It wasn't the best time for us," Roy picked up again. His tone dropped out of caution or shame, but it would not matter to the microphones.

"No, it wasn't," Thiess said gently. "Go on."

"You picked up Felfe in November, 1961, and that did in most of the network around him. We needed new blood, new connections. I managed to arrange two couri-

139

ers who could run material either through the Wall or into Luxembourg. But soon it became obvious that the material they were carrying did not justify the risk. There was a lot of dead wood strangling the operating area. Some of the agents had become so lazy that their information was barely one step ahead of the international news, worthless by the time we got it. There was also too much traffic in intelligence, too many free-lancers, liars and thieves. It was becoming harder and harder to separate the genuine stuff from the fakes. Secret memoranda, not worth the paper they were written on, could be bought in the streets of Berlin at any time of day.

"So in the end I sent the small fry packing, even turned a couple of V-men, Gehlen's recruiters in the eastern zone, who went back to Pullach, but got no results. They probably spilled everything to the case officers. That left me, in early '64, with a nucleus of three good agents and two couriers working out of Bonn. They were still the best people I had when the operation fell apart in '65."

"Your nucleus was five," Thiess said. "That was very small."

"We had the quality, though," Roy said with a touch of pride. "We produced results. And we couldn't risk quick expansion because Sister had invested heavily around Bonn. It was her domain. There were so many agents from KGB Center tripping over one another between Berlin and Cologne that we were afraid ours might be picked up by accident, in a general sweep. But then we were safe, relatively speaking. We had Henlinger."

Roy didn't mind rubbing Thiess' sore. Henlinger, a personal friend of Gehlen's, had eventually been picked up in 1966. The scandal was bigger than the one which erupted during the Felfe trial five years before. Henlinger, who had been protected by Gehlen against counterespionage investigations, had brought his mentor to the ground. Gehlen "retired" eighteen months later.

"Tell me about Henlinger," Thiess said softly.

"We have a saying at Center," Roy said. He was smiling, but his voice was hard. "It is this: Old Nazis never die, they just fade away into the security services of West Germany. True, no?"

Thiess' mouth tightened, but he said nothing.

"It is an elementary fact that the greatest weakness of both the BND and BfV is the presence of many Nazis and former SS and SD officers in the top ranks. Look at how we got Henlinger.

"In '55 two old pals met on the train from Cologne to Düsseldorf. One was called Trepper, more precisely ex-Standartenführer Trepper. The other was Hoffmann, a bull-necked thug who had been the Gestapo's 'military attaché' to Mussolini's OVRA.

"Trepper had been denazified, that double-think process which converts murderers into patriots, and joined Gehlen early in 1952. At the time he ran into Hoffmann, Trepper was deputy personnel director at Pullach. He looked kindly upon Hoffmann, who was then out of a job and broke, and offered him a position as 'collector,' recruiting other former Nazis and using the Karlsruhe office as base. Hoffmann, eager to repay his debt, began scouring the countryside and eventually brought a total of fourteen ex-SS and SD men into the Pullach Org. Among them was Henlinger.

"Trepper helped Hoffmann out, but he never liked him personally. Hoffmann was too crude and vulgar. Henlinger, on the other hand, was smooth, urbane and *korrekt.* After only seven months' service, Trepper promoted him

141

to the position of assistant investigator in counterespionage at Pullach.

"The weak link in the chain was Hoffmann. Trepper must have investigated Hoffmann to some degree, but what Trepper never discovered was that Hoffmann was working for us all along. He had made contact with us in Dresden, where his wife was living. In fact, it was she who brought him in. We gave him a retainer of DM seven hundred and fifty, told him to act poor and get into the Org via the old killers' network. Things had gone very slowly until he caught on to Trepper. But once Hoffmann was inside, he got Henlinger inside, too, and we could not have asked for anything more."

"So it is not only we who use former Nazis," Thiess said.

"But we never trust them, and you do," Roy countered, smiling faintly. "Blood is thicker than water with you. Your service was born under the Nazi shadow and lives in it to this day. That is your weakness," he repeated.

"Did you run Henlinger at all?"

"He was before my time. I used him once or twice, but that was all. Because of the position Henlinger held, his information was always of top quality. Sometimes it was at Center before Gehlen himself saw it. But even more important was the fact that we now had a chance to recruit and place men fairly high up in the service. I took over this second generation in the middle sixties."

"And your Henlinger, your success, was Berg."

It may have been pain which caused Roy's lips to flinch. He remembered that lonely night in Mitko's office as they listened in silence to the tape-recorded words of a man who was already dead. He remembered Berg's last request, that his wife be found and taken care of by the state she had faithfully served. He wondered where Martha

Berg was now and what had become of her. He was not certain he would be able to do even that much for Berg.

"Berg was the best of the lot of them," Roy said softly.

"He brought you a great deal, didn't he?"

"Whatever we asked for. Anything that came in from allied intelligence in NATO, from BND pals not in NATO —Israel, for example—from the Americans, it was all on my desk in a matter of days. We passed it all on to counterespionage and twisted your pathetic little men around our fingers. Some we picked up; others we fed useless stuff, listened in on their radio signals, watched their dead drops and courier runs. Everything, Thiess, bloody everything."

Roy was grinning, like a wolf that has been caught but still manages to take a chunk out of the hunter. Could it be pride? Thiess wondered. Is that what will finally crack him, that along with his hatred for the Germans which fuels his pride at having beaten us? Will this make him reveal all he has been trained never to reveal, speak in a manner which forces his conscience first to revolt, then to acquiesce?

Every defector had a method of weakness peculiar to himself. Some who came over were already dead men. They spoke in low monotones, like machines spinning out their last tapes. They no longer wanted to hear what they were saying. They had insulated themselves against the remorse which accompanied every word, and they prayed that it might be over with quickly. Others spoke up frantically, pushing the information out of themselves as though they were choking on it. These sought shelter and kindness. They needed to have the comfort of another human voice, to share a cigarette, to drink a glass of whiskey in company instead of perpetually alone. They were not the best men to handle. They beat their breasts too much and wailed too loudly. They misreported information, repeated themselves, forgot the most important details, not out of design but out of simple confusion. The interrogators had to be patient enough to sift out, from the hundreds of hours of tapes and reams of transcripts, what was usable and what was fantasy, padding or shameless, desperate lies.

The best men were those like Roy. Their motive was simple: survival. Not any crisis of conscience, change of heart or disillusionment but simple survival. Roy did not pretend to like Thiess or any German. How could he when he had worked so hard against them? And he was still a proud man, not bowing his head to the enemy but challenging him, recounting and laughing at his weaknesses. Roy did not want Thiess' friendship, although he was human and needed it. But he was too proud to ask for it. It would have been a sign of weakness.

Thiess didn't care. He would be with Roy for only a fortnight, three weeks at the most. He would use that pride, prick it on occasion, remind Roy of his weak position, then fall back and let Roy win a point or two. He would lead Roy to the confession slowly, pressing, probing, retreating when he hit a wrong nerve. He would help Roy overcome himself. It was only a matter of time. Roy knew he would have to talk, and Thiess was there to make this as painless as possible.

Roy had been drinking steadily, but when the door opened, he started. A uniformed orderly, submachine gun slung over his shoulder, clicked his heels and saluted Thiess.

"Idiot!" Roy muttered.

The orderly heard but did not look in his direction. He handed Thiess a large brown envelope and stepped back. Thiess did not open it but passed it to Roy.

"The first pages from decoding. Will you have a look at them?"

Roy tore open the envelope and settled the half dozen legal-size sheets on his lap. He turned to the light and read through them quickly.

"It's all right. They've got the hang of it."

"You are certain nothing is missing. No errors?"

"I said so, didn't I?"

Thiess took the papers back, handed them to the orderly and dismissed him.

"You were talking about Berg," he said.

Roy hesitated. "Yes, I was."

And slowly he began to speak of the Bonn operation. He started with Berg's personality, the dedication that enabled him to pass daily through either side of the mirror, by day stepping into his office at the Chancellery, by evening coding and transmitting reports to GRU Center. Roy had met Berg three times and was impressed. The power Berg held had not corrupted him. He had learned that to master power, to remain in control, one must always step away from power, never clutch at it. Power was a means, not an end.

Berg had been groomed as Center's primary agent in West Germany. At first, when Berg joined the Social Democratic Party, he sent nothing, engaged in no espionage activities. He watched and waited. Promoted to district organizer, he sent in minor pieces of intelligence, dealing with party personalities, their private lives, their weaknesses. But Berg continued to play very carefully. He was biding his time.

145

As soon as he was made secretary of the party, Center opened a special frequency for his exclusive use.

Over the next three years Center's patience paid off handsomely. As in Henlinger's case, it was the character of the BND that was at fault.

"The French are stupid at intelligence, no good at all," Roy said. "The British suffer from nepotism and the mysterious old boy network. But the Germans had, until a few months ago, the greatest malaise. It lay squarely with their director, Gehlen."

Gehlen had learned nothing from his experience with Henlinger. Whomever the chief trusted, he trusted blindly and protected from counterespionage investigation. Gehlen had a long history with Berg, who had been one of his agents in East Germany. When Berg came to the West, he did so under Gehlen's mantle. By the time he was finally posted as security adviser to the chancellor he was invincible. Not even Schareck and the BfV could take on both Gehlen and the chancellor.

When Berg was certain of the security of his posting, he asked Roy to organize the satellite network which would speed information through to Moscow in bulk.

At this point Thiess interrupted. He did not want Roy to go into the minor agents until he had all the details about the big one, Berg. Thiess put his questions delicately, playing Roy as precisely as if he were a master violinist. In smooth but unhurried succession he queried Berg's payments, bank accounts, safe houses, the dead drops and the schedules of Berg's couriers, the means of transport Berg preferred, the sequence of delivery dates he chose, the role of Berg's wife. He asked for everything that even remotely had to do with Berg, personally, professionally, as a traitor. And as though both men had come to a tacit understanding, Roy gave him everything.

There was no pause. Roy, drinking slowly and steadily as though fueling himself, pressed on, never avoiding a question, rounding out details clearly. Sometimes he would pace about the room or stare out the window into the cloudy, desolate sky, and the pane would cloud from the warmth of his breath. To the frozen trees and whitened grass he talked of the Essen chemist and the woman of the air force officer, documenting their recruitment, payment, delivery of materials. He spoke of the tennis player and how he had seen him arrive that night in East Berlin. He talked of everything.

It was midmorning of the second day when Roy at last staggered to the couch and collapsed into sleep. He had reached the end. He had given up everything he knew of his own network, that of Sister, and whatever he could think of about the intelligence operations of the Warsaw Pact countries. He had spoken, with few interruptions, for some forty hours, and when he finally stopped, it was Christmas morning.

# CHAPTER NINE

## *Interlude in Byzantium*

"DID ANYONE FOLLOW YOU FROM TWELFTH?"

"Undoubtedly. It was to be expected. But you have invited me here. This is your territory, not that of the KGB. My shadows will be very lonesome."

Valentin Jovanich Ponomarev spoke with an arrogant certainty. He had flown from Moscow to the invisible city of Leninsk that afternoon. A ranking member of the Politburo and expert on the space program, Ponomarev traveled not only with his personal bodyguard, now sitting up front with the driver, but also with two members of the Twelve Department, Surveillance Directorate.

"There will be no obstruction," Mitko said. "Let them stay with you, as closely as they like. I will have some people looking after them. They watch you, we watch them; the game is understood, the rules respected."

Ponomarev nodded and sat back in the cushions of the

limousine. He was the youngest member of the Politburo, a trim, well-dressed man barely into his fifties. His hair was carefully arranged to disguise his partial baldness, his face set in the inscrutable features of a leader, easy with authority. Ponomarev nodded at the glass partition, soundproof and bulletproof, between the rear compartment and the front seat.

"I suggest you tell me about Roy now," he said. "While there is strict privacy." Ponomarev never wasted any time.

"Roy went over on the twenty-third," Mitko said. "He is at Pullach now, quarantined."

"Is there a line of communication between you?"

"Nothing. It would have been a needless risk. Roy will report as soon as he has anything. I leave the when and wherefore to him."

"But you do have someone waiting, if he returns."

"I do."

"I am still concerned about the timing," Ponomarev said. "He has a little over a month. That is not very long, I am told, by operating standards."

"It will be long enough."

"And Bibnikov?"

Mitko permitted himself a tepid smile. "There was a meeting of Committee One on the evening of Roy's defection," he said. "Bibnikov made an unusual mistake in assuring all present he had suspected something like this was going to happen. Andropov shut him up by asking why he hadn't done anything about it. From then on the discussion was routine. We assessed the damage Roy would do to the networks and fell back on contingency planning."

"Didn't Andropov ask you about Roy?"

"He did. And I told him what I had said before, at the meeting of Committee One. We had made a mistake. We

149

had deliberately destroyed a good intelligence agent, and now we were paying for it."

"Did he accept your argument?"

"He had little choice, with the facts staring him in the face."

"I imagine Bibnikov is frothing." Ponomarev laughed.

"He is, but only inwardly." Mitko's tone was soft, but the words carried a rebuke. "Do not ever underestimate Bibnikov. He has lost this round because he was too cautious. He had surveillance on Roy, but for some reason he did not move in for the kill. Something worried him, perhaps because I didn't fight hard enough for Roy. Now he sees he has made a mistake. But it does not follow he will become careless."

"I think you are too pessimistic," Ponomarev suggested. "He is not that dangerous, not now."

"I think I only wish to succeed," Mitko said evenly. "That is what we all want."

Ponomarev let it go. He believed that Mitko was playing it too tightly, but that was only his opinion. Up until now everything had held, and Ponomarev was not about to stir matters up.

"What about Vovchok?" he asked.

Again Mitko gave the semblance of a smile. "Koldakov is very pleased with his progress. There is no question that he will be ready."

"He is the weakest link in the chain," Ponomarev murmured. "As long as he is with Koldakov, there is no danger, but when he is released. . . ."

"There will be someone with him until the very last minute."

"But we are dealing with such an unstable personality."

"Is a patriot an unstable person?" Mitko demanded.

150

"Vovchok's target is the man who destroyed his country, his family and his career. Surely we understand why Vovchok is willing, even glad to act?"

The question was rhetorical, and Ponomarev did not answer.

"You know, of course, that the Politburo has been informed of the, eh, exercise on January 23," Ponomarev said. "They are really quite fascinated by this Blueprint idea."

"They will be even more interested when the recall signal doesn't come," Mitko said tonelessly. "The exercise is scheduled to start at dawn of the twenty-third. Throughout the evening of the twenty-second, our troops will be quietly withdrawn from the forward areas in the east, again under the pretext of an exercise. The first bombers will penetrate Chinese territory at exactly five in the morning."

"With no recall."

"None. The pilots will receive their orders directly from Moscow as soon as the new government is installed."

"God help us if we don't hit them hard enough the first round," Ponomarev said softly. "It will be a nightmare."

"Believe me, we will strike effectively," Mitko said coldly. "So long as the Politburo ceases to exist on the night of the twenty-second, nothing, *nothing* can go wrong."

Ponomarev remained silent. He suddenly thought it a very awesome thing, to start a war.

It was Tamara's second evening in prison. Bibnikov had picked her up at her apartment, on the afternoon of the day Roy had gone over.

They had put her in Cell Block Four of Boutyrky Prison on Voronezh Street. Tamara was the sole occupant of a cell that usually held four prisoners. In the center a scarred wooden table was bolted to the concrete floor, and there were two chairs at either end, also bolted. But apart from these peculiar furnishings, the cell was as filthy and cold, the mattress as lice-ridden and dirty, as any other.

Tamara sat huddled in one corner, on the floor. She would have preferred to sit at the table but was afraid to do so. She didn't think it was there for her use. Her hair, once loose down her back and silky, was knotted again in the bun she had worn before Roy had come to her. For the fortnight they had been together, she had squandered her money on gentle oils for her skin. Now it was itchy once more and beginning to flake. They had given her disinfectant powder, but it had only brought on a rash. Of all the features in that thin, drawn face, only the eyes remained as Roy would have remembered them, huge, brown and liquid. Tamara began to cry once more.

When she awoke to find him gone, she had cried, knowing as only a woman can that he would not be back. She had showered, tidied the flat and left. When she returned to her squalid little room, anger, resentment, fear for him and shame at the emptiness of her dreams swept down upon her. She was confused and alone, vulnerable without her lover. That was how Bibnikov found her—lying on her bed, the pillow clutched tightly against her face to stifle her sobs.

Bibnikov had not been rough with her, only indifferent. He pulled her to her feet without the slightest effort and told her to take a warm coat. She had thrown away her winter coat, it had been so threadbare, so she took a heavy shapeless jacket instead. That was all the ceremony behind her arrest.

In the car Bibnikov formally announced that she was

under arrest. He had sounded like an irate Moscow commuter, annoyed because the bus was late. In the same tone he explained that the man she had been intimate with, Captain Roy, had been engaged in treasonable activity and had fled to the West. Like all cowards, Captain Roy had used honest Soviet citizens, particularly Tamara, to help him in his treachery and dirtied the good name of others to mask his own duplicity. Bibnikov expressed his sympathy and ended by stating that he was certain Tamara would cooperate with the investigating authorities. He sounded very bored by it all and did not bother to explain why she needed to be arrested in order to cooperate with the state.

At Boutyrky, in a small, stuffy office that had been requisitioned for the occasion, Tamara told Bibnikov all she knew about Roy, which was very little. She spoke in a dull monotone; but sometimes, when she remembered something they had done together or a particular evening, her voice rose excitedly, and she twisted in her chair as though she expected him to walk through the door that instant.

Bibnikov listened without interruption, making few notes. He had read all the surveillance reports carefully. The places the girl spoke of and the times correlated almost exactly. But that was not what he was after.

"What did he do at the library?"

Tamara was confused. Roy had clearance to the files she had given him.

"And the evenings? Why did he spend so many evenings there?"

"He was new in the department. His own work wasn't going well. I think there was some trouble with Major Panev. Alexander was trying hard to understand the background of China Section."

153

"That's all?"

Bibnikov's tone was insinuating, and Tamara flushed.

"Yes, that's all," she whispered.

"I do not believe you." Bibnikov sighed. "You saw enough of each other without having to screw in the stacks. But that is not *all* of it."

"I don't understand," Tamara cried softly. "It is the truth."

"You gave Roy nothing but files intended for the D rating?"

"He never asked for anything more."

"And had he, would you have given him whatever he wanted?"

Tamara hesitated for the briefest instant, but it was enough. When she finally said no, her voice was low and uncertain.

"Perhaps, perhaps not." Bibnikov shrugged. "The fact is that yesterday, someone opened the file cabinet, the double A section. Whoever did this was unauthorized, for no one with the proper clearance went into the library either in the afternoon or in the evening. This person could have had only one motive, don't you think, for wanting to look into the double A material?"

"I don't know," Tamara said helplessly.

"Guess!"

She shook her head violently.

"To steal the secrets of China Section—would that be a reasonable explanation?"

Bibnikov waited for the reaction but got none. The girl sat unmoving, barely breathing.

"I told you Roy was a traitor. I said that someone gained entry into the double A material—"

"How do you know this is so?" Tamara asked suddenly.

154

"We took the precaution of installing a small seal on the lock. We did not tell you, of course, or anyone else. Today the seal is broken. Since we know that no authorized person went to that cabinet, we can assume that either you or Roy or both were responsible for breaking it. So I repeat: Did you give him material from section double A?"

"No."

"Then only the key and he went and got it himself?"

"No."

"Then who broke the seal?" Bibnikov screamed. His huge fist pounded the table, inches away from Tamara's fingers.

"I don't know!" she cried. "I don't know! Please. . . ." And again she wept but this time hysterically, from terror.

"Are you so stupid as to believe he was diligent in his work?" Bibnikov kept on. "That it was diligence which made him return night after night for D material which wasn't of the slightest use to him?" Bibnikov towered over her, his voice twisting and tearing at her nerves. "Didn't you *know* he was copying state secrets?"

Had Bibnikov asked that question first, Tamara would have given herself away completely. Now her fear and tears spared her. Yes, she had known Roy was doing more than sifting through old D records. He was not a man to work so hard over nothing, toward a goal for which he had only contempt, to keep precise schedules and concentrate rigorously in order to satisfy a superior for whom he had no respect. The truth was out when she saw him, accidentally, coming out of the double A section. He had looked at her, and she remembered the spark of fear in his eyes. But he had said nothing and moved back to his table. Neither of them ever mentioned the incident.

She should have reported him then, of course. Twice

during the next day her hand was on the telephone. She had the number she could call. It would require only a few words. But she waited all day, and when he walked through the doors at six o'clock and kissed her, she was happy that he was there and no one would be coming to take him away. After that she never thought of calling again.

Her complicity did not change her feeling that what he was doing was wrong. But perhaps there was a reason. She tried to convince herself that he was engaged in very secret research, that he had special orders from the head of Center himself, but nothing could erase the tainted feeling that had slid over her like a soft silk sheen. She was now a criminal, too. In the end she accepted that he would be caught and he would have to leave her. Either they would arrest him or he would flee, and she would be alone again.

Yet she told no one. There was a bond between them, of loneliness and need, which had been born long before she had caught him coming from the double A section. He had been kind to her, but not because he had known he would steal and she would not report him. He had not taken her out on his arm because she was either useful or beautiful, and he had not slept with her out of pity or in the vulgar way other men wanted to. A current of love cannot exist unless there are two poles for it to flow between. Tamara had come to love him, and although he had said nothing, she knew he loved her too. Every triviality which is attributed to love sickness—the touching of hands, the understood silence, the pleasure of another presence—this and much more was real between them. So when the time came, Tamara could not betray the man she loved. She surrendered to the happiness that rose within her when he came through the door, and she would not take away one moment of the time he could be hers. She had gained little in life. This one chance, this one love she had had to take. She had to know once, if never again, what else life could hold, aside from grinding misery and waste.

Bibnikov lit another one of his cigarettes and leaned toward her. "You did know, didn't you?"

Tamara shook her head. "I knew nothing."

Bibnikov nodded and sat back. Before he could proceed further, he had to have a full psychological profile on the girl. He had to know what frightened her, what dreams she had, how deeply she loved, or thought she loved, Roy. Every weakness had to be tabulated, and a method for exploiting it devised. It would take a little time, and Bibnikov did not have much to spare. It would have been much easier if the girl had had some family.

"That will be all for now," Bibnikov said abruptly and walked out, deliberately leaving her with the feeling she had been abandoned.

That same afternoon she was taken to the infirmary, where the doctors were waiting for her. They asked her questions about herself, her family, the circumstances of their deaths and the kinds of men she favored. They led her gently back over her life, asking when she had lost her virginity and whether she had had any pets as a child. Tamara answered honestly, and the doctors were kind to her. It was very late when they finally led her to the cell and let her sleep an exhausted sleep. The next day they began again and they continued without interruption to the end of the week.

During each interrogation, every day, she hardly thought of anything but Roy—where he was now, whether he was safe or hungry, alone and afraid as she was. No, he

157

was all right. Her heart told her that. And he hadn't been caught, and this made her happy. But the nights were the worst. She would reach out for him, crying, and when she awoke and he wasn't there, she would lie mutely, her eyes fixed on the ceiling. The only question her heart refused to answer was whether she would ever see him again.

Finally, the questioning was over, and Tamara was back in her cell. She did not stand as Bibnikov entered. He carried nothing with him and sat down at the table, asking, in his nondescript tone, for her to be seated in the other chair. She obeyed. Then he asked her to repeat her story about Roy.

What Bibnikov did not tell her was that he knew Tamara very well now. He knew exactly what she was afraid of.

# CHAPTER TEN

## *The Mercker Report*

IT WAS THE BEGINNING of Roy's second week in the West. The weather had grown coarser. The sky was a uniform gray with the sun a dull yellow ball high above the clouds. Ice mists hung over the tops of trees, and on the ground, the grass crackled under one's footsteps.

He made himself breakfast from the provisions in the refrigerator. They were good about the food. An orderly had come on Saturday and taken his order for the following week. Even out of season there was melon.

When he finished, he rang up the switchboard and told the girl he wanted to go for a walk. Twenty minutes later Thiess appeared, the same scarred leather coat, the high boots soaked with frost.

"I need some air," Roy said. "Let's walk."

"We would like you to have a look at the China material once more," Thiess said once they were outside. "There are certain discrepancies."

Roy grunted and said nothing. He stepped up the pace, walking briskly in long strides, swinging his arms from side to side. The cold air drove deep into his tired smoke-filled lungs, piercing his tension and exhaustion. After the marathon session Thiess had left him alone for a day, but on Friday they were back at it, the proceedings lasting twelve hours. Roy thought the Americans had probably inspected the bulk of the China material and were coming back with questions.

They reached the wall which surrounds Pullach and turned to the left. This was the northernmost part of the compound, well away from the main buildings and traffic.

"Tell me about Red Spring," Thiess said, "and the Mercker Report. We did not talk very much about that."

Roy, walking a pace ahead of Thiess, was surprised. This was the third time Thiess had returned to the report, the springboard for one of the most significant successes Soviet espionage had ever scored against Germany. Thiess was smelling something, and Roy didn't know what. Perhaps today Thiess would tip his hand.

Roy rubbed his hands together and stuffed them deep into the coat pockets. He had forgotten to bring gloves.

"All right, Thiess, we'll do it once more, and that will be the end, right?" He spoke in a tight voice, hiding none of his exasperation. "I don't know why you're making such a fuss over this. It's very clear."

"Just talk," Thiess murmured. "I am overlooking something."

"The trouble began in '67," Roy said. "Gehlen was on the way out and nominated two people for the succession—Wessel and Wendland.

"Wendland looked like the most likely to get the old man's job. He had the support of the majority of the staff

160

at Pullach, which was impressive but not very surprising, because Wendland was of the old school, the largest petrified tree in the petrified forest. Wessel, on the other hand, was something of a maverick. He had left the BND in '52 and built up MAD, military intelligence, which soon started grazing on the BND's paddock—intelligence gathering. He even wanted to run independent offensive operations, the sin of all sins.

"In the end, the chancellor chose Wessel. Not a bad choice, since he happened to be a good intelligence officer and would have done a good job of cleaning up the BND nest. But the chancellor also appointed a three-man committee to help Wessel along. The chairman was Chief of Section One, Reinhold Mercker, and his committee's investigation lasted some five months. During that time the BND was virtually turned inside out. The investigators spent, I believe it was, five full weeks at Pullach alone. Then they moved to the out stations. If an officer refused to answer, he was threatened with arrest on criminal conspiracy. Nor could you argue that you had been ordered by your superior to remain silent. Juniors were bullied until they talked, and sometimes commanders were brought in to give verbal reassurance that no one would be prosecuted under the Official Secrets Act.

"What came out of all this was the Mercker Report. Four copies exist."

"As I have said before, you are mistaken," Thiess said sharply. "That is not the number."

"Then what about the copy sitting in Mitko's safe in Moscow?" Roy shouted. "How many times do we have to argue about pieces of paper which every senior officer in Soviet intelligence has read three times over?"

"When did the report come to Moscow?"

"I received it exactly seven days after it was handed to the chancellor."

Thiess lapsed into silence, his lips tightening. The Mercker Report was still volatile material in Bonn. Only the most senior members of government had read even parts of it. Fewer than a dozen officials had been privy to the entire text, which evaluated the performance of every cell of the BND structure.

Mercker and his team dissected every department and all the subdivisions of the departments. The report examined intracell rivalries, personality clashes, political pandering, blackmail and budget pleas. It detailed the nepotism that had set into the BND during Gehlen's last years, the misappropriation of budget money to further the political ends and social ambitions of BND veterans, the condescending manner in which young officers, who were technocrats instead of war heroes, were treated.

The rot within the BND had spread so far that very few names from the Org's general roll were absent from the Mercker Report. Those, along with minute details on BND's daily activities and overall scope of operations, provided a virtual tour guide of West German intelligence. It was of untold value to Moscow Center.

"It was Berg?" Thiess asked him.

"Of course."

Roy continued: "The Mercker Report started the run. The old BND guard was worried sick that the government would throw them over without the customary golden handshake which usually amounted to DM one hundred thousand. A lot of them, former SS and SD officers, had nowhere else to go in German society. Certainly no other government service would take them on. Still, the panic could have been avoided if Wessel had been a trifle less zealous. He should have kept on old Wendland, even if it meant creating a figurehead position. But it became clear to Wendland and the hangers-on that Wessel would have nothing to do with them, and then it began.

"On October 18 of last year Wendland put a Belgian pistol to his temple and splattered his brains all over the office. Three hours later Rear Admiral Ludke, whose preference was a shotgun, did himself in. The next week Heinrich Schenk, a senior at the Ministry of Economics, hanged himself in Cologne. The day after, Edeltraud Grapentin of the Federal Press Office died from an overdose of sleeping pills. On the eighteenth Lieutenant Colonel Johannes Grimm, Defense Staff Operations, also died by his own hand, and finally, on the twenty-first, Gerhard Bohm, also from Defense, disappeared. He was found three days later, drowned.

"Apart from Wendland and Grapentin, who were of no interest to us, the deaths of the others were of enormous benefit to our security operations. Although not one of the dead was in our employ, we had agents in all their offices. In the confusion and speculation that followed the suicides—the so-called Red Spring because the press believed all the dead had been working for us—the people whom we controlled moved higher and deeper into the new organization. As the old Nazis ran for cover, our agents quietly took over the vacant echelons and, in one case, a subministerial post."

"I assume we have all the names," Thiess interrupted.

"You have all of mine. Sister's you will have to ferret out yourself."

"So Wendland's death really had nothing to do with your operations," Thiess murmured. "All the panic was over nothing."

163

"That's right."

"And it was Berg who brought you the Mercker Report."

"Yes."

"Forgive me for saying so, but I find that very curious. You see, I know the distribution list. Berg's name was not on it."

"That's impossible." Roy shook his head. "As the chancellor's adviser on security affairs he must have had access to it."

"You are wrong," Thiess murmured.

"Balls!" Roy snapped. "How else would we have got it?"

"I don't know," Thiess said thoughtfully. "Do you remember *exactly* when you received it?"

Roy leaned against a tree, his forehead pressing into the sticky bark.

"The report was commissioned at the end of January. It took about five months, so that would be June . . . June 23 or 24."

"It must have been delivered by courier."

"Some parts were transmitted."

"On the schedule you wrote out for us?"

"That's right. Berg gave us what he thought were the vital parts, in case it should prove impossible to get the full report to Moscow. But we had it seven days later, complete, intact."

"Who was the courier?"

"The mechanic. He used to service Berg's car. Let me ask *you* a question now. What have you done with Martha Berg?"

Thiess regarded him steadily, but he seemed embarrassed at the about-turn. "That is not in my province. You can discuss that with Schareck."

164

"Well, well." Roy grinned. "I wondered if I would ever meet the great man himself."

"What day did the mechanic pick up the report?"

"I told you I can't remember. I gave you an approximate time. You'll have to get by on that. Maybe it will come to me."

"It will be important," Thiess said. "Schareck will ask you about that. You would do well to have an answer ready."

But he did not meet Schareck that evening as he half expected to. Nor did he take up Thiess' offer to play a round of squash. The morning talk had left him drained and dispirited.

He was puzzled by Thiess' skepticism that Berg had provided Center with the Mercker Report. No one else could have done it, yet Thiess was hinting that Berg must have been acting in concert with someone, a source closer to the report than Berg himself. It didn't make sense, and it seemed to Roy irrational that Thiess would suddenly break his smooth procedural pattern to follow a tangent.

He poured himself two measures of whiskey and turned on the television. An American film, dubbed, was playing. He adjusted the volume low and sat facing the screen, alternately reaching for the cigarettes and the glass, wondering if he should have accepted Thiess' proposition. Before leaving, Thiess had offered him a woman. Roy had laughed and declined, thanking Thiess for his consideration. Now the idea came back to him.

He thought of Tamara, remembering her long, hard body. He could picture her lying in the crook of his arm, her face turned upward, hair splashed across the whiteness of the pillow, the pace of her breath as he stroked her

165

breasts and buried his lips in her neck. Tamara was a woman he had discovered. Like that magic swan which hides under the feathers of the ugly duckling, she had come out for him. Now, he thought, she has probably retreated into the stale drabness of an uncaring, unloved woman. Yet her memory gave him a powerful, painful joy, for Tamara was more real for him, more alive and female in her hidden beauty than Anna was in hers, knowing she possessed it, proud and unhesitant to accept the homage it brought. Anna had the power and influence of the new Soviet bourgeoisie, the disdain, contempt and pride which marked the upper echelons of his society. It was a world Roy knew well. Its aristocrats had been born at the time of the Revolution and had emerged alive from the purges and the Great Patriotic War. Unlike Europe, here the aristocrats were the survivors, not the victims.

He did not begrudge Anna's people anything. Good socialists they were not, communists even less, but they were fiercely loyal to their country. Yet in the process of their survival and struggle for accumulation, something had fled from their souls—an implicit joy of life, an honest simplicity and sharing which he had seen flow from Tamara. In high places men developed squints from telling too many lies and overtaxed the medical facilities with nerve-related disorders. Wives kept strict watch not over their own husbands, but over the spouses of their friends. A pass over in promotion, a transfer to a position of lesser responsibility, a failure to attend the rigorous social calls—all were danger signals, warning lights flashing along a dark coastline. The whispered word filtered across dinner tables, opera boxes and management meetings, and soon the unfortunate family would be cut loose by its friends, just as her father had cautioned Anna to set herself free of Roy.

Angels on a pinhead, friends in time of need, in most cases they numbered the same.

He thought of Tamara, whom life, as he knew it, had passed by. Normally a girl without pedigree would never have worked at Center. He had never asked her how she had got her job but supposed there must have been a shortage of librarians at one time. Tamara had been taken on temporarily and installed permanently either out of neglect or sloth on the part of the supervisor.

And he had come to love this girl. She cared for him in the small ways he seldom saw or acknowledged. His shirts were freshly washed without any of the harshness that clung to them from the laundry. At the end of the week his working desk was cleared of the ashes and scrap paper which cluttered it. There appeared a small porcelain jug where he could toss his kopeks, which he did not like to convey around with his other change. Yes, they were small things, but in them Tamara showed her love, and she was not ashamed to offer it in the ways she could.

Yet he had used her. Used her as coldly and methodically as his instinct, training and experience had taught him. Deliberately he brought her into a world where she could not defend herself, and he had known there would come a point when he would not be there to protect her either.

Roy poured another drink and tossed it down, trying to dissolve the choking feeling in his throat. But it was too strong. His head pitched forward, and tears streamed from his eyes and through his fingers as he covered his face with his hands. The importance of the mission, the sweet chase of revenge, sank away, and only the terrible vacuum of time remained. Time—Mitko had said it might be two weeks or two months before he found what he had come for. Two months—that was too long. Tamara would not survive that long. If Koldakov failed to protect her, if Bibnikov hurt her, Roy swore he would make it very difficult for Bibnikov to die. He had to die, that much was written. But if Tamara had been hurt, Bibnikov would suffer as well. As the tears fell, he understood that the responsibility for Tamara's fate would have to be shared between him and Bibnikov.

Yet through his grief he remained the intelligence officer. One part of him, the eternal observer, watched the entire scene. He knew the automatic cameras were recording every emotion. Tomorrow, before coming, Thiess would watch this display, and he would think Roy was beginning to break, that the weight of his defection was destroying him. Thiess would think his work had gone successfully, and he would look forward to squeezing out the last bits of information Roy was still holding back. And he would give Thiess certain information. Roy was acting in full honesty with his feelings, but that honesty would deceive Thiess into accepting something other than what he expected.

And sometimes, as now, honesty was what paradoxically would have the most effect, for the lie.

The next morning Thiess called on him early. Roy had not slept that night. He had drunk half a bottle of whiskey, yet it had brought him no peace. He had paced and thought, smoked and drunk some more.

Thiess brought him his bank statement. The account was in the name of Helmut Strauss. The letter from the Credit Suisse manager, addressed to a safe house in Munich, stated that the bank was very pleased to have received Herr Strauss' initial deposit of DM 50,000 and that this would be invested, as requested, in ninety-day notes.

168

The manager was looking forward to further instructions at the end of this period.

"My services are worth more than that, Thiess," Roy said.

"I have taken the matter to Department Four's Finance Division. They have gone to Wessel, and I will speak to him next week. I am suggesting a retainer of DM ten thousand per month until we are through."

"How long do you keep me?"

Thiess hesitated. "I can't tell you exactly—"

"Well, you had bloody better!" Roy shouted at him. "I'm sick of being cooped up here. I'm also tired of seeing your face!"

"It is difficult, I know," Thiess said quietly. He did not appear to have taken offense. "You have shown great patience. I ask you to hold on for a little longer. I could lie to you and say it will only be another few weeks. But I don't know."

"You're hanging onto me for something," Roy said slowly. "You're saving me. For what, Thiess?"

"Schareck wants to see you," Thiess said. His voice dropped as though he were warning Roy. "He has been kept up to date on your development. He is interested in you. Also resentful for not being able to get to you. But I do not want to let him in yet."

"All right, I'm happy for the lot of you. You are all very pleased mucking about in your sandbox filled with departmental intrigue. What about me?"

"You will have enough money, enough to start with, at any rate, and if you are careful, it will last. Your identity as Helmut Strauss is complete. There are a West German passport and residence papers. You are a political science

169

instructor, educated at the universities of Heidelberg and Berne. With those qualifications you can travel and work anywhere you like."

Thiess' voice trailed off as though there were something else he had to say.

"You're telling me you've kept your part of the bargain," Roy said. "I will have money, papers, I can run. What are you *not* telling me?"

"Are you absolutely certain you want to leave this work? Will you be able to live without it? Will it be safe enough for you on the outside? The KGB is very rough with defectors, you know that."

"You see what this waiting about is doing to me, sitting on my ass," Roy snarled. "I'm killing myself, Thiess. Slowly I am burning the candle at both ends."

"We can give you work."

The offer was completely unexpected. Roy had thought he might be propositioned, but the drift of the interrogations convinced him Thiess had no interest in recruiting him. Then out of nowhere, this.

"If it's the kind you've been feeding me now, analysis, no, thanks. I can't sit behind a desk. It's impossible."

"If you cooperate with Schareck, even active operations might be possible. Not against the Soviet Union. You would never want to work against your own country. But it is a large world, no?"

"Schareck, Schareck, it all keeps coming back to him," Roy said irritably. "I thought you were running this show. If he is, why doesn't he come in and say what he wants instead of sitting back and pulling your strings?"

"You have told us a great deal about the activities of your apparat," Thiess said. "In strict terms you have lived up to your end of the bargain. We have gained a great deal

170

of insight into Soviet operations against us. But there is one thing, and it is very important, which you have not told us: How did the Mercker Report get back to Moscow?"

"What is so bloody important about that paper?" Roy exploded. "All right, it makes the top people at Pullach look like horses' asses and blows apart every rivet in the BND structure. There's no denying its value. But does it matter *how* we got it?"

"Yes," Thiess said simply. "It matters very much. As I said, think about it. Think about it because Schareck will want to know."

# CHAPTER ELEVEN

## *The Second Run*

THE NEXT DAY WAS SUNDAY. Thiess came by early and asked if Roy wanted to come to church with him. The service was nondenominational, performed by a pastor in a small church outside Pullach.

Roy was incredulous. "I'm not in a confessional mood today, Thiess," he muttered finally. "Besides, you've done well up to now without help."

"Sorry." Thiess shrugged. "Even if you don't want to participate, I thought you might like to watch."

"Just the same, no thanks."

"See you in the New Year then."

They began again on Monday, the first of January.

Thiess took him out of the compound. They drove without an escort, turned left on the main highway, followed it for three kilometers, then swung off onto what seemed a quiet country lane. When they reached the cul-de-sac, Roy saw another car, empty, parked up ahead. They got out, and Thiess put on his sunglasses against the glare of the sun off the snow. He took the lead, walking in long, precise strides along the beaten snow path, his hands clasped on the small of his back. Roy narrowed his eyes against the brilliance of the blue snow and followed.

"Why the change of venue?" Roy asked when he caught up with him.

"Venue is a legal term," Thiess observed. He took his breath in purposeful inhalations, like an athlete. "If you don't like it here, we can go back. I just thought a change of scenery. . . ." He left the sentence unfinished and pushed on, the wind sweeping his greatcoat in a gentle arc to the left.

He climbed to the top of a knoll and looked over the snow-driven fields broken by sagging wire fences. The stillness was absolute.

"Soon," Thiess murmured, "soon all the questions will be over with and you shall be on your way."

"Not that soon," Roy said quietly. "There is still Schareck and, after him, probably Wessel. And I am not finished with you either."

"No," Thiess admitted. "There are more, always it seems more."

Thiess seemed full of questions that morning. They were quickly put, seemingly trivial, but taken together, they wove into an intricate mosaic. He wanted to know all the small details of Center. Did they still recruit only from certain classes of society? Did the children of the purge victims find it easier or more difficult to gain admission into the academies? What was the ratio of men to women? Thiess had heard that interdepartmental sex was de facto encouraged so that desires could be satisfied within the service walls and thus not escape outside—was this so? Was there really that much difference between the new "technocrats" and the stalwart generals who had never finished with the Great Patriotic War?

Thiess asked about leaves, transfers and holidays, the pay scale allowances and fringe benefits, as he called them. He queried Roy about the medical services, the psychiatric examinations and psychological testing. He finished with the unexpected.

"And your motivations, your philosophy. Can you tell me about that?"

"Do *you* have a philosophy, Thiess?" Roy demanded. "Does any of us?"

"You should not ask me that," Thiess answered reflectively. "I am of another generation. I learn the new modes of thought about warfare and listen as the classical arguments of strategy are systematically altered. But that is not the same thing as having developed them. You are a child of the atom. I am burdened by what I was born into, as you will be when the next men step up."

"Oh, Christ, Thiess, you speak as though there were a difference in what came before us or what will come after," Roy said. "It's all the same, has been ever since God commanded Moses to go and spy out the land of Canaan. Techniques vary; personalities are molded to fit the requirements of the age; character is bent to reflect the state which employs you. The rest—the fundamental mistrust, deceit and treachery—that remains the same."

"All the same you must have a belief," Thiess said stubbornly. "You cannot live without one."

Roy paused, drawing deeply on his cigarette.

"Lenin stressed that politics is the reason and war is only the tool," he said. "The venerable Marshal Sokolovsky interpreted this to mean that the military point of view is always subordinate to the political. That was and is the official doctrine.

"Let me tell you the unofficial belief. The soldier is the guardian of the nation—not the state, but the nation. The distinction is very important. He is the watch that never rests. Under General Suvorov in the eighteenth century he put down the Pugachev rebellion. Interestingly enough, Stalin invoked the name of Suvorov as hero even though Suvorov was responsible for the liquidation of thousands of peasants. Under Kutuzov the soldier delivered the mortal blow to 'the beast,' as Tolstoy called Napoleon's Grand Army. During the Great Patriotic War he hacked his way into Berlin on a road built from the corpses of his comrades.

"That is the heroism. There was plenty of cowardice and stupidity, like the Finnish War and the obscenities of Hungary and Czechoslovakia. But in the end it is the Russian soldier who is custodian of the nation's heritage and the first defense of its prejudices. By the latter I mean our centuries-old fear of China and, to a lesser extent, the Slavophile mistrust of things Western. The soldier is responsible for both flanks. On the whole I would say he bears more hatred toward the East than the West, but the important question in his mind is which element is the threat at the moment. Which represents the greatest danger to the motherland? History has taught us never to be caught off guard, and we respect that history. But even today the fundamental direction of the military is defensive, not offensive.

"To protect and to preserve, that is the first principle," Roy finished. "And hope to hell that the politicians do not make one suffer any more than is necessary."

"Fear and mistrust breeding in the name of defense, security and patriotism," Thiess murmured. "You may be right—it is not different anywhere. The army is always under the thumb of the politician. . . ."

"Especially with us." Roy laughed harshly. "The leadership will never get over its fear of 'Bonapartism'—the threat of a military coup. And yet we are asked to assume the aggressive defensive posture. We are not to wait for you to come to us. Territorial boundaries cease to exist. We track and hunt each other across Europe and kill whenever we must. Every time I read a message from Berg I thought to myself: There, that is one more sniper position covered, one more line of defense established. Whenever I sent a man in to retrieve an important dead drop, I did not sleep until he returned. He was my man, and I had the same responsibility to him as a commander has to his troops."

"Noble," Thiess murmured, shaking his head. "But still, someone has to lose."

"We have reduced casualties to an acceptable level," Roy said. "We can do no more."

"Acceptable perhaps," Thiess countered. "But to quote Stalin, 'Where a million is a statistic, a few is a tragedy.' Your tragedy and mine because we know the men we send, we know the risk we take with their lives and in part we redeem that risk by taking chances ourselves. That is how we preserve our self-respect. But in the end no argument suffices. You thought differently, I'm sure, when you were looking at the body of Hans Schiffer."

Thiess stopped and looked around him. They had walked to the top of another hill. Around them the countryside was very still, the sunlight sparkling off the frozen trees. Off in the distance Roy could see smoke coming from a chalet chimney.

176

"I think it is time to get back," Thiess said somewhat regretfully. "It has been very illuminating, talking to you this way."

"I wonder," Roy muttered. "I wonder why we ever have to bring this baggage up. We poke at it, sift through the rags, sort them out and gather them all together again, thinking that perhaps we have changed something. But nothing has been added or taken away. The whole never changes."

"There you are wrong," Thiess said. "If that were the case, obviously you would never have defected. Would you?"

The moment they cleared the compound gates Roy sensed something had gone wrong. The car that had been waiting for them when they arrived at the end of the country lane began to follow them on the highway. That was normal. During the drive Thiess had said very little, only the occasional comment about the peculiar habits of German drivers. At the entrance to Pullach their passes were checked as expected.

When they entered the cottage, Roy realized his instinct hadn't erred. Waiting for them were two young soldiers, their weapons at the ready. One stood by the counter, facing the door; the second had taken up position at the far end of the room, the classic crossfire pattern.

From the kitchenette a short, thin man emerged, wearing a gray overcoat of wolf fur. He was Schareck of counterintelligence.

"What's the game, Thiess?" Roy turned on him. "What were you fattening me up for out there? A nice walk, chummy conversation all so Schareck could get in here and wait?"

Thiess pressed Roy's arm as he went by, stepping over to Shareck.

"Ask your men to lower their weapons," he said coldly.

Shareck shook his head. He pulled out a piece of paper, folded many times, from his pocket.

"On Wessel's authority. I am to relieve you of the prisoner."

His tone was dry and careless, implying that Thiess should have known better than to interfere.

Thiess started to read the paper, but Roy was already moving. The soldier by the counter stepped closer. His automatic rifle was slung at the shoulder, the trigger arm brought through the strap so that the hand rested on the casing. Roy caught the barrel with his left hand, jerking it high and fast so that it wrenched the soldier's arm at the socket. His cry of pain was lost in the rapid fire as the bullets traced into the ceiling. Roy swung his other hand around, pressing the fingers together, and smashed it into the soldier's throat.

Then he heaved the man's body in the direction of the other escort and flung himself at Shareck. The heavy coat absorbed Roy's kick, which should have cracked the bones over Shareck's heart. But the same coat impeded Shareck's movements. He aimed a judo chop, and although it did not reach far enough, it glanced off the top of Roy's head, and that was enough.

Roy's left heel began slipping on the waxed parquet floor, and his second kick upset his balance, the recoil sending him heavily on the ground.

"Thiess!" Roy screamed as he tried to roll away from the oncoming soldier. "Thiess, why the charade? Why?"

He was on all fours, his head hanging as the aftermath of pain from Shareck's blow trembled in his skull. He looked up and saw Thiess moving toward him. But before he could reach him, darkness cracked down upon Roy as the other soldier's rifle butt was swung across in a vicious hiss.

The word "charade" kept on repeating itself in his mind. He was burning up in a terrible heat, and through the flames that one question "Why?" reechoed as though a thousand insane voices would whisper nothing else. He heard himself groan, and he rolled over. The coarse material scratched at his face, and he pulled the blanket away. It smelled strongly of urine.

Carefully Roy opened his eyes and focused on the end of the bed. He saw cockroaches scuttle along the edge of the bunk and disappear underneath. The thought that there was a colony within the mattress nauseated him. Pressing his hand against the wall, he pushed himself away, falling over the edge of the bunk onto the floor. He managed to break his fall slightly, but the knees hit hard, causing him to cry out. Overhead a light bulb was glowing sporadically, threatening to burn out. He dragged himself into the corner, moving by instinct toward the light, to the barred window set in the wall. Using the uneven ridges in the concrete, he began to pull himself up to his feet. When he finally stood up, the blood burst from his mouth, choking him.

He fell forward, vomiting blood, the mess running down across his fingers. He inhaled once, then began crawling insanely to the door, his fingers slipping on the floor. He struck at the door once, then again with his fist. It opened immediately.

He did not recognize the shoes, but the coat was the same color as the one Schareck had been wearing. He

179

craned his neck, the sickness sliding back down his throat, and stared wildly into the impassive eyes of Schareck. They seemed so far away, he thought, looking at and through him.

"Get up!"

Roy shook his head.

Schareck motioned to the guards, and two pairs of strong arms heaved him to his feet, dragging him out between them.

"Let him walk alone," Schareck commanded.

Roy stumbled against the wall but remained on his feet. Ahead of him Schareck was marching smartly down the corridor, his padded heels not making a sound. He turned the corner and disappeared into a room.

There was a sink and a white towel on a rack. Schareck had seated himself behind a cheap metal desk.

"Wash your filth off," he said and turned away. Roy moved over to the sink and heaved into it. He stood like that for a long time, then finally turned on the tap and ran some water gently over his face.

"No good," he gasped. "Still bleeding."

"It will stop," Schareck commented disinterestedly. "You were not hit hard, not as hard as you caught the guard. Put a towel over your face, and sit down, and swing your head back."

The cold wetness of the towel felt so good that Roy was tempted to close his eyes and pass away into oblivion. But Schareck's voice would not leave him.

"You killed the soldier, Roy. You murdered him."

Roy said nothing. Schareck waited a moment, then came over and lifted the discolored towel from Roy's face.

"I said you murdered a soldier, a nineteen-year-old boy!"

"Your fault, Schareck," Roy said weakly. "Too stupid bringing them in. He had his rifle on automatic, Schareck. . . . Stupid."

He reached for the corner of the towel and brought it to his lips, sucking on it. Schareck, who had been holding onto it, let it drop in disgust.

"It has been easy for you, hasn't it?" Schareck continued. "You have been treated well. Nothing has been denied you. You have become a capitalist overnight."

Roy was silent.

"You have given us reasonably good intelligence. Everything was going well until the Mercker Report. You won't tell us about that? Why?"

"Nothing to tell," Roy said weakly.

"If you want more money, say so," Schareck sneered. "There is no shame in it."

"You're a fool, Schareck. You've been at it so long you don't know when a man is telling the truth."

"When did Center first learn of the existence of the report? The very first mention."

"As soon as the Mercker Committee was formed," Roy said woodenly. His voice sounded very nasal, the nostrils almost completely blocked. He breathed noisily through his mouth.

"Did Berg tell you when the report was handed to the chancellor, the exact date when it was ready?"

"June 17."

"And you received your copy, so you claim, when?"

"The twenty-third or twenty-fourth, I can't remember exactly."

"But you told Thiess it was *exactly* one week after the report was presented to the chancellor."

"All right, so it must have been a week then! What difference does a day make?"

181

"A great deal, Captain, a great deal. What was Center's reaction? Mitko's in particular?"

"We were incredibly happy!" Roy whispered venomously. "It made our day. We were going to send you a card of thanks."

"That would have been interesting," Shareck said thinly. "But didn't you or Mitko think all this too great a coup?"

"You're completely mad, Shareck. Why should we question what Berg sent us?"

"I did not mean that you should question the content of the material but the fact it had been procured at all!"

"But Berg was in a position to get it!"

"That is what Center believed?"

"Yes!"

"The copy you received—was it carbon or duplicate?"

"Duplicate."

"Did Berg tell you how many copies were made?"

"Yes."

"And how many was that?"

"One master, which was later destroyed, and three copies."

"What part did Berg send over the radio?"

"The major names—who was headed down and why, recommended replacements. A list of all agents operating within the Soviet Union and East Germany, their courier runs and transmission schedules. It was a long relay. We took a chance."

"What was the date of transmission?"

"The evening of the twenty-third."

"Are you certain?"

"Yes."

"How long was the transmission?"

182

"Twenty minutes, perhaps a bit more."

"In the evening?"

"Of course! Around nine o'clock your time."

"That is impossible," Shareck said softly, satisfied as though he had executed a delicate *coup de grâce*. "Our tracking installations indicate that there were no transmissions monitored on that date."

"That can't be!" Roy croaked, starting from his chair. The towel dropped away as he staggered to where Shareck was sitting. "I tell you you are wrong!"

"Sit down, Captain," Shareck said calmly. "There is much more to go yet. You will need your strength."

Roy's eyes were blazing at him, blind with fury. "A joke," he muttered. "Some kind of sick Hun joke."

"Sit down!" Shareck yelled. "No, this is where you are wrong," he said, a little more easily. He picked up a square plastic-bound booklet.

"This is the logbook for June. Every transmission originating in West Germany is recorded here. Our equipment is of such caliber that we do not miss a single one. On pages fourteen, forty-seven and one hundred six we have the grids for three transmissions originating in the area which Berg used. The last was on the thirtieth of the month. You remember that one?"

"Yes."

"And there isn't one between the fourteenth and the thirtieth. There are only three, not four. And since you are so positive about the date of the transmission concerning the report, right down to the hour, I can only presume you are lying."

"That can't be," Roy whispered.

"Oh, but it can," Shareck countered softly. "Tell me exactly what it was that Berg transmitted."

183

Roy repeated the list.

"He told you about *all* the agents operating within East Germany?"

"Yes."

"Not the actual names, of course."

"No, cryptonyms. But that, with the codes that were used, was enough for us to locate them."

"Of course. It would require nothing more," Schareck mused. "But here again, you see, we have a problem. Berg did not have access to that part of the report which dealt with East Germany. It is an elementary rule of the trade, is it not, that one never allows a man to see sensitive information concerning the country of his origin. Berg had come from East Germany. He would never be allowed to see anything relating to it, on the off chance he might come across an old friend who was scheduled for—how do the Americans say it?—termination with extreme prejudice. For execution, in other words. This might have tempted him into an unfavorable course of action, such as warning the individual concerned. So you see it would have been impossible for Berg to have told you all that. Again, you were so certain. You must be lying."

"And if you knew so much about Berg, if the transmission had originated in the area where he lived, why the hell didn't you pick him up there and then?"

"It was too soon," Schareck said. "I had only my suspicions. Perhaps I was wrong. You see, sometimes you made mistakes with the information Berg passed you. You used it too soon. Agents were picked up too quickly; false information was fed back to us literally weeks after a new one-time code had been in operation. It seemed whatever we tried came back on us or failed outright. We knew there had to be an agent in place. We were tracing an abnormal amount of transmission from one area, but we wanted more than the identity of the agent. Equally important were the method of operation and extent of that operation. I was waiting for developments."

"But now you know I had the entire report in Moscow," Roy said dully. "And whatever you say about transmission schedules, I still had part of the contents before the actual paper arrived."

Shareck looked at him very carefully. "Let us assume for the moment that you are telling the truth. That could only mean one thing: that Berg had someone higher than himself working for Center, someone who did have access to the full report."

"Can't be!" Roy hissed. "How could Berg have had anyone working for him that I didn't know about?"

"But that is precisely the point, Captain," Shareck finished neatly. "You must have had that someone. You must have suspected that Berg, no matter how extraordinary his capacities, could not have got this information by himself."

"I never had cause to suspect collaboration,"

"Again you are lying. And we did not spend all this time, risk and trouble just to bring you here to lie to us!"

"Finish it, Shareck," Roy said in a low voice. "Finish because I'm sick of it. I can't take much more . . . I need a doctor."

"What else do you know about Berg?" Shareck demanded harshly. "Keep talking, Captain. It is your salvation, believe me. Who within Center knew of Berg's existence?"

Roy closed his eyes. "Mitko, Accounts, Communications, Special Investigations," he recited.

"And the KGB?"

"They knew we had a very high and accurate source, that's all."

"They didn't know the code name, Madonna?"

"Yes, I think they did."

"Did they ever correlate or substantiate the reports Berg sent in?"

"It was the other way around."

"Always?"

"No, several times we asked for confirmation and received it."

"Did they give their source?"

"No."

"But the material had to do with West Germany and you believed it absolutely reliable?"

"Yes."

Schareck was leaning forward, his eyes boring into Roy. He would not let up until he had what he wanted.

"And who could have had material that was so accurate, so important that it qualified to serve as Berg's confirmation?"

"I don't know. KGB never told, never would have even if we had asked."

"Captain, your agent could not have filed the transmission for the reasons I have made clear. So there had to be a collaborator. I will tell you now that we were closer to Berg than I led you to believe. We were about to launch a program of misinformation through him. Certain facts would have been withheld from him which would have made his reports suspect. As soon as he learned of this, and he would have because you would have told him, Berg might have dropped precautions and checked with his higher source. We were hoping for that. Now we have you, and you say that none of the Red October group worked for you. Very well, that means whoever supplied Berg with the details of the Mercker Report is still active!"

At that moment something snapped in Roy. Painfully he rose to his feet and took hold of the back of the chair for support.

"You're filth, Schareck!" he whispered hoarsely. "You're playing in a fantasy world. There was no one behind Berg, no one, do you hear? But for some damn reason you feel there has to be. All right. Then go and ask your number one source, don't keep pounding me. Ask Iron Mask. It's because of him that I'm here. He blew my network to you. You rolled it up and wiped your hands. So if you believe there is a traitor in your squalid little service, find his control. Iron Mask will tell you. If he knew about Berg, he will know this one, too.

"And now you tell me something," Roy rasped. "You tell me why you butchered my men. What was it in you that wanted to see them bleed, that enjoyed the screams, the smashing of bones? You tell me, Schareck. Tell me who Iron Mask is. Tell me what kind of pervert you had to recruit to do your work for you."

"Later," Schareck was saying. "Later for all that. . . ."

"I can't hear you!" Roy screamed. He clutched his ears at the pain of his own voice. "Can't . . . hear you."

And he crumpled to the floor at Schareck's feet.

187

# CHAPTER TWELVE

## *The Final Run*

ROY REMAINED UNCONSCIOUS during the time they moved him from the underground cells at Pullach to Bonn.

A physician rode along in the ambulance, monitoring the vital life functions and correlating these with the amount of sedative he gave Roy at regular intervals. Schareck had told him he wanted Roy fit for some action, that he didn't care what happened afterward as long as Roy could perform when released. The physician, who had wanted to hospitalize Roy as soon as he saw him, kept his peace.

Schareck rode in the first escort car. He had cleared one radio channel for exclusive communications between himself and the ambulance. The third vehicle of the convoy carried four men from Schareck's BfV office.

Thiess was not permitted to see his prisoner again. A call

from Wessel's Bonn office had made it clear that the defector was no longer of any concern to the "soft" man.

When he awoke the next morning, Schareck was waiting for him, finishing his breakfast. Roy pushed himself up on his elbow and instinctively felt for the lump on the side of his head. It was a heavy gauze bandage sticky from antiseptic cream.

"Are you hungry?" Schareck asked him.

"No." Roy's voice was barely a whisper.

"They will bring you juice and some coffee," Schareck said. "Then you will get dressed. You will see Wessel in one hour."

Schareck watched as Roy drank his breakfast and slowly washed himself. It was obvious he was still groggy from the sedative, but there seemed to be strength behind his movements. Schareck wondered exactly how much amphetamine Roy had been given.

The guard brought in the suit Roy had been wearing in Pullach. It had been cleaned and pressed, and the shirt smelled of lilac. When he was ready, Schareck called for the escort, and they walked across the street to the Chancellery.

Wessel's office was designed to give the impression of solidity and elegance. All furnishings were of wood, highly polished mahogany, ash and ebony. A green leather pad was inlaid on the desk. Wessel himself looked charming that morning. Freshly groomed, he was sitting easily in the high-backed chair, the manicured fingers spread out as though on display, his doughy face slightly pink from shaving. Because of Wessel's love of social functions and manners, the service had named him "the spy in the white tie."

189

"Good morning, Schareck," Wessel said courteously.

"Sir." Schareck gave a stiff little bow.

"Captain Roy. . . ." Wessel's eyes lingered on him. "Sit down, please. Would either of you care for coffee?"

Wessel looked from one man to the other, a waiter taking orders. None was forthcoming.

"Very well, then let us begin. Captain Roy, there is no need to go over old ground. We are indebted to you for the information you have placed at our disposal, and I trust the remuneration and other arrangements have proved satisfactory as compensation."

Roy said nothing. His head was throbbing badly, and he was afraid to move.

"However, there remains the outstanding problem of the Mercker Report and the means by which it came to GRU Center."

"That is old ground," Roy said.

"It is of the utmost importance to us, for reasons you can well understand, to locate the source which passed the report to Berg," Wessel said.

Roy lit a cigarette and threw the match across at the ashtray on Wessel's desk. He missed.

"There is nothing to talk about," he said slowly. "Can't you get it through your thick heads that—"

"One more betrayal won't make any difference!" Schareck stopped him coldly.

"You must admit, Captain, that there are some contradictions in this case," Wessel said more carefully. "As I say, you have been more than cooperative except on this one point of information which you refuse to yield. Although you insist Berg couldn't have had another source, you do admit that had he one, you would have known. Now we tell you there must be another source. So you see, it is quite simple.

190

"What I propose is the following," Wessel continued quickly. "We will go over the Mercker Report once more. It has been some time since you've seen it, read the actual words, gotten the flavor . . . perhaps you will remember something. Even if Berg never gave you the name of the agent, you may come across something about Berg's transmission which you have forgotten. We are looking for the ordinary everyday details which specialization causes us to overlook, things which are there staring at us, a clue, an idea which might tip the balance. You understand?"

If he did or did not, it made no difference to Wessel. He depressed a lever on his intercom. A moment later Cornelia Zolling, the chancellor's personal secretary, entered. She handed one sheaf of papers to Wessel, then paused. Wessel nodded, and she carried over the other copy to Roy.

"We will do this in two stages," Wessel said after the secretary had gone. "From the information you have given us concerning the material Berg allegedly sent over by transmission, we have the list of agents, dead drops and so on. Please have a look and see if any are missing."

Roy took fifteen minutes to study the typescript. As he read through it, he again experienced the rising excitement he had felt when the transmission had come into Moscow. There was a voyeuristic quality to this. Just as a peeping Tom can feel his lust rise at the sight of a woman undressing by an uncurtained window, so Roy derived pleasure by watching the secrets of a rival service come to light before his eyes.

"There are two things I'm not sure of," he said. "Here on the fifth page, second paragraph, and at the beginning of the second section. I don't remember the names or dates. They must have come in later."

Wessel made a note. "And the rest?"

191

"I remember the rest," said Roy.

Wessel scribbled something else on his pad and called in the secretary. This time the material was bound in a black plastic folder. It was the balance of the seven-hundred-page Mercker Report.

"I hope we do not have to go through the entire body," Wessel said. "The portions of the report which Berg could not have had access to, the sections on East Germany, are marked by the red flags. Before you begin, Captain, I will show you into an adjacent room. A telephone has been provided for your use. Call me if there is anything," Wessel added needlessly.

"Thanks."

The room was little more than a closet, cramped and stifling. There was a single small desk and hard uncomfortable chair. An ashtray and lamp were the only decorations.

Schareck saw him in, then closed the door and locked it. Roy took one more look around his cage and irritably flipped open the dossier to the section on East Germany. He had read for almost an hour before he turned a page and discovered the file on Iron Mask.

Roy looked up from the pages. In a rapid angry gesture he tapped out a cigarette and struck a match. Through the haze of smoke he considered the position of the video camera and reckoned the lens could not focus on the page from that angle. He didn't care about the sound equipment.

His first thought was that the addition of the Iron Mask dossier was a trap. He had asked Schareck about Iron Mask's identity and had been brushed off. Now the dossier was there before him, with no introduction, no preamble, no instructions. For the sake of the camera and to gain time to think, he flipped past the section and went on to the analysis of Polish security.

What would Schareck gain by slipping him the dossier? There was no point to it. Yet Schareck must have chosen to include it at this moment. Only he knew that Roy was interested in the Iron Mask report. Was Schareck then the special source Mitko had talked about, who was to provide Roy with the dossier that would send Bibnikov to the firing squad? Of the half dozen people who had access to the Mercker Report how many would *also* have clearance for Iron Mask? According to Berg, Wessel himself was running Iron Mask. Schareck had bullied in on the territory with the chancellor's permission. Three people. Center was not running the chancellor of West Germany, nor Wessel, so it had to be Schareck. And Schareck had played his role well, wrenching Roy away from Thiess and conducting his own brand of investigation, the results of which were not lost on the other two. At the same time Schareck was setting him up to receive the papers, he was also showing what a magnificent interrogator he was. Roy silently gave Schareck due credit. Now he flipped back and began reading about Iron Mask, the cryptonym for chief of Special Investigations, Sergei Bibnikov.

It was there, the whole stinking rotten story. The Germans had got their hooks into Bibnikov shortly after the war. As one of the unit leaders of SMERSH Bibnikov plundered his way into Berlin behind the front-line troops who were dying to free the spoils for him. While other commanders delivered whole trainloads of paintings, artworks, silver, *objets d'art* and furniture to Moscow, Bibnikov took only what was virtually untraceable—gold, bars of bullion stacked in three suitcases.

Since it was impossible for Bibnikov to leave Berlin, the

suitcases were delivered to Switzerland by a man who made his living by courier work. He could be trusted because he knew his clients and understood that they would have him dead if he cheated them. But what Bibnikov didn't know was that the courier was also a Gehlen agent.

When Bibnikov returned to Moscow, he was an anonymous millionaire. But in short order he was contacted by Gehlen's people, informed that the Org knew not only the nature of his account in Zurich, but also its number, and advised that it would be in his best interest to become a dormant agent for the Germans. The threat of exposure guaranteed that Bibnikov would act when needed, that he would become their top man in Moscow.

The following twenty pages detailed Bibnikov's activities in the service of German security. Some of the details were familiar to Roy—agents mysteriously blown, codes broken, lines of communication snapped. The late fifties were the heyday of the Gehlen Org, when Soviet agents were being picked off seemingly at leisure, with no plausible explanation. A good many Center controllers were packed off to do duty on the Volga because their networks fell apart weeks after being put into operation. Later on most of these tragedies were laid at the feet of the traitor Popov.

Bibnikov had done his work well, without having the slightest suspicion ever cast upon him. Even the tumult and housecleaning of the BND under Wessel failed to dislodge him or endanger his position. He was the master piece on the board, above the daily battles and internal intrigues. He served only the top man, Gehlen or Wessel, it didn't matter. He served them for money and, Roy imagined, for the intangible feeling of satisfaction only a double understands, the slow drip feeding an insatiable hatred, a contentment at watching one's own countrymen go stupidly and unwittingly to their deaths. Something in all this, beyond money, had to satisfy Bibnikov. Roy would ask him about that one day.

The final page of the dossier appeared to be a recent addition. The type was clearer, blacker, the margins set differently. There were only three lines on the sheet, giving an address in West Berlin, the name of someone Roy presumed to be a contact, and a series of numbers he recognized as a transmission code and schedule. The name on the page was Thiess—he was Iron Mask's conduit for material which found its way from Moscow to the West. Now there were four who knew of Iron Mask.

Roy looked at his watch and decided he had been closeted long enough to come up with a possible answer to Wessel's question, if he were going to answer it at all. He would have to gamble now. He had to take this one chance of getting the report out of Bonn. If he won, then possibly, just possibly, he might get back to Moscow. If not, well, it didn't matter. He would never see Moscow again. Roy smoked three more cigarettes and picked up the telephone.

"I must go and speak with a man in West Berlin," Roy told Wessel when they were in the director's office.

"Where in Berlin?" Schareck demanded.

"That is my business," Roy snapped. "We will do this my way. I may be wrong, I'm not sure. But there's a chance the man can still be found. If so, we have something. Something which links a third party to Berg, a party I didn't know about."

Wessel appeared very pleased. "So there was, is, a contact."

"Possibly. I don't know yet."

"You will have an escort," Wessel said. "Schareck will take you."

"I must take the report with me," Roy added. "If the man is there, I want to break him quickly before he has a chance to prepare a story or use the one he's undoubtedly got ready."

"But you said you weren't certain this is the man you want," Schareck countered. He spoke slowly, not hiding his suspicion. If he's ours, Roy thought, he's playing a damn good game.

"I told you we must take a chance," Roy said irritably. "If you want to behave like an accountant, that's fine with me. We'll get nowhere."

Even Wessel hesitated. He had not foreseen a request which would include the Mercker Report. But now it was Schareck who came to Roy's aid.

"With permission, Director, I will carry one copy of the report with me. It will be used only after I am satisfied the circumstances warrant it."

Wessel looked up at him keenly. He was not by nature a decisive man. He preferred group deliberations and committee decisions.

"Very well," he said finally. "I presume you would like to leave as soon as possible."

"Yes," Roy answered.

"I will have that," Schareck said, holding out his hand for Roy's copy of the report. He stuffed the entire report into an empty briefcase.

"Captain," Wessel asked him suddenly, "what made you change your mind so quickly? What is it you saw that brought on this illumination?"

Roy did not answer him directly. "It will cost you dear-ly," he said. "If I am right, it will have cost you very, very much."

A cunning smile appeared on Wessel's lips. It was obvious he would be waiting. "We can talk about that when you return, Captain. There is a satisfactory solution to every problem. Good hunting."

Roy looked at Schareck, but the BfV chief's face was impassive. He gave no sign of satisfaction or skepticism and hustled Roy out of the office as rudely as before.

They drove to West Berlin in Schareck's private car, an old but high-powered Mercedes. Schareck handled the machine like a professional, arms flat out against the wheel, downshifting into turns and speeding off into the straights of the autobahn. They rode in silence and covered the distance in less than three hours.

They might have done it faster, but Schareck slowed down twice, turning into the right lane and driving with one hand, the other resting before the radio set. He repeated the procedure just before the corridor to West Berlin.

The stop at the East German border was very brief. The document check and currency control were done at the car. Schareck passed the guard papers for both of them, his manner that of the disgruntled salesman his passport said he was. Roy had been given an equivalent cover. One of the Vopos asked for the keys and opened the trunk. He poked around for a minute, tapping for a hollow space that would indicate a secret compartment, a fake gas tank designed to carry drugs. The East Germans were very keen on drug checks these days. The guard paid no attention to the luggage. He handed back the keys and sauntered to the barrier, the rifle bouncing on his buttocks.

The passports were returned, money chit signed for, and the car was waved through.

Shareck continued to drive in silence. As they approached the outskirts of Berlin, he pulled over to an emergency telephone. "Do you have twenty pfennings?" he asked gruffly. He was annoyed at not having remembered to get the correct change.

"You know I don't have any money at all," Roy said.

Shareck grunted, resenting having to pay more for his call than was necessary, and left the car. The conversation was very brief, and when he returned, his lips were turned down in obvious disgust.

"Should you have an idea about killing me, I would advise against it," he told Roy once they were on the autobahn again. "We shall be parting company shortly." He sounded regretful, as though he wished it were to be different, but that something stood in the way. Roy shifted in his seat to give his left arm maximum swing. He did not believe Shareck, not yet.

They drove into the city through falling darkness. Shareck used the side streets only a Berliner would dare to navigate. He avoided the heavy traffic on the main roads and twice had to swerve sharply to avoid cars which had the right-of-way on the one-way alley he had chosen.

"Wait here."

They were about a hundred yards from the Wall. Roy could see it up ahead where the last building, part of a printing complex, ended and the bare stubble of no-man's-land began. Beyond were the shadows of the Wall itself, ugly, scarred and splattered generously, on the West Berlin face, with political slogans. Shareck shut off the engine and reached for the briefcase lying between himself

198

and Roy. He opened it and, taking out the report, flipped through it to the pages of the Iron Mask dossier. In one motion he neatly took the sheets out.

"These are yours, yes. They are what you came for," he said tonelessly. But his eyes were looking at the Wall. "Get out and walk to the American checkpoint. Everything has been arranged. They will let you pass without inspection. Go now."

Roy held back, his hand resting gently on his lap.

"I know what you are thinking." Shareck laughed at him. "You do not trust me, and so it should be. But the dossier is what Mitko sent you for. You must admit that. Now take it and go, quickly. I would have liked to have this one end another way but. . . ."

Roy stuffed the papers into the inside pocket of his coat and stepped out, slamming the car door. He did not look back but started running, weaving from side to side, his body hunched forward. He did not stop when he reached the side of the printing warehouse but kept on, setting pace for himself. At the end of the building he turned left and ran parallel to the Wall, twenty yards to his right.

He was thinking whether Schareck had set him up for a kill and, if so, why. It would be a stupid killing, so near the Wall and its politics. Nothing was what it appeared. But all he had to concern himself with was the Iron Mask dossier. He had that, and he had to finish the mission successfully by getting back safely.

The first bullet went over his shoulder, hitting the wall and splattering chips of brick into his face. Instinctively Roy dived into a roll, twisting his head up to get a glance at the sniper's position. The yellow-black sky cast no light for shadows. He could make out the vague forms of buildings in the eastern sector, the window frames bricked in, but that was all. He picked himself up and ran on. He was fair game now.

The second and third bullets passed just behind his back. The rifleman was reloading rapidly, desperately. Roy guessed the gun was not equipped with a night scope; otherwise, even a beginner would have wounded him by now. The fifth bullet did, gouging a piece of the bone off the shoulderblade. Roy was spun about, but his feet refused to stop moving. He staggered forward and was thirty yards from the checkpoint when the floodlamps went on, isolating him like an actor on an empty stage.

The American guards were pointing their weapons in his direction, but the machine-gun unit had its weapons trained on the eastern sector.

It didn't make sense, he thought, no sense . . . unless the east! The path of the bullets passing behind him at an angle had come from the east. And he had instinctively known where the rifleman was; he had looked in that direction.

An American leveled his rifle and stepped forward, moving cautiously.

"Schareck," Roy screamed at him. "I come from Schareck!"

From behind the guard two plainclothesmen appeared. One of them said something to the American, and the automatic was lowered.

"Quickly, quickly!" the German called. "They are waiting for you!"

The barrier on the western side was already open. Roy slipped on the cobblestones and flung his arms out to regain his balance. The German tried to help, but Roy shook him off. He kept on doggedly, reeling like a punch drunk

200

across no-man's-land. Then the lights in the eastern sector went on, and the sirens took up their demented wail.

He was standing in the center of a dirty little strip of land called the bridge between East and West, frozen in the glare of the spotlights. Suddenly he felt very tired. The wound on his head began to throb viciously, and he was conscious of the pain now that he had stopped running. He stood there, waiting for the last shot which would kill him. The rifleman couldn't miss now.

But the gunfire had stopped, on both sides.

Slowly Roy walked to the Vopo checkpoint and stood face to face before a youthful soldier whose weapon was trembling in his hand.

"Let me through," he whispered harshly.

The Vopo hesitated, then raised the barrier, and Roy walked through. He cleared the second barrier, and two men came running up to him. One of them grabbed him roughly by the shoulder.

"Let him be!"

The voice in the darkness was familiar, but Roy couldn't place it. He strained to see the figure that was approaching. It was Ivatushin. Gently Ivatushin put his arms around Roy and held him, pressing the wounded man to his body as though trying to give him strength.

"We have it," Roy mumbled, trying to pull himself away. "We have everything."

Ivatushin straightened up and, still holding Roy by the shoulders, looked into the face of his friend.

"The evidence."

Roy nodded.

"It has come too late," Ivatushin said softly. "Bibnikov arrested Mitko yesterday."

The light fled from Roy's burning eyes, and his body

slumped forward into Ivatushin's arms. There was a smile on his lips as he turned his head up.

"No better than the tennis player," he said. "He was too late—dead. . . ."

The words came forth plaintively as they would have from the mouth of a child facing a reprimand.

Even if he had an answer, Ivatushin could not have given it before Roy's head turned slowly, held for an instant, then hung low between Ivatushin's arms. Looking down, he saw Roy's back was covered in blood.

# CHAPTER THIRTEEN

## *The Trial*

"IT WAS STUPID, DANGEROUS AND UNNECESSARY for you to have called me," Koldakov said quietly. "I did not think you one to panic."

The rebuke had no effect on the Politburo member Ponomarev. He remained motionless in his stuffed chair, staring into the design of the Oriental rug at his feet. The flat was chilly. Koldakov had said so twice, but Ponomarev had neither acknowledged his words nor moved to accommodate his guest.

"It was not a question of panic," Ponomarev said slowly. "There was a risk in bringing you to my house, but it was calculated and, contrary to what you say, very necessary.

"It is a most ironic situation, don't you think?" Ponomarev continued casually. "We have won and lost at the same time."

"Nothing has changed," Koldakov said emphatically.

"Ivatushin was in Berlin when Roy came through the day before yesterday. How he managed to bungle it I'll never know, but still he has secured the Iron Mask file. We have our weapon against Bibnikov."

"And Bibnikov has Mitko," Ponomarev rejoined softly. "Queen for queen, and we have fewer pieces on the board."

"Wrong, we have another queen," said Koldakov. "The file sitting in your safe. All you have to do is get it to the Politburo, and Bibnikov will at least be suspended from his duties."

"You are presuming Mitko has held out against Bibnikov's interrogation," Ponomarev said. "And will continue to do so. But for how long—a day, perhaps two or three. Bibnikov will not kill him. He will not reduce him to a madman. You know what medicines are available in Lunts' laboratory. The drugs will tear Mitko's mind apart, but they will permit him to talk lucidly nonetheless."

"Mitko will not talk," Koldakov said shortly. "He has a secret. I know it because the same dentist worked on me. There is poison in one of his teeth. An antiquated method—that's why no one looks for it in these sophisticated days. But it is very reliable."

For the first time Ponomarev's face showed signs of life. He grasped the implications of Koldakov's words.

"In which case there may be hope yet. If Mitko uses his weapon—assuming that Bibnikov has overlooked it," he added pointedly, "there is hope yet. We might not even have to move the operation to a closer date. If no one else is touched. . . ."

"Why should anyone else be touched?" Koldakov asked mildly. "Mitko understands what is at stake. He will do what any one of us would be expected to do."

"But why did Bibnikov choose to go after him now?" Ponomarev asked suddenly. "Why, when Roy was heading back?"

"He must have been desperate," Koldakov said. "With
Roy gone he was forced to react rather than act. He came
very close to us—too late, but very close."

"But isn't it curious how lax Bibnikov was with Roy,
sending two strongarms who weren't smart enough to get
hold of the dossier? Another thing—how did he know Roy
was heading back?"

"You were always one to question your good fortune,"
Koldakov said dryly. "God knows what sources Bibnikov
has. They're good, that is all that matters. He was waiting
for Roy."

"Could we move up the strike date?" Ponomarev asked.
"If at all necessary?"

Koldakov shook his great head. "Vovchok is ready, but
not the other party. There will be no other opportunity."

"You are still willing to gamble on a single date, even
though the odds have shifted?"

"We have no choice," Koldakov repeated. "Name another date when the target will be available. You know the Politburo schedule."

"I am frightened of Bibnikov," Ponomarev confessed
suddenly. "I wonder if the dossier is enough. . . . Christ,
how could Roy have been good enough to get to the dossier and escape as well? That seems impossible!"

"It has been done," Koldakov said impassively. "Either
way it would have worked out. Roy would have kept Bibnikov running in that direction, after him, or else he
would have returned with the evidence. We have the second of the two situations at hand. Now I suggest we go to
dinner. In the very unlikely event we are arrested, I would
rather it be on a full stomach."

205

"And if we *are* arrested, everyone, including Ivatushin, what will become of Vovchok, of the whole plan?"

"Vovchok will be at the correct place at the correct time," Koldakov said. "Nothing will stop him. He will act regardless of what happens to us. He is a human bomb. It would be a pity if no one were to witness whether he is successful or not.

"And as for the bombers," Koldakov finished, "I have already passed word of Roy's return to Katchachurian on the General Staff. If Vovchok succeeds, he will assume authority, and the strike against China will proceed as scheduled."

The crippled woman who wheeled the supper trolley stopped before Cell Four and clumsily slopped some watery soup into a bowl. She dug around the pot with the ladle and brought up the mashed turnip which held fast to the bottom. But instead of pushing the bowl through the slot, the crone unlocked the door. She pushed her way into the cell and placed the bowl on the table, spilling some of the foul-smelling liquid on the floor.

"There is a message for you, my dear," she said breathlessly.

Her eyes blazed at the girl lying supine on the mattress, unmoving, her eyes fixed on the ceiling.

"Do you hear, I said there is word for you!" the old woman shrieked.

Tamara did not stir.

"The message is from Comrade Bibnikov," the crone said triumphantly. "He told it to me himself. He told me to say your lover is coming back. Your lover is back, and he will be coming to you. He will be joining you. Do you hear, he is coming back!"

206

Confronted by the silence of the girl, the crone was seized by a fit of rage. Her body trembled as she leaned forward on the table.

"He's coming back to you, fool!" she screamed. With a sweep of her hand the bowl was sent flying in Tamara's direction, spilling over the mattress. The old woman paused, then appeared satisfied at the ugliness of her work.

Tamara moved her eyes to the old crone. The woman's eyes were wild. She was quite demented. The prisoners were afraid of her because it was rumored the guard allowed her to carry a knife to protect herself from other inmates when she entered the cells.

The crone shuffled away, muttering, and slammed the door behind her. Tamara did not move, nor did her eyes lose their glassy catatonic fix. Her sign of understanding the crone's message came in the form of silent tears.

He remembered his coat being pulled off his back, quickly, without thought for the wound. He was laid down on something soft and covered with a blanket. It was very cold, and he was shivering.

He rose into semiconsciousness, wavered, seeing vague outlines and shadows surrounding him, then drifted back down to oblivion. For a long time there was a burning sensation on his back as though his skin were on fire. He tried to reach behind and somehow soothe himself, but his arm would not move. Finally, the pain dissolved into a dull, persistent ache. Kindly hands reached out for him, dispelling the demons wailing before him, and he was carried off, helpless and uncaring, but feeling strangely comforted. When he awoke, Mitko was sitting at the side of his bed, smoking.

Roy surveyed the room. The walls were done in a cheerful color, bright yellow with orange trim. There was a tray of medicines on a gleaming metal stand at the foot of the bed. Beyond the white curtains lay the blueness of a crisp January morning. He could almost feel the cold from the icicles that hung from the awning. By contrast the sheets were warm and soft to the touch. Mitko was looking at him thoughtfully, a kindly smile playing beneath his thick mustache.

"How are you feeling?"

"All right," Roy said. He was still dazed from the drugs and uncertain. "What happened?"

"You came home safely," Mitko answered.

"But you were arrested," Roy said. "Ivatushin . . . he told me Bibnikov had gotten to you. . . ."

"So he had." Mitko nodded. "He had me for three days."

Roy pushed himself up on one elbow, wincing from the pain at the shoulder. "What happened?" he repeated.

"Bibnikov had been told you were coming home," Mitko said. "He had his final card to play before we could bring the evidence against him. That was to arrest me, to break me and to have a confession ready when you arrived."

"A confession about what?"

Mitko turned away and very deliberately crushed the cigarette in the tray.

"He hasn't changed," he said softly. "It was exactly the same as it was twenty years ago, when he was just a boy and he interrogated me. Again he almost broke me, he came so very close.

"I am sorry for him. He has utterly lost. He kept on whispering 'old man' at me, as though my age were somehow offensive to him, that I had lived too long and he was going to correct that mistake. He stripped me and tied me and fed me on the floor like an animal."

208

Mitko stopped and lit another cigarette. "And he beat me in his own particular way, slowly, exactingly, with great precision and concentration. He did not use drugs. Perhaps there wasn't the time or he didn't care to use them. Perhaps if he had had more time, he would have hounded me to my confession and destroyed me completely. But I had told myself I would survive. I had to survive after all you had gone through to come back alive. I would not betray you."

"Ivatushin managed to bring the dossier?"

"Yes. I had been arrested as he left Moscow, but I told him what to do. At all costs he was to reach you before anyone else. Just as Special Investigations was watching us, so we were trailing them. We managed to find out that Bibnikov had dispatched men to Berlin. Ivatushin followed. He was to make copies of the Iron Mask dossier and deliver it to Ponomarev, who would get it to the Politburo. Yes, something you did not know, Ponomarev was also working with us. I had already taken the precaution of sending the preliminary investigation report. The Iron Mask file was the final touch."

"So they believed you."

"I don't know what happened within the Politburo. Obviously Ponomarev carried the day although there was probably reluctance, great reluctance to deal with Bibnikov. Otherwise, I should not have spent three days in his hands." The bitterness in his voice was unmistakable.

"Who arrested him?"

"It was all very dramatic." Mitko laughed quietly. "Andropov himself came, with a special team. They were armed with machine guns, thinking that Bibnikov might have protection even in his own office. After Andropov had him, he came for me, to the cellars. He said it was a mistake." Mitko laughed.

"But what did Bibnikov want from you, this confession?"

"He was going to turn the tables. According to him, I was a traitor and you my collaborator. Together we had been working for the Germans for years and had destroyed the network. He had fabricated evidence to that end. I haven't seen it, but Ponomarev told me it exists. That was another reason the Politburo hesitated to arrest him. After all, Bibnikov was their protector, almost one of them. Only Ponomarev and later Andropov realized the threat Bibnikov represented—the power behind the throne, dreaming of usurpation."

"What will happen to Bibnikov?"

"There will be a trial." Mitko shrugged. "Socialist legality will be satisfied." He hesitated and looked at Roy. "Bibnikov has not chosen to defend himself. He has asked for Shevchenko. You know him?"

"I have heard but can't remember." Roy shook his head.

"Shevchenko is very tough," Mitko said. "He has administered labor camps and spent time in them as well. Like Bibnikov, he has an extraordinary capacity for survival. He will not be an easy man to deal with."

"He has nothing to save," Roy said. Suddenly he felt very tired. For him the mission had ended. "Bibnikov is guilty. We have the evidence. . . ."

"Yes, we have the evidence," Mitko said. "And it has cost us so very, very much."

But Roy did not hear him. He closed his eyes and began to dream of Bibnikov. As sleep overtook him, the smile on his lips betrayed his satisfaction. Soon, very soon, Bibnikov would die, and the idea pleased Roy very much.

The tribunal convened in the middle of January. Three

judges had been appointed by the Politburo, one from the Supreme Court, another from the provinces and one from the military. Each man had been informed of the circumstances leading up to the hearing, and from each a pledge of eternal secrecy had been extracted. It was agreed that Savelev of the Supreme Court would direct the proceedings.

For reasons of secrecy the tribunal chose to meet in a courthouse on the outskirts of Moscow. This was not to be a show of pomp and circumstance. There were no spies to parade before the nation, no foreign journalists to accommodate, no propaganda to be gleaned. No demonstrators would be organized to spit on the accused as he was led in. The room would be empty of recruited spectators. There would be no breast-beating by a politically rabid prosecutor, no self-righteous pronouncements about the vigilance of State Security. The defamation of Western imperialists would take a different tone.

Here in the damp room on the third floor of Proletarsky District, Soviet judges would try one of their own, a man who once exerted more power than they could dare dream of. And they would hide this man from the people he had betrayed. The courthouse had been requisitioned under the pretext of conducting an inquiry into black-market speculation. Even the local police, who had been ordered to spread the rumor in the streets, believed this.

The judges came from their sanctum and took their places on the bench behind a blazing portrait of Lenin. The accused was brought in.

Bibnikov walked slowly but with the air of a man who is undefeated. He did not slouch or cower. He seemed annoyed at the furtiveness with which the proceedings were being conducted, resentful of being sneaked in like a thief through the back entrance. His guards, armed, walked on either side of him, looking straight ahead, not touching him. They are afraid of him, Roy thought. They cannot believe that Bibnikov is their prisoner. And he is wearing a blue suit, not a prison uniform. That is his own suit.

After Bibnikov came Shevchenko. He was a tall man with a shuffling walk, rimless glasses and unruly white hair. His face was sunken and tired, but the eyes, sparkling and roving, constantly roving, betrayed a hidden, inexhaustible energy. Roy noticed that Shevchenko's right arm was withered. It hung uselessly at his side, the tips of the twisted fingers visible under the sleeve of the jacket.

He took his place at the accused's desk, whispered a word to Bibnikov and opened his briefcase. Across from him Mitko was sitting, waiting for commencement. He had only one dossier before him, that of Iron Mask. The rest of the details, Roy assumed, everything that constituted Bibnikov's treachery, were clear in his mind. He had no need of notes to remind him.

At a signal from Savelev the security escort locked the front door and those leading to the consulting rooms in the rear. The sentry then stationed itself before the doors. There were no windows, and the light bulbs, encased in dirty fixtures, could not completely dispel the gloom.

Savelev began speaking. His voice was strong, but it echoed off the bare walls and across empty benches as though mocking him. There was no audience, no need for a display of stentorian verbal fortitude. Savelev lowered the tone of his address.

"This tribunal has been convened and its members chosen directly by the Politburo of the Central Committee. I remind the accused, his defense, the prosecutor and the witness that these proceedings are secret. There will be no discussion, no mention of any details concerning this trial at any time. The security escort is thus reminded and cautioned.

"In this trial the office of prosecutor is taken up by Comrade General Mitko, chairman of the GRU military intelligence. The prosecutor seeks, for the crimes of Sergei Bibnikov, the full *exceptional* punishment permitted by Article Twenty-two which governs this case. For the benefit of the accused I shall read both the article and the rationale of its application as put forward in the Commentary to the Basic Principles of Criminal Legislation of the Union of Soviet Socialist Republics and of the Union Republics.

"The commentary reads as follows:

"'The Soviet state is forced to preserve the death sentence. Article Twenty-two of the Basic Principles permits the application of this sentence only for the most serious crimes against the Soviet state and individuals.'

"Article Twenty-two reads as follows:

"'*An Exceptional Measure of Punishment—the Death Sentence.*

"'As an exceptional measure of punishment until its full abolition, the application of the death sentence by shooting is permitted for betrayal of the homeland, espionage, sabotage, terroristic acts, banditism and intentional murder.'"

Savelev stopped and looked at the accused.

"There is no need to enter into the economic, speculative regulations whose breach is also covered by Article Twenty-two. We are dealing here with betrayal of one's country and intentional murder."

Savelev continued reading.

"'Persons not having reached the age of eighteen before the commission and women in a state of pregnancy during

213

the commission of the crime or at the time of sentence may not be sentenced to death. The death sentence may not be applied to a woman in a state of pregnancy at the moment of the execution of the sentence.'

"Since the accused does not qualify for either of the above categories, Article Twenty-two stands in his case. Does the accused challenge this?"

Shevchenko looked up sleepily and waved his good hand. "The accused acknowledges his circumstances to fall within the limits of Article Twenty-two and that his alleged crimes are covered by Article Twenty-two," he said softly.

"Very well, Comrade Mitko, I think you had better begin."

Mitko rose and walked to the foot of the judicial bench. He stood facing the side wall, in profile to the tribunal, his eyes looking past Bibnikov but never directly at him.

"Comrade Bibnikov—or, forgive me, simply Bibnikov, for he's anything but a comrade—Bibnikov has committed treason," Mitko stated simply. "In itself treason is a heinous crime, possibly the worst our judicial machinery has to deal with. But Bibnikov's treason has facets which take it out of the category of conventional betrayal. Bibnikov's treason led him of necessity to premeditated murder.

"It is well known by all concerned that Bibnikov has for many years been entrusted with the duty of watching over the security organs of the state. His office, head of Special Investigations, has given him extraordinary powers. These powers were confirmed upon him by the very men who today have ordered his trial. I mean no disrespect. A viper is not always visible, particularly when that viper is as cunning as Bibnikov, who can serve and protect the leadership, yet at the same time carry out acts of betrayal against them.

"It would be instructive, I think, to look back over Sergei Bibnikov's meteoric and highly visible career.

"It should be recalled that Bibnikov was first exposed to foreign influence as a member of a special NKVD squad which operated against treason within the ranks of the military. Bibnikov followed the assault on Berlin and spent almost four months within postwar Germany.

"After a brief eclipse we find Bibnikov again in Germany, where he is controlling a number of minor KGB agents. But he is not satisfied with his work. He expands his operations into infiltration of nationalist émigré groups. In itself such infiltration was very important to our intelligence gathering. However, Bibnikov also began killing. In the files which record this period I have found no effective reason for the elimination of nationalist leaders. Nor can I understand how Center could have benefited from them. A dead man cannot give away his secrets, however unwittingly. Moreover, I have found no orders which explicitly called for these killings.

"In short then, Bibnikov took upon himself the role of executioner. He was operating in a foreign territory under conditions not always known to his superiors. He could thus manufacture an excuse for the killings and use them to raise himself in the estimation of his superiors. Again, a third party's unwitting help—in this case the oversight of the KGB to query the executions—allowed Bibnikov to proceed without explanation.

"Let us always remember the most important factor: Bibnikov is operating in a foreign climate.

"We continue and find that in 1958 Bibnikov returns to Moscow and singlehandedly unmasks Lieutenent Yuri Popov as a paid agent of the imperialist powers. Bibnikov never reveals the source of his information, but that is all right. The interrogations of and subsequent confession by

215

Popov are sufficient evidence for a tribunal to sentence him to death before the firing squad.

"After Popov's death Bibnikov is rewarded with the nominal control of the new Special Investigations bureau. He does not return to Germany but settles in Moscow. He takes up his old wartime profession of hunting traitors within the security organs. Four years later his work bears fruit with the arrest and subsequent execution of Colonel Oleg Penkovsky. The year is 1962.

"For fifteen years, then, Bibnikov has been behaving as a model Soviet intelligence officer. He has succeeded in unearthing a pair of traitors deep within the GRU security apparat. He has penetrated and worked within enemy territory, bringing back hard intelligence. And no one asked for details; results had their own justification."

Mitko paused. "And their terrible mistakes, as we see now.

"I would ask the court to open the file code named Iron Mask." Mitko remained standing. He did not consult his own copy.

"The first entry was made by a German case officer named Funke. He is unimportant except in one respect: He is the first to mention the existence of a potential double, a man whose name he does not know but who operates within Soviet intelligence, among Soviet troops.

"Two weeks later, in late September, 1946, Funke reports he has talked to this man, has helped him convey money into Switzerland and is prepared to turn the matter over to Foreign Armies East.

"Appended to Funke's report is a comment by one of Gehlen's subordinates. The file is receiving special attention because of the particular position of the Gehlen Org at the time—it was mobilizing all its resources for a major espionage assault on the Zone, East Germany. But curiously there are no additions to this dossier until 1954, the same year in which Bibnikov reappears in the West.

"In the four years between '54 and '58 the dossier, now bearing the code name Iron Mask, grows with alacrity. At the same time Bibnikov is liquidating nationalist terrorist elements directing propaganda against the Soviet Union, West German intelligence is debriefing Iron Mask. Given the great mobility Bibnikov had and the casual liaison with his control, it was ridiculously easy for him to meet with the Org men. On the appended sheet the court will note that Bibnikov's movements correspond exactly with the dates and debriefings of Iron Mask. It might be instructive to note that there is not very much intelligence substance here. Iron Mask provides background details on the leadership succession, on the political climate of the country, whatever military and economic data he has gathered or remembered. There is a large section on Soviet operations against West Germany. At first glance it is curious that Iron Mask had not been asked to give specific details. However, the explanation is to follow.

"There is a note in the file concerning spring, 1958. The dossier on Popov, code named Cherub, has arrived at Pullach. Sent to BND by the Americans, it details all of Popov's knowledge about Soviet operations in West Germany. Gehlen, sensing an opportunity to elevate Bibnikov in the eyes of his superiors, at the expense of the Americans, allows Bibnikov to read the Popov dossier. Three days later Bibnikov returns to Moscow without prior notification to his control. Seven days later a report is delivered to the chairman of State Security concerning the traitorous activities of Popov. The document is detailed and thorough and places in the hands of the KGB unquestionable evidence of Popov's guilt. The case is closed after Popov's confession is extracted by Bibnikov.

"Only now, a decade after the event, are we able to compare the striking likeness between the BND report on Popov's activities and the papers Bibnikov handed to State Security. There is a simple explanation for these parallels. Bibnikov merely copied the BND report, altering style and phraseology to give his own particular flavor to the words.

"Thus, the events of spring, 1958, represent the first quantum advance Western intelligence made into the ranks of State Security. Bibnikov was to be more than just an agent. The BND, after much thought, decided to gamble on Bibnikov. They had the option of using him safely, in a limited fashion—that is, being content with whatever he brought them and hoping that he would remain close by, in the European theater—or they could nourish him. Support his rise. Give him intelligence which, if carefully used, would ensure his promotion. I do not think Gehlen dared dream he would ever get an agent into the most senior echelons of the service, but certainly he had grand plans for Bibnikov. And for those plans Gehlen was willing to sell his own established agents, and those of other Western powers, in Moscow.

"So the Germans sacrificed Popov in 1958. They put him up as an offering to our security apparatus in the hope that Bibnikov would reap the rewards. He did. The treachery and charade were repeated in 1962, when Bibnikov got Penkovsky."

Mitko held back as the tribunal's collective eyes shifted to Bibnikov. Then he plunged on.

"Now it will be noted that up to this point Bibnikov's name as such never appears. Is this so exceptional? A source as valuable as Bibnikov had to be protected against the remotest possibility of treachery. Iron Mask thus remained nameless, anonymous, without a face or a past. Iron Mask did not exist for the service. Only for Gehlen. Even our greatest agents, Felfe and Henlinger, did not know of the existence of Iron Mask, much less his identity.

"From 1962 on the extent of Iron Mask's treachery swells. Note how perfectly Gehlen's records of the receipt of information from Iron Mask correspond with the arrest or execution of both GRU and KGB agents operating in West Germany.

"But treachery is finite. Even the greatest, most effective traitor at one point exceeds his intelligence and planning. Had it not been for Berg, Bibnikov might still be operational. It is a dead man, Otto Berg, who is primarily responsible for our success today.

"Berg was in many ways similar to Sergei Bibnikov," Mitko continued. "He was a German working against Germany; Bibnikov a Russian working against the motherland. Berg was a deep penetration man, as was Bibnikov. Berg had worked his way up through the echelons of the German political structure and became security adviser to the chancellor; Bibnikov was the disciplinarian of our security apparatus. But there was a major difference in the character of these men. Berg was not ruthless. Bibnikov was a trained executioner.

"Berg's control was Captain Alexander Roy. It was he who retrieved Berg's last tape recording, a transcript of which has been provided for the tribunal, from Geneva.

"Again coincidence was showing its hand. The time of Iron Mask's arrival in West Germany was paired exactly with the killing of Roy's first agent, the mechanic. Now for some time I had suspected that there was a high-level traitor within the Soviet security apparat. My suspicions were heightened by the death of the mechanic and confirmed by the destruction of Roy's entire West German operation. Note once more how neatly Bibnikov's journeys into West Germany correspond with the dates and locations of the killings. Bibnikov was present *every single time*. The only question that remains is whether Bibnikov carried out the killings himself or had them done by the Germans.

"These deaths propelled Berg to intensify his investigations. In the end Berg managed to tell us the name of Iron Mask. He was not able to save himself from Bibnikov. Otto Berg was a hero. He stayed in the line even though he had every reason and opportunity to flee. He stayed because he believed it more important to uncover a traitor than to think of one's personal safety.

"Now, even though we possess irrefutable evidence of Bibnikov's treachery, it was understood Bibnikov could never be convicted on the basis of the tape recording alone. It was necessary to get what Berg would have obtained had he had the time—the Iron Mask file, Bibnikov's record of treachery as penned by the BND itself, mostly in Gehlen's hand.

"To say that this was a most hazardous assignment is understating the case. Captain Roy risked not only his life, but also, should he have failed, the reputation of the GRU apparat, which would have been damaged beyond words, and Bibnikov, still safe, could have demanded its complete reorganization or at the very least subjected it to a special oversight committee of which he would have undoubtedly been a member.

"I would like now to recount a part of the rationale behind Roy's operation. At a meeting of Committee One, shortly after the destruction of the network, Roy was relieved of his duties as control for West Germany. He was de facto demoted and disgraced. By disciplining him in this fashion, Committee One unwittingly gave birth to the idea of an intelligence operation against West Germany, for who would be more convincing as a traitor than a man who has been callously and unjustly treated by his own kind?

"Throughout the course of the operation the Germans suspected nothing. They believed Roy was genuine. No doubt they followed his decline and osmosis in Moscow very carefully. They watched as closely as did Bibnikov, who smelled what he thought was a traitor. And for all intents and purposes Roy was evolving into a defector.

"But to ensure that he at least got within the parameters of his target, the Iron Mask dossier, it was necessary for Roy to defect with information valuable to the Germans. His transfer to China Section and the work at the library made that possible. There he did in fact read and copy double A material, to which he did not have direct access because of his security rating. He aroused the suspicions of Bibnikov by his late hours. He also absorbed material on China which he would further use as barter to penetrate the BND or BfV, whichever came for him.

"It should be noted here that I personally authorized Roy to take whatever he felt was needed from the double A section. I was willing to allow the Germans a glimpse into the condition of our armed forces on the eastern border in the hope that when he revealed this classified material, Roy's credentials as a defector would be established beyond reproach. The gamble succeeded. Through Thiess, then Schareck of BfV, Roy found himself dealing directly with Wessel, and it was in Wessel's own office that the file of Iron Mask appeared, appended to a report Berg had already conveyed to us.

221

"Finally, we come to the last step of this operation: the insertion of the Iron Mask dossier into the Mercker Report. It was not chance, not in the least, that the dossier was contained therein. Over and above Berg there was, and is, an individual who remains as our agent in the Chancellery. Only I know the identity. The name was not given to Roy because if the operation ran afoul, he would be subjected to the severest interrogation and might give out this name. This person was the one who passed the report to Roy. As far as the identity of this person is concerned, the Politburo has agreed that it should, in the interest of security, remain secret. I believe the tribunal has been informed of this.

"To sum up then. The evidence against Bibnikov, chief of Special Investigations and trusted guardian of the state, is overwhelming and complete. There is nothing missing. No effort has been spared in procuring those documents which seal his guilt. Perhaps the tribunal feels that an investigation could have been initiated at an earlier stage. I beg to differ. A high-ranking traitor is like the mythical vampire. To extinguish him takes an extraordinary instrument. A man who for the duration of fifteen years systematically betrayed his country, who had sold his birthright for money, who so brilliantly engineered himself into a position where *he* was responsible for unearthing treachery within the ranks of the security apparats, such a man, comrade judges, is no ordinary individual.

"Therefore, I seek and call for the extraordinary measure, the death sentence for Sergei Bibnikov on the grounds provided by Article Twenty-two—treason and espionage and premeditated murder."

The judges, Roy noted, had written very few notes in

the course of Mitko's presentation. They had watched him intently, listening, although they had already read much of what he was saying. Occasionally their eyes would move to Bibnikov, who sat quietly, smoking one cigarette after another. If the judges were seeking some sign of Bibnikov's feelings, they received nothing. If they expected repentance, they did not get that either. Bibnikov had removed himself from everything around him.

The fact that Bibnikov was smoking bothered Roy. Normally this was not permitted. Yet Bibnikov was behaving as though he were in his own office.

Savelev said to Shevchenko, "You may begin your defense."

Shevchenko nodded and got up slowly. He looked down at some notes, then shuffled across to the same spot where Mitko had been standing a moment before. He glanced up at the judges' bench and called out, "I summon Captain Roy as witness."

Roy had been told by Mitko to expect this. Shevchenko would go heavily on him. Schevchenko waited until Roy was in the box before coming up to him.

"Do you hate the accused, Captain?" he asked as though his curiosity had to be satisfied.

Roy hesitated. "He is a traitor. I have no love of traitors."

"That is understandable, naturally," Shevchenko agreed. "I suppose I meant, do you have any *personal* reason for hating Comrade Bibnikov?"

"No."

"Tell me under what circumstances your father died, please?"

Roy turned to the bench. "I do not understand this question. What relevance does it have?"

"Comrade Shevchenko?" the military justice inquired.

"I merely wish to know whether Captain Roy has any reason to bear personal animosity against the accused," Shevchenko said. He appeared hurt. "After all, the captain has admitted he hates traitors and so probably hates the accused. This is a very powerful emotion. Captain Roy also knows that his father died under a disciplinary sentence executed against him by the accused in the course of the Great Patriotic War. I want to know if Captain Roy hates the accused for that reason also."

Shevchenko waited. Neither Roy nor the judges said anything.

"Very well, I will not insist the witness reply. It is evident that if a man hates a traitor, he would not hate the man responsible for his father's death any less so.

"Captain Roy," Shevchenko said, "this operation you agreed to undertake, did you think the odds were greatly against success?"

"In some ways."

"Explain, please."

"Penetrating a foreign service within a limited time period is at best very difficult to achieve. Any one of a number of things could go wrong, a leak, a physical accident, whatever."

"Yet you agreed to undertake this hazardous mission."

"The mission was necessary. Bibnikov had succeeded in eliminating Berg. He was a traitor by the evidence, yet he was also hounding the GRU over the failure of the West German network. His power had grown so great and the evidence against him was so overwhelming that we had to act, taking whatever risks were necessary."

"I see. So force of circumstance led you to accept and plan for certain dangers which, had they arisen in the course of a, shall we say, normal operation, would have been subject to debate and possibly revision."

"That is correct."

"How long were you in the West?"

"A little over two weeks."

"Two weeks! This is phenomenal. Truly. To have achieved a successful mission in that time, in enemy territory, is magnificent."

"The groundwork had been carefully prepared," Roy said coldly. "There was luck, yes, and no operation can be successful without it."

"Two weeks," Shevchenko murmured thoughtfully. He tugged at the sleeve of his jacket, pulling it down over the twisted fingers. "Not only do you penetrate the highest echelons of the West German secret service, but you literally run away with a file so heavily guarded that even your best agent could not get his hands on it. How, Captain, did you manage that?"

"There was a contact."

"Of course!" Shevchenko exclaimed. "The mysterious hidden agent whose name even you, who were risking your life, did not know. You knew of the existence of this man or woman, but you were not told how or when contact would be made or if in fact it would ever be made. Is that not correct?"

"Yes, but—"

"You did not think such arrangements unusual?"

"I couldn't have known the name for security reasons!" Roy snapped. "Also I didn't know how far I would get in the penetration."

"Of course, you are quite right." Shevchenko smiled. "And for these reasons"—he suddenly turned at the bench—"for these reasons a man whose life hangs in the

225

balance cannot confront *all* his accusers, meaning this mysterious agent," he finished viciously. "I find this abominable.

"Comrade judges," Shevchenko spoke more easily, "there is really no need to continue. Captain Roy will tell us only what General Mitko has already stated. We have the facts of the operation that GRU Center ran. Nothing will change them. I have at this point only one comment: When you look at the operation Mitko devised and Roy executed, you say to yourself, But this is brilliant. Daring, cunning with a formidable follow-through. To penetrate German intelligence so thoroughly within the space of two weeks, to obtain a file which was beyond the reach of the highest placed agent of the GRU, to steal this file and execute a successful return from the heart of enemy territory, why, such an operation ranks with the highest achievements in State Security history!

"Or,"—Shevchenko's voice became dangerously soft—"you may think, comrade judges, as I think, that perhaps this operation was *too* successful, its execution *too* flawless, its results *too* convenient."

Shevchenko turned to the doors of the courtroom, and his voice rang out harshly.

"That is all, Captain Roy. I am not quite convinced of your innocence. You will return to your seat. You see, it is you, not Comrade Bibnikov, who is on trial here!"

He paused and shouted at the security escort, "Bring in the second witness!"

The man who came through the doors was very large, a barrel chest supported on thick, powerful legs. His hair was sandy and close-cropped, the face immobile save for pale-blue eyes which roved unceasingly around him like the eyes of a predator. He came directly to the witness box and stood facing the empty courtroom.

"Your name?" Shevchenko asked.

"Slavko Sulok."

"What was your former occupation?"

"Head of interrogation, the People's Police of Hungary."

"When did you leave that post?"

"Four years ago."

"For what reasons?"

"My methods were no longer needed."

"And what were those methods?"

"The physical sustainment of torture in interrogating prisoners," Sulok said calmly.

"What did you do upon leaving the AVO?"

"I emigrated."

"Where to?"

"I chose West Germany."

"And what trade did you engage in?"

"I discovered there was a need of men with talents such as I possessed."

"And so you became—"

"An independent executioner and interrogator."

Sulok's voice never changed. It remained quiet, precise, deadpan. He reminded one of the obsolescent hangman, who considered himself nothing more than an exemplary civil servant, with a necessary state function to fulfill.

"Who was your last client?"

"I did not know him by name. We never met. The offer came through East Berlin. My contact told me only that a doctor required my services."

"And what were those services?"

"I was to execute a specific number of people in West

227

Germany. Before killing Hans Schiffer, I was to ask if he had any knowledge of an operation against those in the same network as he, information which I had been told could have been provided by Madonna, a code name I believed belonged to the man who was Schiffer's control."

"Did you make inquiries about the actual identity of Madonna prior to undertaking the assignment?"

"No. I asked for the money, and the first fifth was deposited into my bank. Every time I undertook an execution another fifth would be deposited the day after the mission was completed."

"So there were five missions, or five persons to be dealt with?"

"Yes."

"Can you give me the dates and locations of these executions?"

Sulok looked up and read off the dates from memory. When he was through, Shevchenko turned to the bench.

"I beg to point out that the information Comrade Sulok is providing corresponds approximately to the date and places when and where the accused was also in West Germany. A day after the second killing Comrade Bibnikov undertook a trip to Koblenz to investigate the death firsthand. Further journeys were made after the subsequent executions."

He turned to Sulok. "And the names of those executed?"

Sulok gave the name of all the agents in the West German network.

"And you are certain you never chanced to get the name of the man who employed you?"

"Never."

"But he was from the Soviet Union."

228

"He was from East Berlin. That is all I know."

"No reasons were given for the murders?"

"I do not require explanations or motivations. If given, they are lies anyway."

"Do you work alone?"

"Mostly. On that particular job I had someone with me."

"A final question. Was your arrangement to eliminate six, not five, people?"

"It was. The figure changed at the last moment. But we never got the sixth."

"That is all, thank you."

The big man nodded and stood down. He did not leave the room but took a seat in the last row.

"I call a third witness," Shevchenko shouted.

The doors opened, and a stout middle-aged woman entered the room. She marched briskly to the podium, her heavy shoes resounding on the floor. She was carrying a tape recorder which she placed beside the witness box.

"Your name," Shevchenko began.

"Lizevta Ivanovna Pervushina," the woman replied smartly.

"And your occupation?"

"Electronics technician, Third Division, Fourth Directorate, Committee for State Security."

"Specialty?"

"Deciphering high-speed electronic transmission."

"Set up your equipment, please, here on the table beside the bench."

Pervushina easily lifted the machine onto the bench, unlocked it and unwound the electrical cord. A guard helped her find an outlet.

"Now the tape, if you please," Shevchenko said.

The technician inserted a cassette. There was a silence,

then a series of incoherent whines and noises. Finally, the last message Berg had sent to Center was played for the court.

"When did you come into possession of this recording?"

"Last Wednesday."

"And who brought it to you?"

"Comrade Andropov, chairman of State Security."

"Did he tell you what it was?"

"No. He only asked for an analysis of the recording."

"And you provided him with one. What was the result?"

"There are two messages on the same tape," Pervushina replied briskly. "The first is the obvious one. The second is contained in what sounds, without the proper equipment, like a jumble of noises."

"Before we proceed," Shevchenko interrupted her, "I must ask the tribunal to read this statement given by Chairman for State Security Andropov. It explains why this tape recording was stolen from General Mitko's vault and comments on the hidden message on the tape. There is also a note to the effect that the Politburo was notified in advance of the chairman's actions."

Shevchenko distributed four onionskin sheets to the judges and passed one copy to Mitko. The diminutive general did not touch it, nor did he look up.

"Does the prosecutor challenge the authenticity of this tape?" Shevchenko demanded.

Mitko stirred as though aroused from a reverie. "No," he said softly.

"Does he admit that the tape was the same one held in his private safe at GRU Center?"

"Yes, it is the same."

Shevchenko faced the tribunal.

"The tribunal is satisfied that the Politburo did in fact

230

authorize Comrade Andropov's actions," Savelev said. "Proceed."

Shevchenko turned back to the technician. "Kindly explain to us this jumble of noises, as you call it, and how it can be construed as a message."

"The ten and three-quarters seconds of 'noise' represents in fact a high-speed message that had been recorded on the tape previous to the other message," Pervushina explained. "Reduction of communications is a common procedure and has been refined to the point where other means are obsolete."

"Could you explain the procedure by which this is done?"

"The message is recorded on a separate tape which is then treated electronically in order to compress the message. The principle is the same as that applied to tape-recorded music. The original recording may have been done on twelve or sixteen tracks. These tracks are then compressed to eight or, usually, four to make the tape suitable for ordinary machines.

"Once the tape has been treated in this manner, the normal procedure is to 'squirt' it over radio transmission. But in this case the agent chose simply to incorporate it on the same reel as the longer untreated message."

"Is it possible to reverse the procedure, to unscramble the text?"

"Of course."

"And you have done this?"

"In accordance with Comrade Andropov's instructions."

"Would you play the message, please, unscrambled?"

The technician removed the first cassette and inserted a second and adjusted the volume. Berg's voice was coming through again.

231

"November 18, afternoon. Madonna to Bibnikov. The courier Schiffer is dead. Roy will learn of this tomorrow, but I doubt anything will be done to protect me. I am Roy's last senior agent in West Germany, and he believes I am his hope to find an answer for the killings. He could not be more mistaken, as I shall explain.

"This morning the chancellor had me in his office for a private security meeting. We discussed the three operations which have cast doubts on the security of the West German government and which pointed to the existence of a deep penetration agent within the Chancellery. The chancellor, aware his party could not afford another scandal, told me that a double operating within the Soviet Union was going to be brought to Bonn, to pinpoint the leak if possible. This was an extraordinary measure, and the man, code named Iron Mask, was, until today, known to *only* two people, the chancellor and Wessel, his control. The name the chancellor gave me was yours, Sergei Bibnikov.

"What all this implies is clear. Schareck of the BfV must have convinced the chancellor that I am the deep penetration agent. To flush me, the chancellor has thrown out a name he claims belongs to Iron Mask. Obviously I am now to try to take some action against this person and in so doing expose myself. Ironic, is it not, that Schareck should have chosen your name?

"The chancellor's gambit, however, puts an end to my effectiveness, both for you and for Roy. I will not mention my demise to Roy but exercise the emergency procedures and try to get back to the East.

"My final report to you is as follows: On your instructions I have checked all counterintelligence operations run by the BfV in the last three months. There is no report of

232

any action taken against this network. The deaths have remained unlinked. No conclusions on their sequence have been reached. There was only the routine check the BfV carried out for the police, and this did not bring in results which aroused any suspicion.

"Therefore I must concur with you—the operation against this network is not only premeditated but is being executed by someone with intimate knowledge of the network, its agents, their functions and locations. We can eliminate all services in West Germany. Nor is there any indication that the Americans or NATO are behind the killings. Your conclusion is, thus, the obvious one: Someone within the Soviet Union is deliberately destroying the West German network for reasons thus far unknown. There is no other possible explanation.

"Because my usefulness to you in Bonn has come to an end and I cannot further investigate the source of the network's destruction, I shall activate the procedure we had arranged—namely, I shall, on the tape to be sent to Roy, repeat exactly what the chancellor told me, that you are the traitor, Iron Mask. According to our plan, if all else failed, I was to identify you as such and this accusation would be used by you for the flush. However, Schareck has, by choosing your name for Iron Mask, done the work for me. Possibly, if I had been him, I also would have picked your name.

"The reaction at GRU Center will be predictable. Roy and Mitko will have no choice but to attempt to retrieve this dossier themselves since I will no longer be operative. That the Iron Mask dossier is a fabrication on Schareck's part is irrelevant. Our concern lies with the traitor within GRU Center who, upon hearing of your 'guilt' may show himself too confident and therefor become careless. Quite possibly, these bizarre circumstances offer the last opportunity for Special Investigations to uncover the conspiracy against this network.

"I offer two personal observations. First, the destruction of the network appears to be a means rather than an end. This, because no logical purpose is served by the slaughter. Neither the West German security services nor Center could possibly benefit from the silent executions of the network members.

"Secondly, I cannot believe that Roy as control is involved in these events. On the contrary he has done everything possible to safeguard me. Since the range of suspects, those who stand over Roy, is small, it should not be difficult to establish the identity of the traitor within Center."

The tape spun, and the machine stopped automatically.

"Comrade Pervushina, that will be all."

The technician nodded and left the table. She took her place on the same bench as the Hungarian.

"I call my last witness," Shevchenko called out relentlessly. "The sixth and intended victim of the executioner Sulok."

For the third time the doors opened. Two plainclothesmen strode into the room. They turned on their heels and allowed their charge to pass between them. She was a small gray-haired woman of a delicate, almost fragile figure. She wore a simple gray dress with a string of pearls around the neck. She walked in slowly as though reluctant to come in. Roy recognized her immediately. She was Martha Berg.

Mitko, who had maintained a rigid composure, slumped forward.

"What is your name?" Shevchenko began again. But this time his voice was kindly, the tone almost regretful.

"Martha Berg," the woman answered softly.

"And you are the widow of Otto Berg?"

"Yes."

"Did you work for the GRU?"

"Yes."

"Who was your control?"

"Captain Alexander Roy."

"Did you know of your husband's collaboration with the accused?"

"Yes. Otto became very uneasy after the second killing. He was at his wit's end for an explanation. Although he never told me specifically, I believe he and Bibnikov saw each other one of the times Bibnikov was in West Germany. I say this because there was only transmission communication between them on tape. Yet to have established this, they met each other at least once."

"You were aware there was a traitor in the apparat?"

"I shared my husband's belief."

"Were you ever in contact with the accused in West Germany?"

"Only in the final days."

"Explain to the tribunal please."

"I was the one who discovered my husband, dead. He had been shot twice. This was about half past two. I first suspected the federal police had come for him, but that was illogical. There had been no cordon around our house. No one came in after me. I then remembered the deaths of the others. They had been tortured first, but otherwise, my husband's fate was very similar.

"I remained for a moment in the kitchen where he lay. Then I went upstairs and began to pack. I had no idea of where I would go. I had to get to the East, but I was afraid to go there. There was an enemy in the East, a very powerful man who would have me dead as well. Yet there was little choice. Eventually the BfV would come, if for nothing ·lse than on account of Otto's position. His death would be heavily investigated. Something of our activities might be revealed.

"I was about to leave the house when a man arrived who helped me."

"Who was he?"

"Sergei Bibnikov. He had come too late for my husband but in time to take me over the border and on to Moscow."

"And you have been in Moscow since December 26?"

"Yes."

"One last question. Did your husband receive any special message from Center before his death?"

"Yes," she whispered. "Two days before, a priority message arrived from Center, from Mitko himself. This was unusual since Roy controlled all communications. Otto had not heard from Mitko for several years. The message read that Otto should check the BND files for any mention of an operation against his network. Mitko referred to my husband by his code name, Madonna.

"Today, when I heard the Hungarian say he had been given the code name Madonna to work with, I realized only one man could have been responsible for the massacre. Mitko himself had given my husband that code name."

"Thank you, I am grieved to have brought you here. It was necessary."

Martha Berg nodded and walked slowly past the prosecutor's table to the benches. She paused and looked at Mitko, her expression a horrible contortion of hatred, confusion and grief. She stared at him mutely and moved on.

"I believe the circumstances of the plot are at last clear,"

Shevchenko said, addressing the court. "At least in respect to the accused.

"The guiding hand behind the destruction of the West German network was General Mitko of GRU Center. The tribunal has heard Martha Berg's testimony. She has corroborated the mention of Madonna by Sulok, a word which only Mitko could have passed on to the assassin.

"It is clear that Mitko, for reasons known only to himself and others who were plotting with him, planned the extermination of the West German network of which Roy was the control. Systematically and coldly Mitko arranged to have his men, one of whom he had known for more than a decade, butchered by an anonymous killer. Heinous as this crime is, it reflects an equally great offense: that of leading Comrade Bibnikov astray in his investigations.

"As Berg deduced, there seemed to be no rationale behind the killings. They did not appear to benefit anyone or anything. Yet Mitko must have had a reason. There must have existed, and I say there still exists, one very important reason why an operation of this magnitude was carried out. I stress the term 'magnitude' and employ it with care.

"*Mitko was and is involved in a conspiracy the proportions of which dictated that he use extreme means to prevent its detection,*" Shevchenko shouted. "What better way to ensure that vigilance is not cast upon him or his plot than by having the man responsible for protection against terror and revisionism, Sergei Bibnikov, chase after a hare in the opposite direction?

"I put to the tribunal the proposition that Mitko's major aim was to deflect the attention of Comrade Bibnikov from the real conspiracy. Secondly, the killings would also silence those who might have by chance come to suspect that they, within the West German network, were being eliminated not by enemy counterintelligence but by their own masters.

"Mitko was also prepared to sacrifice the man he had handpicked to run the German network, Roy. He knew that after the destruction of the network Roy would be severely punished and that there would be a demand for Roy's demotion, if not outright dismissal. He also realized that these demands would come not from the GRU but Special Investigations and the Committee for State Security. And Mitko was right. But Comrades Andropov and Bibnikov thought it advisable that Roy be removed from the running of active operations. However, the fact that Bibnikov supported such a measure did not mean that Special Investigations discontinued its inquiries into the shootings, an element Mitko either did not count on or believed was of no great importance.

"Mitko's true genius, evil but charismatic, is shown in what he did after Roy's demotion and removal. Mitko could have stopped there. He might have contented himself with having blame for the destruction of the network removed from his desk. But he was not satisfied with that. He was too cautious. So he played on Roy's anger at being unjustly treated and gathered him, on the strength of Berg's information about Iron Mask, into the plot. What better way to keep Special Investigations running in the wrong direction than by setting Roy up as a defector? Brilliant and simple. With Roy's suspicious behavior at China Section and the library and finally his flight to the West, Mitko believed Bibnikov would have no choice but to chase on. All of which, of course, would result in leaving Mitko in peace. The bait was too tempting for Comrade Bibnikov to swallow, tempting but too tantalizing.

"There remain two points," Shevchenko said. He

paused as though gathering his thoughts. "The first concerns Mitko's motives, the underlying reasons for his actions. The second is the real Iron Mask. Let us look at them in sequence.

"Why did Mitko do what he did? What could have prompted him to start a trail of deceit and butchery? What was so important to him that he was ready to sacrifice everything, including the life of his most trusted lieutenant? I fear that Mitko himself will be obliged to tell us, for my reasoning and imagination cannot conceive of such things. I offer only one thought: In 1937 Mitko was subjected to extensive interrogation by Comrade Bibnikov, then a junior investigator for the NKVD. I believe the memory of that confrontation has never dimmed. I believe that over the years Mitko has fed off it and embellished its details in his mind. That he has systematically come to loathe and despise everything Bibnikov, as a civilian servant of the state, did to him. Mitko, I believe, embodies the often unspoken tension that permeates our security services. I am referring, of course, to the enmity which exists between the KGB and GRU, between civilian and military intelligence, between the government of the Soviet Union which serves the people and the military, whose ranks are filled with fanatics who believe that the military is best qualified to lead the country. But I reiterate, Mitko will have to tell us the details. Only he knows.

"And there remains Iron Mask—not the personage spoken of in those papers, forged by Schaveck, whose existence encouraged Mitko to engage in further deception and persuaded Roy to go to Bonn to seek them out. The real Iron Mask is a highly classified file. I have received the following recommendations from the Politburo as to the advisability of discussing Iron Mask here."

Shevchenko walked to his table and from a worn brief-case slid out an official document. He passed this to the bench. Savelev glanced at it, then read it aloud.

"'If the evidence against Mitko is sufficient without the disclosure of details concerning Iron Mask, then there is no need to divulge it. Alternatively if the court feels the evidence is insufficient, then Iron Mask must be intro-duced.'

"I believe the evidence is overwhelming," Savelev said harshly.

The military judge rose and called out, "General Mitko will rise."

He came to his feet with dignity, slowly but unhesitating-ly, and stood facing the tribunal. His face did not appear troubled; only the eyes hinted at some confusion, at some-thing he did not understand.

"Do you wish to reexamine any of the witnesses?" the military justice demanded.

Mitko thought for a moment, and the whole of the court hung on his silence.

"No, there is no need to call witnesses," he said finally.

Roy leaped to his feet, seizing Mitko by his slumped shoulders.

"What do you mean?" he whispered. "For God's sake, tell them this is a pack of lies. Tell them!"

"Captain Roy, you will sit *down!*" Savelev roared. "Now!"

But Roy did not move. His eyes blazed into Mitko's and would not let him go.

"Please sit down, Alex," Mitko said quietly. He released himself from the younger man's grip and walked to the front of the bench.

"I ask the court to overlook Captain Roy's outburst," he said. "Under the circumstances it was a natural reaction. And as for the question put to me, no, I repeat:

There is no need to bring back any of the witnesses."

"Do you wish to answer Comrade Shevchenko's charges?"

"I admit to the charges the defense has placed against me. Certain details need clarification, but the gist of the argument is correct."

He turned and faced Roy.

"I am sorry, Alexander, very sorry. In time you would have understood everything. The deception was necessary, yours, Bibnikov's. Although in one respect I did not lie to you. If things had turned out differently, either after the trial or when it was all over, Bibnikov would have been dead. You did want that, didn't you?"

Roy said nothing.

"But," Mitko continued regretfully, like a man who understands all is lost and so there is nothing lost in admitting to everything, "Bibnikov played his last desperate card. He arrested me and the precise time—"

The words died, choked in this throat. Mitko brought his hands to his lips as though to stifle a cough. He pitched forward to the floor.

"Motherfucking bastard!"

Bibnikov rose and overturned the table at which he had been sitting. Jumping over it, he leaped at the prostrate form of the diminutive general and tried to shove his fingers into Mitko's mouth. But Mitko's teeth were clenched. Bibnikov raised the man and hit him violently in the stomach to make him vomit out the poison capsule. Mitko gasped, and his eyes opened briefly, rolling. He nodded stupidly at Bibnikov, who stared at him, then let him drop.

"The trial is finished," Bibnikov said savagely. "He did not come unprepared."

# CHAPTER FOURTEEN

## *Bibnikov*

FROM THAT MOMENT ON everything seemed to move in slow motion for Roy.

Bibnikov was still standing over the body, his chest heaving, his mouth working in vicious anger, a panther that has been robbed of its kill by the hyena. The guards came running in from their posts by the door, but Bibnikov flung his arms out, holding them back from Mitko's inert form. Savelev had risen and was leaning over the podium, his hand raised as though to pound for order, but he was unable to bring it down. Only Shevchenko remained unperturbed. He was sitting at his desk, surveying the madness. He had seen it too many times before.

"The trial is over with," Savelev said finally. "Comrade Bibnikov, you will assume responsibility for this situation. The witnesses will be dismissed unless further inquiries are necessary."

242

"There is no more need of witnesses," Bibnikov snapped. "The corpse will be taken by a regular ambulance to the State Security hospital." He turned to one of the escorts. "Arrange it!"

"As for Captain Roy?" Savelev asked.

"He is mine," Bibnikov said coldly. "I will deal with him."

"I think you have seen enough," Bibnikov said to Roy. "He has left you a fine pile of shit to clean up!"

They did not speak on the way back to the city. Bibnikov drove quickly and brutally, ignoring traffic lights. He braked before the GRU headquarters on Quai Maurice Thorez and motioned for Roy to get out.

"We will go up the back way."

They arrived just after the day shift had gone home. Bibnikov had Roy admitted on the strength of his Special Investigations pass. After the security checkpoint they took a special elevator from the garage to Mitko's quarters.

The office was in a shambles. The floors had been ripped up methodically, leaving splintered planks gaping at the ceiling. The cupboard door hung pitifully on one hinge. The curtains had been torn away, their rods unsheathed, then bent three times over. The chairs' back and seat supports had been torn apart, the frames broken. In places the wall had been sledgehammered from floor to ceiling, and ancient insulation spilled over into the rubble of plaster and wood that littered the floor. Mitko's one piece of handsome furniture, an ancient desk that probably once belonged to a wealthy lawyer, had had its guts ripped out. Even the tooled-leather top had not been spared the knife.

Roy looked up at Bibnikov, who was calmly lighting a

cigarette. The state of the room reflected so well the methodical madness of the character concealed within the heavy body.

"We found nothing," Bibnikov said.

"Nothing?" asked Roy. "After all this you found nothing. Then perhaps you discovered something from the interrogation, Bibnikov. Did the interrogation slip your mind when Shevchenko was performing his mental acrobatics before the tribunal?"

"You're a fool," Bibnikov said in disgust. "A man has been proved a traitor, but that is not enough for you."

"Give me a cigarette," Roy said.

Bibnikov tossed him the package and walked around the ruins, kicking at chunks of plaster at his feet.

"It was well done, Bibnikov," Roy said, "really. I could almost admire you for it. Whoever included the Iron Mask file into the Mercker Report had to be working for you. That was the only way it could have been done."

Bibnikov said nothing.

"It was Schareck? Why did Schareck let me run? Because you had made an arrangement with him, hadn't you? He would give me the phony dossier and let me run if you . . . what? Handed him the real Iron Mask—not Berg, not Bibnikov, but the one agent I in fact did not know about, that I never suspected could exist? Someone working very close to Berg, yet not touching him, never. That was it, wasn't it?"

"It was the chancellor's secretary," Bibnikov said harshly. "The Zolling woman. She was one of Andropov's best people, and I was willing to sacrifice her to get your rotten carcass back to Moscow. Do you hear, Captain Roy? I had to sacrifice her for you.

"You never did know, did you?" Bibnikov sneered at

him. "And neither did Mitko. Mitko only knew that KGB Center had a high-level source within the German government, but he did not know its identity. I did. So I threw him bait he couldn't resist. I had Zolling's name leaked to him. You see, it was too perfect. First Berg tells him there is a BND file which will destroy me completely. Then he learns of an agent who might be able to get this dossier for him. How he got in touch with her I don't know. He didn't go through Andropov. But obviously there must have been a hitch because she couldn't get the report directly to him. Someone had to bring it over. Mitko chose you.

"Your plan was to get the Iron Mask dossier through the Mercker Report. You would play coy with Thiess, possibly even with Schareck, but you would remember to drop the tantalizing hint that you *knew* of an agent, higher than Berg, through whom the report could have arrived in Moscow. You played your role well, and Mitko had made it easy for you. Because he himself believed it, Mitko assured you that there was another plant, not the military but from the KGB, and that he or she would pass you the dossier once you had got as close to Schareck as possible.

"Andropov got wind of Mitko's knowledge of his agent. He didn't know how Mitko had discovered Zolling's identity. I advised him to let Mitko play her. Perhaps he would lead us into some interesting places.

"Andropov agreed. But he too did not know everything—that I had already made my own arrangement with Schareck, for example. If Schareck would get the dossier to you, the Iron Mask file which he had in fact manufactured to trap Berg, then I would give Schareck Zolling's name. Schareck would have a chance to strut success in Wessel's face, and he badly needed some points after Red October, and I would have you where I needed you, here in Moscow, with the evidence that Mitko wanted to use against me. He would go ahead and arrest me, and perhaps, just perhaps, this would make him overconfident. He might be too hungry for my death and make a mistake."

"And Schareck, once you had given him Zolling's name, would escort me to East Berlin . . ." Roy murmured.

"Not quite. He would take you there and release you; then he would get the name. Not before. Schareck would have double-crossed me—kept you after I had given him the name—if I were to trust him."

"But how could you have been so certain I would go after the file?"

"You heard Martha Berg say her husband was in communication with me. Berg and I had already instituted the contingency plan Berg mentioned on the tape, and you needed what was on that tape to get rid of me. Oh, yes, you would go after it."

"You were staking everything on finding that second message, weren't you?" Roy said softly. "Everything."

Bibnikov nodded. "To protect Berg as far as possible, I simply borrowed your method: If there was any information and he couldn't wait for our normal contact, he was to record his message on the same tape as he would be sending to you."

"It was risky for him to have done that. We might have found it by accident."

"That was possible. But I expected you and Mitko would be totally absorbed in the open message. I was right."

"So when you were in prison, you had Andropov ransack Mitko's safe. You were looking for that message. Should it not have been there, you always had Martha Berg."

"I don't know if she would have been enough," Bibnikov said slowly. "I doubt it. But she was valuable to confirm that the message had been put there by Berg himself."

"And the Hungarian Sulok?"

"He was a problem," Bibnikov admitted. "I had my people working without stop, checking the method of execution of your network against the methodologies of known assassins. The field was slightly more limited because of the interrogation. Normally an assassin would not subject his victims to questioning. The list came down to forty candidates. I began with those in Eastern Europe. Sulok and his leaving the AVO seemed to fit. We found him in Germany, confirmed that he had been the killer and persuaded him that it would be in his better interests to cooperate with us."

"It is incredible," Roy murmured. "So intricate, so precise, like a work of art really, deadly but beautiful. I was manipulating Schareck, and he was returning the compliment because of his arrangement with you. And for what? The irony of it all is that there never was a real Iron Mask dossier. Zolling did not enter into it until the very last."

He turned to Bibnikov. "And me? Why was the rifleman waiting for me when I came over?"

Bibnikov did not answer immediately. He lit another cigarette off the dying butt.

"I was told about the shots," he said. "My men said they originated in the eastern zone. They would have gone after the rifleman, but they had orders to stay with you.

"Mitko butchered off your network, and you were the last calf. It wouldn't have been good for you to appear in Moscow, not really. They needed the dossier, not you. You might have learned something in West Germany, something which you were never meant to know. Perhaps you

247

might have even come to suspect someone shitting in your own nest. Mitko couldn't take that chance, not with his operation running and winding down quickly. Ivatushin probably had orders to take the dossier off your corpse. But my people kept him from really hurting you."

"You're insane," Roy whispered. "Completely mad! It was you we were after, Mitko and I were after you!"

"Then why didn't he tell you whom to contact in Bonn?" Bibnikov said coldly. "Why did he send you to the West if not to get rid of you altogether? You were his fool. You were the bait I was meant to take. I was to institute a plan for your execution before you had a chance to blow everything you knew. That would have kept me very busy and well away from Mitko, who would go on plotting and plotting until it was too late to stop him. But the fool is always the last to know, eh? Whether in love or faith." Bibnikov spat out the last words.

"And the trial . . . " Roy whispered.

"That was all for his benefit. I wanted to bring him to the tribunal so I could watch as he led himself into the dock, letting him think he was going to do me in. I didn't have to prove my innocence. Instead I would become his prosecutor." Bibnikov gripped Roy by the shoulders. "Don't you understand, fool, I led him to the rope! I watched him break apart as Shevchenko brought in the witnesses, and I wondered how long it would take before there would be nothing but the pieces."

"Stop it!" Roy screamed. "Stop it!"

"There is more proof," Bibnikov shouted back. "I have it, but it will have to wait. I need you for something else."

"For what?" Roy turned on him. "Your plot. What Shevchenko was raving about?"

"It is a fact," Bibnikov said. "Deny it if you want, but I have brought you here because I need you and I will make

248

use of you. Mitko would not have faced death so willingly, so gladly had his plan not been completed, already running. He had come so far that he bought as much time as possible. Even under my methods he said nothing and waited as day after day passed and we got nothing. What was he waiting for? You must tell me," Bibnikov said very deliberately, "what his vision was."

Roy was silent for a moment, then laughed softly.

"Do you really believe a plan built on the lives of so many men, his own men, would be told to me?" he asked. "Would a mere tool, as you have called me, be permitted to see anything of the grand design? No, Bibnikov, you are wrong. There is nothing I can tell you. There never was."

"By arresting Mitko, I had hoped to panic his cohorts," Bibnikov said. "I did not entirely fail to do so. The thought of sending you into Mitko's world, where after all you would be greeted like a hero, had also occurred to me. But I am not prepared to throw your life away cheaply. The rifleman may come again. I have guarded you thus far, and I must continue to keep him away from you. But whatever Mitko has set in motion cannot be stopped unless you help me."

"I am finished," Roy said. "I have nothing to give you, can't you see that?"

"Somewhere, at some time, Mitko must have told you something," Bibnikov persisted. "A word, a single sentence . . . he must have allowed you a glimpse."

Roy shook his head and went over to the window. Between the inner and outer frames he saw a shriveled piece of lemon. On the floor below was an overturned refrigerator. It had finally been delivered after all. Suddenly he turned to Bibnikov.

"It was not Mitko," he said. "You are right, but it was not Mitko."

# CHAPTER FIFTEEN

## *Flower of the Frozen Spring*

THE MAN DISEMBARKING among the passengers of Aeroflot Flight 23 from Tbilisi attracted no attention. Dressed in grease-stained overalls, red woolen jacket and sailor's tuque, he appeared to be nothing more than another oil rigger on leave in Moscow, probably a technician, judging from his youth and slender frame.

The man stopped at the bottom of the ramp, wiped the thick lenses of his eyeglasses on a handkerchief and put them back on. His face was wide and smooth, with the beginning of a golden mustache. He walked briskly toward the baggage counter and picked up a single knapsack. His documents were routinely stamped at passport control. He checked the date on his papers—January 22.

He took a taxi into Moscow and got off at Sverdlov Square. From there he walked down Petrovka Street, past the dingy shops and apartment houses, some of which were more than a hundred years old. He moved through the bustle around him as though it did not exist, ignoring the bazaars of clothing, dry goods and God knows what else that spilled into the streets—the women peddling greasy cakes, the policemen who were busy trying to keep pedestrians on the sidewalk and out of the road where delivery vehicles jerked spasmodically through a medley of horns and curses. He passed the Moscow Criminal Police Station at Number 38 and turned off into an alley that emptied onto a dilapidated courtyard, strewn with cabbage leaves and garbage tied together in old newspaper. He checked the building directory and went up to Room 24 on the second floor. He did not have a residence permit, but he knew the metropolitan area very well and had a key for Number 24.

The room was very cold. The only window, facing the courtyard, could not be shut properly. He tried to bring it down all the way, but the frame refused to meet the ledge. The previous tenant had kindly left a pile of newsprint in a stack on the floor.

He moved away from the window toward the cupboard. The shiny lock on the door was out of keeping with the general condition of the room. He took out another key and pulled the door back. The items he had been told he would find were on the floor: an alarm clock which gave the time as three thirty and a leather rifle cover. He carefully set the clock on the floor across the room, where he could see it at a glance, and unzipped the leather sheath.

The weapon was a Kalashnikov assault rifle, a modification of the model that had won great fame in Vietnam and was prized by American troops as a trophy of war. The barrel was shorter and made of heavier metal, sealed with heat-resistant chemical. The magazine feeder and ejection opening had been enlarged and reinforced with the same chemical. The stock had remained untouched.

At the bottom of the sheath were three clips of armor-piercing bullets. He loaded one of the clips immediately and held the rifle out, feeling its balance. He had trained with this kind of weapon and knew the mechanism thoroughly. The changes did not upset his handling. Still, he checked the firing points carefully and took special care to examine the trigger. There could be no last-minute jam.

He glanced at the clock and drew out the last item from the closet. It was a seaman's duffel bag, with straps sewn in to hold the Kalashnikov firm. Inside was the uniform of a Kremlin Guards Directorate officer. Quickly he stripped and put on the uniform. When he was through, he stuffed his clothing and the rifle sheath deep into the bag and carefully strung in the rifle. He piled up the clothing on either side of the barrel, padding the weapon securely.

He did not bother removing traces of his presence from the room. When he was safely away, others would come and remove the conspicuous lock, the clock and the rags soiled with gun grease.

The rifleman shouldered his burden and left the room. He walked carefully down the staircase and into the courtyard. He came out on Petrovka and disappeared in the direction he had come from an hour ago. In Moscow, a city of uniforms, one more went by unnoticed.

The planning of the operation had deliberately allowed for no time lapse. Starting with his arrival in Moscow, everything had been calculated to the minute. Traffic, weather conditions, official schedules—all had been carefully scrutinized to ensure that the rifleman's concentration would not stray from the assignment. He had been assured, repeatedly, that there would be no mistakes from the other side.

The man passed down Kuibyshev Street and along the GUM store, went past the Place of Skulls near St. Basil's and turned into Red Square. Darkness had descended on Moscow, and the wind, bitter and unyielding, drove people from the streets. They huddled in tramway queues and let out a collective sigh of relief when the trolley at last appeared. The cars would pause, then shunt off into the night, the sparks from the electric wires mingling with those that came off the icy rails.

The Kremlin was deserted. The mausoleum of Lenin looked very cold and gray. The rifleman glanced at it briefly and turned to the path along the wall, looking neither to the right nor the left, keeping his head down against the wind cutting through the greatcoat. But his hands were warm, for he was wearing thin chamois gloves under the heavy mitts.

He leaned against a doorway cut into the massive stone and brought some cigarettes from his pocket. He had been warned that he might be challenged and that the best way to avoid notice was to do what the other guards did—huddle in doorways until the leadership had almost arrived. He smoked slowly, staring sometimes at the sky, massive and black, and at the proud pillars of the Council of Ministers Building and the Central Committee Chambers. He remembered Lenin's tomb and wondered what Lenin would think if he might see the events that were to unfold at his grave.

He finished his cigarette and opened the duffel bag. Removing the clothing, he took out the Kalashnikov and shouldered it. Then he placed the bag back in the recess. When he emerged, he appeared to be another sentry, although an experienced eye would have noticed that his weapon was not the detail's standard issue.

The rifleman began walking to Borovitsky Gate, through which the official vehicles would be coming. He was thirty yards short of the entrance when he saw the figure of a man step forward, stop briefly and move off. That was the final signal, and a second later the first of the headlights appeared. The operation would proceed according to plan.

The rifleman had been told to expect the routine convoy. The first escort car was a black Volga with four Guards Directorate men. Then came the series of ZIL limousines that were used in winter, leaving the Rolls-Royce for the summer runs. The target, the rifleman had been told, was riding in the first car. The escort was completed by another Volga.

The rifleman stepped back as the first Volga appeared. He let his rifle strap slide down along his arm and raised the weapon slightly. The ZIL limousine was following slowly, like a lumbering animal suspicious of the dark. The rifleman stripped off the heavy mitts and held his weapon at the waist. In the force of the wind he did not hear the safety come off. The distance between the gun barrel and the approaching car was only thirty-odd feet and narrowing as the driver concentrated on following the taillights of the Volga. The rifleman's last thoughts were of the sequence: windshield first, then systematically the windows along the side, then down to the gas tank. He estimated the car would be an inferno within ten seconds. In one motion the rifle came up and the finger tightened on the trigger.

The burst that bisected the rifleman came from the right, passing well in front of the oncoming limousine.

The rifleman twitched and danced as the bullets hit him, picked him up and pushed his body with their momentum. The weapon dropped away, its stock shattered.

The driver of the limousine reacted instantly. The powerful engine revved up and hurled the car through the darkness, the headlights spinning a crazy arc, the tires spewing snow, then gripping fast. The other vehicles followed suit. But no security men emerged, guns at the ready. The convoy twisted and slithered to the wall.

Alexander Roy, holding a Kalashnikov rifle, emerged from the darkness. He was walking to the statue where the second man, who had appeared so briefly to signal the rifleman, had run. Now he had come out and was looking in the direction of the fallen rifleman.

"It's finished, Ivatushin," Roy called out against the wind.

Ivatushin straightened up and turned, revolver in hand. The hand swung in a lazy arc, and the barrel centered on Roy, who walked on until he could see his friend's face more clearly.

"Finished, nowhere to go," Roy repeated.

Ivatushin looked down at the gun in his hand but did not lower it.

"You should not have come back, Alex," he said. "Everything had gone so well. You had done exactly what we wanted, but you had to survive. You had to return. You have cost us everything."

"You failed," Roy said. "You had your chance to kill me in Berlin. I thought you were a better shot."

"There was no choice, Alex," Ivatushin called back. "I tried to have Mitko change his mind, but he wouldn't. He said that you weren't hard enough, that you would never understand what had to be done and the means that were necessary. He said that you would never forgive him for the network and that, by taking you in, we were taking in a serpent. He was right in the end.

"And I will tell you more," Ivatushin shouted.

But Roy did not want to hear more. His body was immobile, conscious only of the gun pointed at him. And his finger moved, squeezing the trigger of the Kalashnikov, watching as the bullets spat out through bluish green flame, as they hit Ivatushin again and again, releasing him only when the clip was empty. Roy turned and walked away in the direction of the cars.

From the rear of the first ZIL Bibnikov emerged. He came around to Roy, but Roy did not stop and headed in the direction of the gate. He did not see that despite the protests of the other security men, Party Chairman Leonid Brezhnev had got out of the car and was standing looking after him, his hand raised in a futile gesture for Roy to come back.

He was brought back, though, twenty minutes later, when a Moscow policeman took his life into his hands and arrested Roy for walking the streets with a rifle.

Roy was speaking. "They wouldn't let me see you. Neither Mitko nor Bibnikov, each for his own reasons. Mitko knew what had happened to you. He had to keep me away because I might somehow falter and interfere with his plans. Bibnikov, who knew how the trial would end, needed me for that end. He had to have the information I carried."

He was holding Tamara's head against his chest, half sitting on the bed beside her, her full weight lying warmly along his flank. His fingers stroked her hair at the temple, brushing at the stray wisps.

"After the trial Bibnikov kept hammering the same question over and over again: What was the conspiracy Mitko had been involved in? What was it? Bibnikov wanted to know, and I would not tell him, not yet. Then he said he had had no reason to shoot me at the Wall, that his men had been there to protect me. The only other person who was there was Ivatushin.

"But then I remembered Koldakov. I tried to recall exactly what Koldakov had said. Finally, it came back to me, how he had gone on about Stalin and the killing of Kirov, how the NKVD had recruited an unstable man, given him precise instructions on where Kirov was staying and how vulnerable he was and set him loose. Thirty-five years later Mitko, with the help of Koldakov, Ivatushin and God knows who else, brought the same plan back to life. The military would finally create its Golem, give life to the specter of a military coup."

He brought one arm around her shoulders and easily lifted her forward. Roy propped himself up against the iron pipe that served as a headboard and brought her head back to his chest, her face looking directly at him.

"I explained none of this to Bibnikov. Instead, I checked the chairman's schedule. He was due back from Helsinki on the twenty-second. His first meeting at the Kremlin would be that same evening. From the Kirov plot I knew he wouldn't be attacked en route. The killing would be patterned to the last detail. That meant someone would be waiting for the chairman as he arrived at his offices. The rifleman would either be outside in the darkness or inside. I took the outside.

"I asked that all guards continue on as usual. There was nothing wrong with men sheltering themselves in that kind of weather. I told Bibnikov where I would be that night and asked him to ride with the chairman. But he was to do nothing. There was to be no reinforced escort, no change in the convoy route. Nothing was to be betrayed.

"I picked out the rifleman immediately. He was very good, but he was too attached to his gun. He held it as though he were about to use it. I also saw another man going over to the statue. That was Ivatushin, the safety man who would kill the rifleman after the job was done. There would never be any witnesses, and Ivatushin undoubtedly had a good reason for being at the Kremlin that night, as a cover story."

He leaned forward and brushed her forehead with his lips. Her hair was loose again, gathering under her neck, and it smelled faintly of wild spring flowers.

"To serve the security of the state is perhaps the highest privilege for a citizen of our country. It is a privilege that breeds privilege and creates an elite that is believed to serve the people as a whole. Yet it is the people who are afraid of us.

"People think our world is completely different from their own. They are afraid of the violence, the treachery and deceit we practice, even encourage and exploit. Yet I do not think there is much difference between our world and the real world. The human qualities are the same; only in my world they are sharper, clearer. Under strain, courage and cowardice, love and hate, patriotism and treason become more defined. There is little room for subterfuge, for the philosophic padding, the comfort of allowing time to take care of matters, the luxury of inaction. Every decision a man makes reveals more of his true character. Sometimes he is led to see more of himself than he wishes to. Reality is that stark and cannot be manipulated, forgotten or really excused. One's actions and their results remain to face one with the full weight of their consequences. There is no escape. Men age very quickly in such a world. There is almost no time left to correct the mistakes. One must forget them and get on with the job. But now the job is done, and there is still a little time to make something right. Not very much, not very much at all. But perhaps enough so that one could say at least that much was done."

He rose from the bed and walked over to where his jacket was draped across a chair. Tamara, motionless, was lying almost diagonally across the bed, her head hanging over one edge. He returned and moved her so that she would lie properly, her head on the pillows.

Tamara had not understood a word he said. The doctors said that she could hear but that there would be no response. Nothing anyone could say would register in her mind. Her eyes stared out perpetually in the gaze of the blind, unmoving, never blinking, the muscles frozen in the fear that had overwhelmed her. They would not tell him exactly what had been done. They really didn't have to. The rat bites had left scars, and the punctures along the arms suggested heavy and frequent doses of drugs, probably Scoline, which creates in the victim's mind an unspeakable fear and dread of everything around him. Nor would they tell Roy how long she had been that way. There was no medical opinion on her recovery, which meant there was no chance of recovery at all.

"I have to go now, but only for an hour or so," Roy said. "I will be back this evening. We will eat together the way we used to and afterward play chess. Or listen to some music, whatever you like."

He went over and kissed the cold, unfeeling flesh of her lips and left.

\* \* \*

He was admitted to Bibnikov's office without question. The security man led him in and locked the door behind him. Bibnikov always locked the doors during calls.

Bibnikov was sitting behind the desk, his massive bulk lit by a solitary lamp. He glanced up at Roy and went back to reading a report. The perpetual cigarette hung from his lips, and he was frowning in concentration.

Roy took off his coat, hung it up and from inside his tunic brought out a gun, the Hanyatti he had never returned to Andrushin, the armorer. He waited until the silence made Bibnikov look up once more.

"You have seen the girl," Bibnikov said. He closed the file and tossed it into a tray.

"Yes, I have."

"I could have prevented that," Bibnikov said. "Perhaps I should have. I knew what it would do to you."

"When Mitko called me into the office that first time and explained the operation, he said its conclusion would mean your death," Roy said quietly. "I have longed so much for your death, perhaps of even killing you myself. I will satisfy myself now."

"You're not so stupid," Bibnikov answered. "You are a good intelligence officer. You can even kill men. But you are not an executioner. An executioner is one who kills on orders, without thought whether his act is good or bad or if the powers that be have all the correct reasons for demanding that this act be carried out. You would demand such reasons, even from yourself. They were given you in the case of the rifleman and Ivatushin. But you have no reason to kill me."

"She is lying in the hospital," Roy whispered. "A helpless

260

girl whom you methodically tortured for how long . . . and for no other reason than you enjoyed it."

"I told you you have a weakness," Bibnikov said harshly. "She was that weakness. Perhaps you had said something, a word or a phrase you would swear had never passed your lips, but it had. If Mitko had succeeded in getting to you in East Berlin, I would have had only her. I had to use her. In the end it was futile, but that is not the point. I had to interrogate her. I had to be sure! And you know it!"

"I only wish I could make you suffer," Roy said softly. "I wanted you to suffer so badly, very badly."

"Only a fool carries on such a dialogue." Bibnikov laughed at him. "A convinced man would have walked in and pulled the trigger without further nonsense, as you did at the Kremlin. Why will you not admit that you are afraid to kill me? It is not shameful. Not that you are afraid of your own execution. No, death you will accept. What eats at you is that you have no home anymore. The GRU will never accept you. Of course, they cannot refuse to take on a hero, but they will never trust you. You have acted against them, your own soldier comrades. A military man has helped in the arrest and execution of a superior! What general will ever trust you again? How will he be certain you are not working for me or Andropov? You will be feared, hated and respected for that hate as I am. You know you have been cast in my image now, and that is what you hate. Killing me cannot erase the image I have left on you for the rest of your life.

"But I propose that you should live," Bibnikov continued. "You have seen the girl. There is no chance she will recover. There is no riding away into the sunset for the two of you. So I ask you: I have crippled her; now let me make her end merciful. Her life, what she could have given to you, that, too, has been taken away. Yes, she can live out the rest of her days crippled and mute. Or else one injection can be administered, and she will be spared her agony and, with that, you as well. She will remain for you in memory, which is kinder than living with what you have lying on the bed.

"As for yourself, I have instructions and traveling orders which have been personally approved by the chairman. You will continue your work elsewhere."

He stood there with the weapon still in his grip, staring at the pale-blue eyes that remained fixed on his. A thousand times in those moments he felt the metal of the trigger, warmed by his finger. He imagined Bibnikov's head exploding into bloody redness as the bullet entered. He felt within him a desperate need to prove his loyalty to the one person alive who still mattered to him. Yet when he thought of Tamara, he remembered only the screaming madness that arose within him as he lay by her, the madness that gripped him in the knowledge that she would never be his again. And still he wanted to confirm his loyalty to her, to answer for the living death to which he had condemned her.

But it was her memory, too, that would not allow him to do vengeance. He had thrust her from the sad peace of her world into the violence of his own. She would never have asked him to kill for her. He would not do so now.

Bibnikov rose and crushed out his cigarette. He did not approach Roy but remained standing behind his desk.

"You are dismissed, Roy," he said curtly. "The chairman and Andropov are ready to receive you at the Kremlin. You need not keep them waiting."

"I will bury her myself!" Roy said fiercely. "I want no one else to be there, do you understand, no one!"

"She doesn't have anyone else," Bibnikov said. "Never did. She was alone before you came."

As he left, Roy saw Tamara's face as it had been when she slept in his arms, her hair scattered across the pillows, the lips pressed into a tiny smile. He saw this, and he understood he was condemned by it.

# TERMINATION REPORT

# SPECIAL INVESTIGATIONS—POLITBURO

## MOST SECRET

**FEBRUARY 4**

The Bonapartist plot of General Mitko, former chairman of GRU military intelligence, has been dealt with.

Through the interrogation of party member and Politburo member Ponomarev this department has learned the identities of the instigators of the plot and their cohorts.

TURCHEVSKY, IVAN VASILEVICH—Marshal of the Soviet Union, party member

KOLDAKOV, PIOTR DENISOVICH—psychiatrist, party Member

KATCHACHURIAN, BORIS ILLYCH—general of the Air Force, commander of Leninsk bomber Squadron Delta Four

These three men, along with Mitko and Ivatushin, formed the nucleus of the conspiratorial nest. All have been interrogated and dealt with by a military tribunal under the leadership of Marshal of the Soviet Union Grechko. The sentence handed down has been carried out with extraordinary measure.

All interrogations reveal that Blueprint was a plan to launch a surgical strike upon the People's Republic of China on January 24, after the shooting of Party Chairman Brezhnev (January 22, 1969) and the subsequent arrest and detention of remaining Politburo members, Ponomarev excepted.

Ponomarev would have assumed nominal control of the government at that time to create the impression that the events which had occurred were part of a radical, but entirely civilian, change in the leadership.

In reality Ponomarev would have been acting as a puppet for the military.

With Ponomarev in Moscow, Turchevsky, on Mitko's counsel, would have launched the strike on China, with no prior warning or an issuing of an ultimatum. Blueprint, *a theoretical plan*, was in fact a plan of war, to be used on the specified date.

Special Investigations has undertaken to seal the Leninsk base. All officers and technicians have been quarantined for investigation. A parallel team, chosen by Comrade Marshal Grechko, has been dispatched to assume duties at Leninsk.

Special Investigations considers the situation there secure.

Special Investigations strongly recommends two courses of action to reduce the chances of another such attempt at a military coup:

**A.** All documents relating to Blueprint as related to intelligence be sealed and deposited in the time vault, for a period of not less than one hundred years.

**B.** That Special Investigations have its mandate extended to the creation of a special unit which would keep surveillance on the military exclusively.

As regards course "B," this officer proposes the following plan. It is ironic to be sure but no less effective for that.

The so-called mission on which Captain Roy had been sent to West Germany had its foundation on his disgrace within the GRU. This disgrace was to be aggravated by Roy's becoming a traitor in the eyes of his comrades when word of his "flight" spread through the departments. Everything proceeded as Mitko had planned except that in the end Mitko's gambit failed and Captain Roy, by returning safely, became the chief architect of his commander's destruction. So now Roy has in fact been discredited. What senior officer would take Roy into his unit knowing Roy had been responsible for the demise of a former superior? Which rank, assigned to Roy, could guarantee his commanding officer that Roy wasn't watching him or that he represented no threat? Of course there could never be such a guarantee and no officer will ever trust Roy again. It is ironic that the man who set out to save his country by slandering himself wound up achieving his goal but in the process made himself untouchable.

In view of these circumstances, I propose that Captain Roy be seconded to the new Special Investigations unit which will oversee internal security within the military organs. His experience in the GRU, giving him a comprehensive overview of intelligence operations as well as an understanding of its techniques and psychology, will prove valuable to this new body. That Captain Roy will bridle at

266

the suggestion of such a posting is noted. However he understands, if not readily admits, that he could never again belong to that community. The military will not take him back, yet he is a man who cannot live without his profession. So in effect he has no choice. This will ensure his service and obedience to Special Investigations in a manner more binding than any personal loyalty.

BIBNIKOV